"I already have a career, Mr. Hanson, and it doesn't involve Labrador."

"No," he said. "It involves other people's weddings. I got that part. But this place'll grow on you, I guarantee it, and the fishing lodge will generate enough income to make you happy even if you're an absentee business partner living and working in Maine."

He towered over her, his eyes intense. "We're only two weeks away from opening. I just need to find another fishing guide or two. At least think about keeping your grandfather's half. But know this," he added. "If you decide to sell out, I'm not going to make it easy for you. I've worked my ass off to help make this place what it is. This is my future we're talking about, not to mention your grandfather's lifelong dream."

Before Senna could respond, he strode away, leaving her standing on the dock staring after him.

Her life, up until this very day, had been fairly steady, safe and predictable, but suddenly she found herself in the middle of a whole bunch of unknowns—and in spite of the dubious circumstances, she found herself looking forward to exploring them, even if it was just for two weeks.

Dear Reader,

I am haunted by Labrador. I first saw this wild and lonely land
in 1991, behind a team of Alaskan huskies while running the
Labrador 400 sled dog race. The race began in a snowstorm
that ended two days later and found my team and me lost
in a kind of wilderness we'd never experienced before. This
is a land of caribou and wolves, of Innu and Inuit, of savage
shrieking winds that both humble and exult. This is a land
of brilliant displays of northern lights, a land where the
silence—when the storm finally passes—is so still that it's loud
to the ears.

We eventually found our way out of that wild place, thanks
to a bush pilot my parents hired to find us, but we never
found a way to escape the pull of it. That pull brought us
back to race the following season, and the memories of those
two journeys tugged at me throughout the years and caused
endless discussions of "going there again" with my father, who
had been equally taken by the truly wild character of the land.
In fact, one of the last conversations I had with my dad was
about Labrador and buying a cabin there. I bought a place in
Labrador last year, on the first anniversary of his death. It's
a remote cabin fifty odd miles from the nearest road, on the
shores of the same wild lake that scrambled me and my team
so badly in that first race. Wolves and caribou travel the gravel
strand in front of the cabin, the wind blows free and the
waves lap up against the shore. It's a beautiful, lonely spot, a
place that heals the spirit and nourishes the soul.

This story is about two people from different worlds and
different backgrounds being thrown together as business
partners in this remote wilderness. How they adapt to this
reluctant partnership and come to terms with each other and
with the land itself is a tribute to their characters, and perhaps
even more than that, it is a tribute to the healing power of
nature and love's eternal optimism.

Nadia Nichols

SHARING SPACES
Nadia Nichols

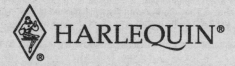

HARLEQUIN®

TORONTO • NEW YORK • LONDON
AMSTERDAM • PARIS • SYDNEY • HAMBURG
STOCKHOLM • ATHENS • TOKYO • MILAN • MADRID
PRAGUE • WARSAW • BUDAPEST • AUCKLAND

ISBN 0-373-71317-7

SHARING SPACES

This edition published by arrangement with Harlequin Books S.A.

® and TM are trademarks of the publisher. Trademarks indicated with
® are registered in the United States Patent and Trademark Office, the
Canadian Trade Marks Office and in other countries.

www.eHarlequin.com

Printed in U.S.A.

Books by Nadia Nichols

This one's for you, Dad.

CHAPTER ONE

LIKE MOST WEDDINGS held at the Inn on Christmas Cove, this one had been in the works for well over a year, but unlike most weddings, this one had been under Senna McCallum's sole charge right from the start. She was personally handling this wedding because Sheila Payson, the bride's mother, had asked her to, and nobody said no to Sheila Payson, who was heir to the Payson dynasty and used to getting her own way in all things. Senna had been working at the inn her mother's sister owned for the past five years, her first two as a sales associate, learning the ropes, and then as head of the sales department, the person who oversaw each and every function and made sure everything down to the smallest detail was perfect. At twenty-nine, Senna had already garnered enough of a reputation to have attracted the attention of Mrs. Payson, which was quite an achievement for someone with a bachelor of science in wildlife biology.

The details had been endless, and the phone calls and visits from the bride and her mother had become more and more frequent, as many as two or three a week as the date drew near. Now that the big day had finally arrived, Senna was relieved. The weather, which was iffy in late June on the Maine coast, was bright and clear.

Fogs could shroud Christmas Cove, creating a damp gray mood not at all conducive to nuptial festivities, or it could be stormy and rainy. But luck was with them, and the dark, sparkling cove with its rugged granite ledge and wind-stunted evergreens had never looked more beautiful.

The ceremony itself was held beneath the arbor in the rose garden and had gone off without any problems. The first hour of the reception before the guests moved into the ballroom for dinner was in full swing to the accompaniment of a string quartet. The wait staff were passing crab cakes with rémoulade, lobster salad in endive spears and chicken satay with peanut sauce. The first and second hors d'oeuvre stations were abundantly supplied with jumbo shrimp, Jonah crab claws, mahogany clams and oysters on the half shell. The reception was progressing more smoothly than Senna had dared hope when the inn's general manager took her aside.

"Senna? You have a call from your mother," Linda Sherwood said, handing her the portable phone.

Senna thanked Linda and moved around the corner of the building for privacy. "Hi Mom, what's up?"

"I'm afraid I have some bad news," her mother said. She sounded upset, and Senna's grip on the phone tightened. "Your grandfather passed away on Wednesday. His lawyer called a little while ago."

Senna closed her eyes with relief that her brothers were okay. "I'm sorry to hear that, Mom. I wish we'd been closer to him, but—"

"Senna, I know you're busy so I won't beat around the bush," her mother interrupted. "According to the lawyer, the admiral named you as his executor."

"*What?* Are you sure? Why not Billy or Bryce?"

Senna caught a glimpse of movement. The banquet director hovered nearby, an apologetic look on her face, and tapped the face of her wristwatch. It was time to move the wedding party into the ballroom. Senna nodded that she understood. "Mom, I'm sorry, but I have to go. We're right in the middle of a big wedding. I have tomorrow off so I'll come over right after I get out of work tonight and we can talk in the morning. Love you, and leave the porch light on for me."

Senna stood for a few moments, collecting her thoughts before rejoining the wedding party. It had been five years since she'd last seen her grandfather. A lean, stern man, gruff to the point of being scary and used to being obeyed after a career in the Navy, Senna had always been more than a little afraid of him. Secretly she'd pitied her father, the only child of a man who had probably never dispensed a word of praise or a heartfelt hug in his entire life. Maybe that's why he'd turned out to be so aloof himself. With the admiral as a role model and a mother who'd died when he'd been a boy, what choice did he have? But why on earth would the admiral, a chauvinist to the core, have chosen her over one of his grandsons to settle his estate?

The banquet director sneaked another questioning peek around the corner of the building and Senna drew a deep breath. "I'm coming," she said, and stepped out into the golden sunlight. The scents of rugosa roses, freshly mown grass and the salt air mingled with the tantalizing aroma of foods. Servers in black and white circulated among the guests, carrying silver champagne and hors d'oeuvre trays, and the strains of the string quartet gave the afternoon an elegant, romantic mood.

Senna's practiced eye took in the dynamics of the reception and was satisfied with what she saw. Everything was going exactly according to plan. She approached the bride, who was radiant in her satin Reem Acra gown, and touched her arm gently. "Excuse me, Sophia," she said, "but we'll be moving into the ballroom shortly. It's time for everyone to be seated."

FIVE LONG HOURS LATER, just after eleven, she arrived at her mother's house in Castine. The lights were on in the kitchen and her mother was up, waiting for her. She opened the door in her flannel nightgown and bathrobe, her hair plaited in a long braid over one shoulder. "You must be exhausted," she said.

"It's been a long day," Senna admitted, relishing the feeling of coming home. She no longer lived here and hadn't since she went away to college, but the old homestead had been in her mother's family for over two hundred years. There was something about the place that always made her feel comfortable and safe. The kitchen was just the way she remembered it as a young child, when Gram and Gramp were still alive. Her mother had kept the teakettle on the back of the wood cookstove, and she poured two cups. They sat at the table together and nibbled on gingersnap cookies.

"So, tell me everything you know," Senna said.

Her mother sighed. "That's not much, I'm afraid. Your grandfather died in Labrador. He was living near a place called North West River. Apparently he was diagnosed with cancer a year ago and the doctors didn't expect him to live this long."

Senna took a sip of tea and sighed, easing a cramp between her shoulder blades. "Labrador. You'd think he would have named an executor who lived in the area, and one who was a little bit closer to him."

"The funeral was held today and the admiral is being cremated, per his wishes. The lawyer would have called you directly with all of this information but the only phone number he had was this one."

Senna took another sip of tea. It was strong and good. She was tired to the point of feeling dizzy. "I'll call him first thing Monday morning."

"There's property that will have to be disposed of," her mother said.

"What kind of property?"

"The lawyer mentioned a house, a vehicle, an airplane and a fishing camp."

Senna frowned over the curl of steam that rose from her mug. "Maybe he'd sell it all for a consignment fee. He could mail or fax me all the legal forms I need to sign, I could notarize them and send them back...."

"You'd better go and look the situation over so you know exactly what the estate consists of before making any decisions," her mother advised.

Senna shook her head. "Mom, I don't think I can get away from work. We're just getting into the busy season."

"You haven't taken a vacation in several years," her mother pointed out. "Labrador sounds like a wild place, and you like wild places, Senna. I'm sure your aunt would let you have some time off."

"Yes, she would, but that wouldn't be much of a vacation. Are you *sure* the admiral wasn't married?"

"Positive. He called it quits after wife number three. If you took two weeks off, you'd have time to explore some of the country and time to think about some important things, like your future with Tim, and your job as sales director at the inn."

Senna lifted her chin out of her palm and blinked the sleep from her eyes. "What makes you think I need to do that?"

"I'm your mother. I know how much you miss being a wildlife biologist, and I know you aren't in love with Tim Cromwell even though he's hopelessly in love with you and has been for years."

Senna gazed at her, amazed. "As a matter of fact, Tim and I broke up a few weeks ago. We're still friends and probably always will be, but you're right. I wasn't in love with him."

Her mother's eyebrows raised. "How did Tim feel about that?"

"He took it pretty hard. He still thinks I'll eventually realize that he's the man for me. Tim's a good guy and he deserves to have a woman who's crazy about him. He'll be a lot better off without me. And yes, I miss being a biologist, but I like working at the inn. I've learned a lot, and the pay is a lot better than what I was making working for the state."

Her mother wisely refrained from commenting. She took a sip of tea and continued, "The lawyer told me your grandfather's been living in Labrador ever since he retired from the Navy shortly after your father died."

"Why Labrador?"

"Apparently he was big into fishing, and the fishing's quite good there."

"Fishing." Senna dropped her chin back into her palm with a sigh. "That figures. The old sea wolf couldn't stay away from the water."

Her mother stirred another dollop of honey into her

tea. "Senna, the admiral's last request was that you handle his estate, and I think you should honor it. You *are* a McCallum, after all."

THE JOURNEY FROM CASTINE to Labrador was a circuitous one at best, and expensive to boot. From Bangor, Senna flew to Quebec City, from Quebec City to Wabush, from Wabush to Goose Bay. It didn't seem too difficult to connect the dots, but flights to Goose Bay weren't like flights to Boston. One didn't have many choices, so she had to lay over a night in Quebec before catching the flights to Wabush and Goose Bay. Arriving at 2:00 p.m., she immediately phoned the lawyer to find out where her grandfather's house was located. There was no point in racking up more expenses at a hotel if she could stay there while she got his affairs in order. Two weeks was two weeks, though with any luck she'd have everything done in half that time.

"Well, m'dear," the lawyer, an older-sounding gentleman whose name was Lindo Granville, said upon hearing her out. "The thing is, your grandfather's house isn't exactly in Goose Bay, y'see?"

Senna tried to place the accent, which sounded very Celtic. "Well, if you could tell me how to get there, I could stop by your office for the key."

"Key? I doubt the place is locked up, m'dear. Do you have a car? I'd be happy to drive you over if you don't."

"I've already rented one, thank you. I'm at the airport now. I thought I'd stop by your office first, if that's all right. I'd like to start settling my grandfather's estate as soon as possible."

Lindo Granville was as pleasant in person as he'd been on the phone. He was a ruddy-faced man in his late sixties who looked as if he'd spent much of his life out of doors, not ensconced in an office pushing papers around his desk. He invited Senna in, poured her a cup of strong, black tea, finally found what he was looking for on his cluttered desk, and handed her the admiral's last will and testament. "It's up to date, he was in town just last week," Granville said. "We had lunch together and he made a few amendments prior to that."

"He must have known he was going to die soon," Senna said, steeling herself as she looked down at the legal papers.

"Yes." Granville nodded. "Didn't feel the least bit sorry for himself, though. He was more worried about his business partner."

"Business partner?" Senna glanced up. This was a new twist.

"John Hanson. They were good friends. Hanson stayed with him 'til the very end, so's the admiral could die at the lake house. He didn't want to die in a hospital, y'see, and I don't blame him one bit for that, but he needed a lot of care towards the end. You'll meet John Hanson by and by, if he survived your grandfather's wake. The last time I saw him he was full of screech and dancing with my sister, Goody."

"Screech?"

"Screech is Labrador's own brand of hooch. Rum. Powerful stuff, and he'd drunk a powerful dose, y'see."

Senna pictured a drunken old man clasping a drunken old woman at a classic Irish wake and inwardly winced. "What kind of business did they share?"

"A fishing lodge. Outfitting and guiding," Granville said. "They were just getting started when the admiral was stricken. If you read the will, you'll see that he left everything to you."

The lawyer's words struck like a bolt of lightning. *"Everything?"*

"Yes, m'dear. Everything. A word of caution, there's very little remaining in his bank account, the lodge's construction costs took the most of it, and there are some liens that need to be paid, but the properties are worth a considerable sum."

Senna scanned the words rapidly. Sure enough, there it was, in black and white. Admiral Stuart McCallum had left all his worldly possessions to her. Senna sat back in her chair, dumbfounded. "May I take a copy of the will with me? I can read it more closely tonight."

"Of course, m'dear, and as soon as you're ready, I'll help you through the probate procedures. You'll need to be legally appointed as his executor and we can start that process right now if you want to sign a few papers. Because we're dealing with international paperwork, everything will take a little more time, I'm afraid. Do you have a lawyer you'd like me to work with on your end?"

Senna nodded and handed him the business card of the firm who had handled her father's affairs. "I'd like to fast-track this process and I'd appreciate your help. I'm hoping to sell his share of the business as soon as possible."

Thirty minutes later the legal matters were in the works and Senna was ready to leave. "Now then," Granville told her. "You'll need to drive to North West River and ask anyone there where the admiral's house is. They'll tell you." He hesitated. "Do you have a place to stay?"

"I plan to stay there, of course," Senna said briskly.

Granville paused. "The thing is, m'dear, the admiral was a bachelor and for that matter, so is John Hanson."

"I'm sure I'll survive whatever state of bachelorhood his house is in, Mr. Granville. I grew up with two brothers who were the biggest slobs on earth. Really, I'll be fine. Thank you again for all your help."

There was another pause. "Well, you see, m'dear, the lake-house property was part of the business, and half belongs to John Hanson."

"Don't worry," she reassured him, because he did seem genuinely troubled. "I'm sure I'll find the half that was my grandfather's."

Granville's frown of concern deepened, and Senna wondered if perhaps John Hanson was so old as to be a little bit daffy. "You're welcome to stay with the wife and me, m'dear. We'd love the company."

"That's very kind of you to offer, Mr. Granville, but I need some closure, and I'm hoping to find it at my grandfather's house. Besides, Mr. Hanson and I have some business matters to discuss, and the sooner we get that dialogue started the better."

Twenty minutes later, Senna was driving through a land that was wilder than any she'd ever seen. She was used to the rocky coast of Maine, but Labrador was much more remote and far less populated, and once out of Goose Bay there was only one road. She caught glimpses of the water through the fringe of black spruce on her right. The highway map designated this as Lake Melville. The drive to North West River didn't take long. By 4:00 p.m. she was there, and, heeding Granville's directions, she pulled to a stop across from the first person she saw, rolled down the window, and asked,

"Excuse me, but would you happen to know where the admiral's house is?"

The towheaded blue-eyed boy was pushing a bike with a flat tire. His expression was lively and open, and he said, "Take the next left that leads up the south shore of the lake. You'll hear 'em, when you gets close. The admiral's dogs," he explained, noting her expression. "You'll hear 'em, but you're too late. You missed the wake by a day. It was a good one, too, from all I heard." Then off he went, pushing his bike along the gravel road.

She followed the directions he'd given, and drove cautiously up a narrower road that appeared to be bereft of human habitations. She wondered, after a few kilometers, if the boy had been pulling her leg. There were tire tracks, to be sure, and she could see the gleam of the lake through thick stands of black spruce from time to time. But no houses.

Senna stopped the car and turned off the ignition, rolling down the window again. She listened intently in the silence and heard eerie, undulating wails reverberating through the forest. Wolves, and not that far away. She felt a tingle of excitement at the thought of actually catching sight of one. There were wolves here, and one of the biggest caribou herds in the world, and the native people were called Innu and Inuit. She knew as much from reading the literature on the Air Canada flight this morning. What she didn't know, as she sat in the rental car and listened to the wild howling, was why her grandfather had chosen to live out his last years here, far removed from the Navy's elite social circles and manicured golf courses. Why had he chosen to live in such a remote land and *why* had he named her as his executor? She was hoping she'd find some answers when she reached the house, but even if she didn't, seeing a pack of wolves or a herd of caribou would definitely make this journey north worthwhile. Her mother had been right.

As usual.

She started the rental car and crept cautiously forward, keenly scanning both sides of the road and hoping for a glimpse of the wolves she'd heard. She caught the flash of lake water and a bright opening up ahead in the forest of spruce. Sunlight spilled into a clearing. There was a building and a truck. Make that two buildings and two trucks. She stopped again, assessing the place. This had to be her destination, since the road ended here. The big building was somewhat of an architectural oddity, grander than many she'd seen since her arrival and resembling one of Maine's old Rangely Lake houses. With its big center chimney and gabled roof, log construction and a spacious porch that faced the water, it had all the earmarks of a tranquil lakeside retreat.

A second, smaller structure nestled back into the trees, was also built of logs, but had a broad, low Alaskan-style roof with deep eaves. Perhaps that was the place where John Hanson lived, since the admiral, possessing an ego the size of the Atlantic, would surely have lived in the bigger of the two cabins.

Senna stared, trying to take it all in. The lake was vast. She couldn't see the end of it by a long shot. There was a dock that jutted into the water, and a float plane was tethered at the dock's T-junction. The wolves were howling again, but even as she sat there, engine idling, the noise faded. She drove a little closer, feeling foolishly timid. She had every right to be here, after all.

There didn't appear to be any phone or electric lines anywhere near the place, and the property looked neglected. Upon closer inspection she could see trash scattered here and there. Beer cans and bottles. She cut the ignition again and immediately the whine of hungry mosquitoes filled the silence. That, and the rhythmic wash of lake water against the dock pilings and the gravelly shore. She got out of the car, closing the door quietly and standing for a moment, swatting at the mosquitoes and wondering if it might not be a good idea to retreat to Goose Bay and come back early in the morning. She was tired and the land was unfamiliar to her. She'd like to get something to eat and read through the stack of legal papers Granville had given her.

First, though, she wanted to make some connection with her grandfather, whom she hadn't seen since her father's funeral and would never see again. Besides, in this northern latitude the sun was still high. She had plenty of time to find her way back to Goose Bay. She kicked a Labatt can out of the way as she walked up the path, climbed the weathered steps and opened the screen door, entering onto the porch and peeking through a window that could have stood a good polishing. It was dark inside, and gloomy. Senna hesitated before trying the front door, glancing around and trying to imagine her grandfather living like this. The porch was littered with pizza boxes, paper napkins, cigarette butts, more beer cans and bottles. The boy had mentioned that the wake had been a good one, but it would have been nice if they'd tidied up afterward.

She knocked sharply at the door and predictably received no response. The doorknob turned easily and she stepped into the entry hall. To her left was a living room with four big double-hung nine-over-six windows looking out on the lake and a handsome stone fireplace. A staircase in front of her ascended presumably to the second-floor bedrooms, and she glimpsed a large kitchen through the doorway to the right. She closed the door on the whine of mosquitoes and almost immediately became aware of another noise, far deeper and much more ominous than the frantic hum of hungry insects. Senna stood quietly for a moment, analyzing the rumblings, which sounded very much like loud snoring being rhythmically and robustly delivered from upstairs.

She hesitated again. Could she possibly be in the wrong house? Could the smaller cabin belong to her grandfather? She glanced around furtively while upstairs the snores resonated like thunder. There was only one surefire way to find out. Senna crept into the living room, feeling a bit like a criminal, opened a corner desk, riffled through a stack of papers and spied several bills and correspondence with her grandfather's name on them. She breathed a silent sigh of relief. At least she was in the right place, but if this *was* her grandfather's house, then who was upstairs? Could it be that John Hanson had drunk so much hooch at the wake that he'd been unable to make it back to his own cabin?

She stood at the foot of the stairs and thought about calling out, but couldn't bring herself to deliver more than a tentative, "Hello?"

Her voice sounded woefully feeble, and she got no reply. If the snoring *was* being generated by the admiral's business partner, a man probably well into his seventies or better, he might be completely deaf. She crept up the stairs. At the top were two bedroom doors, one opening to the left, the other to the right. She froze with uncertainty, heart hammering against her ribs, then peeked cautiously around the left-hand door from whence the hearty snoring noises emanated. Senna noted the small bedroom, the double bed with a brightly colored Hudson's Bay candy-stripe wool blanket laid atop, dormered window that looked out on the lake. Pine bureau, mirror, chair, braided rug. There was a simple, rustic charm to the room. On the bed, sprawled upon its side, was an enormous furry dog. Some kind of northern breed closely related to a wolf, by the looks of it, old and grizzled, paws twitching in the midst of some lively dream, and snoring with deep and absolute contentment.

She backed quietly out of the room, relieved, and drew a deep breath. The lawyer hadn't mentioned animals, but that husky certainly looked like it belonged on that bed. Senna peered warily around the other door, preparing herself for another wolf-like creature, and nearly gasped aloud when she saw what was lying on the bed in the second bedroom.

Definitely not a dog, and most definitely not her grandfather's elderly business partner. A man was sprawled crosswise on the mattress. He was face down, head and shoulders hanging over the edge, arms dangling, knuckles brushing the floor. Naked to the waist, blue jeans, bare feet.

Silent and unmoving.

She took a step forward, studying his form for any signs of life even as the newspaper headlines flashed through her imagination.

Executor Discovers Body in Bedroom of Deceased Grandfather's House.

But no. There was movement. The man was breathing. Not snoring, like the dog, but sleeping with the same deep stupor. This bedroom, however, in stark contrast to the first, was a mess. Beer cans were strewn on the floor, clothing was flung everywhere. The bureau drawers were ajar, the top cluttered with more trash and paraphernalia, and the mirror so plastered with pictures that hardly any glass remained exposed. She studied the chaos for a moment in disgust, then glanced back at the unconscious man, unable to squelch her curiosity.

She couldn't see his face, but his hair was dark, glossy and tousled. His back, shoulders and arms looked strong; smooth well-knit muscles tapered into a lean waist. In spite of the fact that the man was completely relaxed in sleep, she sensed enormous power, the same power she'd once witnessed in a mountain lion dozing in the sun on a rock outcrop in the mountains of Montana. Senna swallowed a nervous laugh. What a thing for her to be doing, standing here staring at a strange man sleeping in her grandfather's house and comparing him to a mountain lion. What on earth was the matter with her?

More to the point, what was she to do? This man could be a mass murderer, for all she knew, and this place was remote enough to make her uneasy at the thought of confronting him without some means of defending herself. She backed out of the room, returned to the kitchen, and picked up first thing she saw that would qualify—a cast-iron frying pan on the stovetop with about an inch of bacon fat solidified in the bottom. Returning to the second floor, she cleared her throat and knocked briskly on the door frame, neither of which had any effect in rousing the man.

"Excuse me," she said in her most professional Do-not-argue-with-me-I'm-the-sales-director voice—which had an equal lack of effect.

"Ex*cuse* me," she repeated, louder this time.

One dangling arm twitched and she tensed for the ugly confrontation, but all the man did was shift slightly, groan as if the effort cost him, and then resume his sleep.

Senna lifted the frying pan and rapped it against the door. The sharp gunshot of noise was impressive. *"Hello!"* she said. "You need to wake up, please. Tell me who you are and what you're doing in my grandfather's house."

The man thrashed weakly, moaned and rolled over. One arm flung out, hand groping blindly for the pillow to bring it over his face to shut out the daylight…but not before she caught a glimpse of a dark, unshaven jaw and a rugged profile. "Goway," a deep voice rumbled, muffled beneath the pillow.

On his back now, baring his broad chest, flat stomach, dark line of hair disappearing into the belt line of his jeans. Arms and shoulders definitely well-defined with muscle, hands strong and calloused as if he worked hard for a living. Sexual, in a very primal way—not that she was noticing.

"Look, mister, I'm warning you right now, you'd better vacate these premises. This is Admiral Stuart McCallum's house, I'm taking possession of it, and if you don't leave right now I'll call the police, or the Mounties, or whatever you call them up here."

"Goway." The man's second gruff utterance was an echo of the first.

Senna heard a noise behind her. A stealthy sound, soft

and menacing. As she turned her head she saw that the large and grizzled husky, who moments before had been snoring quite loudly on the bed in the other room, was now standing in the doorway behind her. Its eyes were yellow and its stance was rigid and threatening. Senna realized that in the great beast's eyes she was the stranger here, the trespasser, and she remained very still.

"Easy," she said, her mouth suddenly dry and her grip tightening on the frying pan. "Good boy. Nice dog. Easy…"

"Chilkat, down." The man's voice, muffled by the pillow, was nonetheless authoritative. The husky immediately hunched to the floor, but its eyes never wavered from Senna. She swallowed and glanced toward the bed. The pillow was no longer over the man's face but his eyes were closed tight on a pained expression.

"He's lying down now," she said, wincing at the quaver in her voice.

"Uh-huh." Spoken as if he already knew.

"Is this your dog?"

"Uh-uh." Uttered as if she should know that, if she had half a brain. One hand lifted, rubbed his face, then he shifted sideways and squinted up at her. "Who the hell are you, and why are you threatening me with a frying pan?" he said, speaking slowly, as if the sound of his own words caused him great suffering.

Senna's chin lifted. "My name is Senna McCallum and I'm the admiral's granddaughter. Who are you, and what are you doing in this house?"

"I'm John Hanson, I live here, and I'm trying to get some sleep."

Senna was shocked. "But you can't be my grandfather's business partner. You're not old enough."

He made a noise that could have passed for a groan. "If it's any consolation, I feel very old right now." He struggled onto his elbows. "I don't suppose you could make some coffee and bring me a cup? Coffee's in the lower cupboard to the left of the stove. And you better put that damn frying pan on the floor before Chilkat grabs it out of your hand. He's the pot licker around here and you're driving him crazy."

CHAPTER TWO

THE ADMIRAL HAD KNOWN he was sick long before he was diagnosed with cancer. His energy levels had been dropping steadily, and the pain that he used to hold at bay with handfuls of aspirin began to cripple him up. He'd finally sought professional advice. Aside from announcing to Jack with blunt matter-of-fact realism, that the doctor had told him he wouldn't live out the year, McCallum never spoke of his illness. The two of them carried on as if by ignoring the bad news, eventually it would go away. This was fine with Jack. He'd come to like the admiral very much in the eight years he'd known the man, so he'd just as soon avoid any discussions of the unfair and untimely fate that awaited his friend.

Jack knew the admiral came off as a cold-hearted bastard to the multitudes who had dealt with him in the military, but he had an advantage that most people didn't. He knew the admiral was a dyed-in-the-wool fly fisherman who lived and breathed to cast his lines upon some of the greatest fishing waters in the world, so when Jack's commanding officer had asked him eight years ago for some advice about where to take his father fishing, Jack never missed a beat.

"Labrador," he said. "That's one of few places left on this continent where fish are still the size God intended them to be, and the wilderness is still wild."

His commanding officer wanted to know more, and Jack was happy to provide any and all information. When his CO asked if he'd like to come along as an informal guide, all expenses paid, Jack could scarcely believe his luck. "Yes, sir," he'd said, immediately. "I'd be glad to."

"My father's an admiral," his CO had warned.

"I know he is, sir. I'll be on my best behavior," Jack promised.

Jack's CO was Stuart McCallum, Jr., son of Admiral Stuart McCallum, the Sea Wolf, who had long been known as the toughest, meanest admiral in the fleet. But if he was a genuine fly fisherman, Jack was sure he'd find some common ground with the crusty old man. He'd been prepared for the worst, but on that trip with the two McCallums he'd made a good friend of the old admiral. They'd fished annually in Labrador until his CO died in a plane crash and the admiral retired that same year. Two years later Jack had taken a midnight phone call on board a ship in the middle of the Persian Gulf.

"McCallum here," the gruff voice said. "I'm in Labrador, looking at a piece of property, and I need your advice."

It took him a while, the Navy being the way it was about unscheduled leave and all that, but the old sea wolf, though retired, still had some pull. Two weeks later Jack was standing on the shore of Grand Lake, a major jumping-off point to all of Labrador's intriguing wilds, and the admiral was saying in his raspy voice, "I want to retire here, Hanson. I want to build a place right on this lake, and I want to build a fishing lodge in the interior that's only accessible by float plane for people who care enough to make the effort. I'm looking for a business partner, if you're interested. How long can you stay?"

Jack stayed as long as he dared, being as he was only a captain himself and not ready or willing to be court-martialed, but when he left, the admiral was already beginning construction of his retirement home. One year later, Jack's marriage was over and he decided to end his naval career as well. True to his words, the admiral readily allowed the younger man to buy into his Labrador dream.

And what a dream it was. That the admiral could harbor ambitions that required such vision and herculean physical effort astounded Jack, who believed himself to be unique in that regard. But the admiral's tireless strength had played out rapidly near the end of the project on the Wolf River. His doctor advised him to return to the States for further tests and chemotherapy treatments, but Admiral McCallum had no use for doctors or hospitals. "I'll die in my own place, and in my own time," he said. "I want to see our lodge on the Wolf River completed. I want to sit on the porch and sip my scotch and watch the river run past. I want to see the salmon come up it to spawn. I need to know that life goes on, no matter what."

They'd both worked hard toward making that vision become a reality, though Jack shouldered the brunt of the work in the final year of the admiral's life. As his health steadily failed, McCallum lost energy but he never lost sight of his dream. The last time Jack had flown the old man into the interior and landed on the river just below the lodge, McCallum had known he'd never live to see it up and running.

"Put my chair on the porch," he said that evening, laboring for each precious breath. "I'll sip my scotch and watch the sun go down."

One week later, the admiral was dead. All of North West River gathered for the traditional Irish wake the old admiral had requested, though McCallum was only half Irish, the other half being pure bull-headed Scot. All of North West River attended the party, a grand send-off the old man would have enjoyed…all except the part where the wedding planner showed up, and Jack won their last bet.

It was one of the few times he and the admiral had spoken about what would come after.

"I've named my granddaughter executor of my estate," McCallum had said. Jack was feeding the sled dogs, and the admiral walked out to the dog yard to smoke his pipe and watch. Retired from the team, Chilkat was his constant companion, but the admiral's faded blue eyes softened as he looked upon the dogs. Clearly, he loved them all.

Jack straightened from ladling soupy dog food into a bowl. "The wedding planner?" he said. "Why not one of your grandsons?"

"They're city boys. They wouldn't want anything to do with a place like this. Senna's the only one who might feel something for it."

Senna McCallum was the only person the admiral regularly spoke of in his family, though he also had two grandsons living somewhere on the East coast and a spinster sister out in Oregon. He'd told Jack about Senna right at the outset on that first fishing trip. "She's a good girl. Spirited, but lacks guidance. Makes all the wrong choices. She'll end up the way most girls do, paying homage to a man that's not good enough for her, raising a bunch of spoiled brats that want and get everything for nothing. Too bad, because she's sharp. She could go places, if she'd just take some good advice, but she doesn't think much of her old grandfather. Never listened to a thing I said."

Since then, he'd made brief but frequent references to Senna, which Jack had strung together into this general assessment: She makes her living planning other people's weddings. Got her degree in wildlife biology, wrote a brilliant paper on the Yellowstone wolf pack and landed a good job with the Department of Inland Fisheries and Wildlife, but couldn't hack the politics. Couldn't compromise what she knew to be right with what would keep her employed. She's too brash, doesn't know when to pull her horns in. Was let go for stirring up all kinds of controversy and bucking the big hunting lobby over the snaring of coyotes and the baiting of bears with stale doughnuts. Spunky. She made the front page of the paper at a big legislative hearing in Augusta. Shortly after that she was conveniently laid off. Her mother's sister owns a country inn on the Maine coast, and her aunt gave her a job there, so now she's nothing but a wedding planner.

A wedding planner was someone who dealt with weepy, emotional brides, bossy overbearing mothers and grooms who didn't realize what the hell they were getting into. Queasy. Jack couldn't imagine a more insipid career, and knew from listening to the admiral talk that he wouldn't like his granddaughter at all. He hoped she never showed up in Labrador.

"She doesn't give a hoot about me," the admiral alleged not a week before his death, puffing on his pipe with a contemplative gaze, "and that's not her fault. I was never a very warm and friendly grandfather. I didn't know how to be. And after her father died I didn't visit them anymore. Senna's mother never liked me much, nor did the boys. It was easier to stay away. I doubt Senna will come to Labrador when I die. But I've made it all nice and legal. Did it yesterday, in Goose Bay, with Granville. Just so you know."

"Yes, sir."

"Wish you'd quit calling me that, son," the admiral said in a quiet voice, gazing out at the dogs.

"Yes, sir."

"She won't come."

Jack stood, holding the five-gallon pail and the dog-food scoop. "She'll come."

The old man shook his head. "Not in a million years."

"Bet you a thousand bucks she shows up."

McCallum's eyes flickered momentarily with that old fighting man's gleam. "You're on, but you'll lose," he said, extending his hand to seal the pact. "Give my winnings to Goody Stewart. She needs the money more than you do, and she's a damn fine woman."

"You should've married her," Jack said.

The admiral turned away with a shake of his head, shoulders bowed beneath the weight of the years and the pain that had beaten him in the end. "I've never been able to make any woman happy. Goody deserves to be happy."

But Goody wasn't going to get the admiral's money, not that there was any to give, because Jack was at this very moment looking into a pair of angry eyes—gray, pale blue?—that belonged to the admiral's grand-daughter.

He struggled up onto his elbows, trying to focus his eyes. Not easy, after the past few days. Damn hard, in fact. Better just to go back to sleep. Sleep it off. Sleep off everything, but she was right in his face, pointing her finger, waving a frying pan, and threatening to bring in the Mounties. Sergeant Preston and all that. He squinted and blinked. She was wearing a dark conservative skirt suit that showed off a pair of the shapeliest legs he'd seen in a dog's age.

He rubbed a hand over his face and wished she'd shut up before his head exploded. There was nothing like a good old-fashioned Irish wake to bring out the best and the worst in a bottle of booze.

She should be planning her own wedding. That's what the admiral had told him about his granddaughter. "She deserves to be barefoot and in the kitchen if planning weddings is all she aspires to." The admiral had set very high standards, and woe to the granddaughter who lowered the bar, intentionally or not.

"Or not," Jack muttered, interrupting Senna McCallum's diatribe about how she was here to settle the admiral's estate and had no intentions of playing cook and housekeeper to a hungover heathen who couldn't even sit up in bed. He was pleased that his words had startled her into momentary silence, giving him another chance to eye those slender, feminine legs.

"Or not what?" she said, spine stiffening, frying pan lowering a bit. Her hair was gorgeous, the rich gloss of mahogany framing an equally beautiful and expressive face that just now was scowling on the stern side, but he bet that when she smiled her radiance would shame the sun. And damn, those legs of hers would rival any high-paid model's...

"You didn't deliberately get yourself discharged from your wildlife job just to spite the admiral. It was purely accidental," Jack said. "I'm sure of it."

"What are you talking about?" She recoiled as if he were rabid.

"Your grandfather told me all about you, but he never mentioned how good you looked in a skirt."

If anything, her demeanor became more hostile and her eyes narrowed with suspicion. "Then you really are John Hanson."

"I prefer Jack," he said. He extended his hand. "Pleased to meet you."

She declined to shake his hand, taking yet another step back instead. "We need to talk," she said.

Jack needed aspirin, strong coffee and a lot more sleep, but since obviously none of these mercies were forthcoming, he sat up, very slowly, and attempted once again to focus his eyes on the young woman standing in his bedroom. "We threw a wake for your grandfather yesterday…or was it the day before? I've lost track. Damned sorry you had to see the place in such a mess, but it was a good old-fashioned Irish wake, just like the admiral wanted, and I'm not sorry about that. He deserved a good send-off."

In spite of the effort this explanation had cost him, there wasn't an ounce of sympathy or understanding in her expression. "That explains all the trash. I'm here to settle his estate and I had hoped to be able to discuss this with you as soon as possible, but I can see that's not going to be any time soon." She paused to glance down at the dog. "Is your dog about to attack me?"

Jack glanced at Chilkat, who was still eyeing her intently. "Like I told you before, he just wants to clean the grease out of the frying pan you're holding. That's his job and he takes it very seriously. And for your information, that dog belongs to you now, Ms. McCallum. His name is Chilkat, and he was your grandfather's lap dog. A real cuddler. I'll introduce you to the rest of the pack when you're ready, but there are some things you need to understand. The admiral and I were full business partners, the lake house was part of the business, and you're standing in my bedroom."

The admiral's granddaughter looked confused. "Do you mean to say that the two of you shared this house? You lived here together?"

"Even Steven."

"Then…who lives in that other cabin?"

Hopeless. He'd known it would be. Who could understand the bond between himself and that irascible stiff-backed admiral who had scoffed at Jack's plan to build a separate cabin for his own use, and then, when the cabin was complete, had suggested using it for a workshop. Who would understand that gruff old admiral was a lonely soul who *liked* sharing the lake house? Certainly not this young woman with the mahogany hair and the beautiful face which unfortunately seemed to be marred by a permanent and disapproving scowl.

"Nobody," Jack said. "We use it for a workshop."

She digested this as cheerfully as she had everything else. "And just how am I supposed to sell my grandfather's half of this property while you're living here and the place looks like a pigsty?"

Jack's headache was getting worse with every beat of his heart, as was the day in general, or what was left of it. He sat up and swung his legs over the edge of the bed with a silent groan. "That sounds like a personal problem to me. Tell you what. If you're that hard up for a quick buck, I'll pay you a dollar if you make a pot of coffee for me," he said. She was still brandishing the frying pan as though she'd like to whale him with it, and her nervous movements were making him dizzy and more than a little nauseous.

"This is not a joking matter," she said.

"I'm not joking. I'll pay you up front if you don't believe me." And then, as she began to erupt, he raised his hand. "Look, lady, like it or not, I own half of this house, half of the smaller cabin, half of a very mangy pack of sled dogs, half of the plane, half of the fishing lodge, and one half of each of those rusted-out trucks. Get used to it." He gave her as challenging a stare as he could, given the circumstances. "The admiral and I were full business partners. I sank everything I had into it, and have no regrets except two. Your grandfather up and died on me, and he left his half of the business to you."

Jack stood cautiously, holding onto the headboard. The room remained still. Good. If he could just get some fresh air, he'd be able to keep his stomach down. He reached for a clean undershirt. Rummaged in the bureau for a clean pair of socks, donned his favorite flannel shirt, and pulled on his boots. All the while she stood in the doorway, holding that big, greasy frying pan and watching him with the wary expression of a prison guard getting ready to move a dangerous prisoner into a maximum security cell.

"I'm sensing a streak of voyeurism in you, Ms. McCallum," he observed as he picked his wallet off the bureau and removed a dollar. He held the coin out to her enticingly, but she clearly had no intentions of playing along. He sighed, stuffed it into his pocket, and looked around for Chilkat. "C'mon, dog," he said. "She isn't about to let you lick the pan." Chilkat stood. "Chilkat can stay with me, at least for tonight. That'll give you some time to settle in and take a reality check, but don't think I'm hauling anchor permanently. I'll be back tomorrow." He glanced around, wincing. "Hope you'll have the place cleaned up by then. Feel free to start with my room."

"Where are you going?" Still frowning, still suspicious.

"I have a sweet-natured friend in Goose Bay. She's always glad to see me, and she makes a great pot of coffee. I'll save myself a buck and get a smile for a change."

She had to turn sideways to let him out of the room, and he heard her footsteps following him down the stairs and out onto the porch. At the bottom of the porch steps he glanced back. She was watching him with that same wary stare and still gripping that damn frying pan. "Oh, and by the way," he said. "The sled dogs'll need to be fed pretty soon. We feed them twice a day, meat stew or frozen fish in the morning and a soupy kibble mix at night. Water morning and night. The feed's kept in the small cabin out back, along with everything else you'll need. There's a list of the dogs' names pinned to the door, and their names are on their dog houses, too. Follow the path behind the cabin. The dog yard's just beyond the treeline, no more than a hundred yards from here. If you get lost, just listen. They howl like a pack of wolves." He gave her legs one final appreciative stare. "I suggest you change your clothes before tackling that job."

He turned and started for his truck, Chilkat trotting at his heels.

"Wait!" he heard her cry out as he reached for the door handle. Jack paused then turned. "You can't leave without showing me how to take care of the dogs." She was looking and sounding a tad distraught.

"Right now, I need a gallon of strong coffee and a sympathetic friend. The dogs probably won't bite you as long as you put the frying pan down before you go into the dog yard. They don't like being threatened any more than I do."

The color in her cheeks deepened as she looked at the skillet, then back at him. "I'm sorry, but when I first arrived, I didn't know who you were." She waved her free hand about her head to drive off the mosquitoes. "I'll make you a pot of coffee, Mr. Hanson, if you'll just show me how to feed the dogs before you go. Please."

Jack stood for a moment, considering her offer. "I dunno," he said, rubbing his jaw. He thought for a few seconds just to make her suffer a bit more. "I'll stay, but only if you promise to serve that joe with a pretty smile."

"Thank you, Mr. Hanson. I'll put the pot on." She spun on her heel, still wearing that disapproving scowl and carrying the greasy frying pan. The screen door banged shut behind her.

He shook his head and glanced down at Chilkat, who never did get to lick the pan and so understood completely when he said, "No sense of humor."

"THIS IS BANE," Hanson said, speaking over the collective howls of twenty impressive-looking huskies less than thirty minutes later, having consumed an entire eight-cup pot of black coffee and looking marginally improved. "He's an Inuit husky, like the others, only he's considerably smarter than the rest. He was your grandfather's lead dog. The admiral ran him up front with Belle, the dog next to him. Just remember, you can't run Bane next to another male. He'll kill him."

"I believe it," Senna said, keeping her distance from the thick-coated, yellow-eyed and very muscular sled dog. "And I have no intention of running any of them." All of the huskies were behaving as if they would cheerfully tear each other apart if their stout chains didn't keep them from doing so. "Are they always this aggressive?"

"Only when they're awake. Here, I'll show you how to scoop the food, and in what order the dogs should be fed," he said, taking the heavy five-gallon bucket out of her hand. He held a one-quart ladle in the other, and he made a rapid circuit of the dog yard, emptying two buckets before he was done and making frequent asides as he bent over each food dish. "This is Tiny. A real hard worker for her size and a sweetheart, too, aren't you, girl?" The small slender husky's ears flattened back at his voice, her eyes gleaming with pleasure. "And this is the mighty Quinn. My lead dog. The best of the best, better than Bane, and he knows it, too. Look at him. He thinks the world's his dog bone."

Senna laughed in spite of herself as Jack filled Quinn's dish and the sled dog dove in. "They sure like to eat."

"These dogs likes to eat almost as much as they likes to fight," he said with a touch of Granville's rough Celtic brogue. He grinned at her for the first time and Senna felt an immediate whole-body response. "So. Think you can feed them by yourself tomorrow morning?" he asked as she struggled with an erratic heartbeat.

Senna shook her head, feeling the heat rush to her

face. "No. I mean, tomorrow's different. Mornings, the dogs get meat, right? I haven't seen that yet. You'll have to show me at least once, so I can get the hang of it."

He picked up the empty buckets. "Okay. My friendly friend in Goose Bay awaits, but I'll plan on being back here by 7:00 a.m."

Senna followed him through the gate. The dog yard was completely enclosed by a seven-foot-tall wire fence to keep the dogs safe from the wolves, or so Jack had informed her. She closed and latched the gate behind her and had to practically trot to keep pace as he strode back down the path toward the lake and the house. "Look, it's getting late," she blurted, swatting at clouds of mosquitoes as they emerged into the open and lake water sparkled through the black spruce. "I'll fix you another pot of coffee, if you like. We have lots to discuss. Business-related things. You could tell me something about my grandfather's life here, all the things he did, and give me an idea of all the affairs I'll need to straighten out before I leave. Maybe you should just stay…."

He acted as if she hadn't spoken, kicking open the cabin door and setting the buckets on the floor by a deep laundry sink. The cabin brimmed with all the paraphernalia of an arctic expedition. Several dogsleds were suspended from the purlins, except for one which was on a work bench apparently having some maintenance done. Snowshoes, pack baskets, fly rods, two large canvas canoes, sacks of dry dog food, two big chest freezers, countless five-gallon buckets, shelves filled with tools and paint cans… Senna gazed about her in awe as Jack washed his hands at the laundry sink, wondering at this secret life of her grandfather's.

"I'm sorry we got off on the wrong foot. Maybe we

should start over," Senna began again as he reached for a towel. "I'm a very good cook...."

He leaned his rump against the sink as he dried his hands. That grin of his kick-started her heart again. "Is that so?" he said, his gaze holding hers a little too closely for comfort.

"I'll fix supper for you," she said, suddenly feeling uncomfortably warm. "You'll feel much better with some food in your stomach."

His grin broadened. He turned and hung the towel back up then went to one of the chest freezers and lifted the lid. "How are you with wild beasts?"

She moved to stand beside him and peer into the dim recesses. Half of the freezer seemed to be allocated to blocks of dog meat, the other to packages wrapped in freezer paper. She picked one up. "What kind of wild beasts?"

"The smaller packages are caribou. The larger are moose. Your choice. The cuts are written on the package."

"I've never had caribou."

"Have you ever tried moose?"

"I'm from Maine, Mr. Hanson. Of course I have."

"If you liked moose, you'll like caribou even better. And please don't call me Mr. Hanson. Jack works just fine for me."

Senna lowered her eyes. "How many packages?"

"Two if by caribou, one if by moose."

Senna chose two of the caribou steaks. "Caribou it is, then, and whatever else might be in the kitchen."

"No promises. Your grandfather was particular about his fare, but he didn't eat much in his final weeks, and I haven't paid much attention to the larder since he died. My guess is that the wake cleaned the cupboards out." He gave her a quizzical look. "What day is it, anyway?"

"Tuesday," Senna said, and then, wondering, asked, "What day did you have the wake?"

"It began Saturday afternoon, right after the service," Jack said.

"Did many people attend?" Senna asked, curious as to what kind of friendships her grandfather had made in this faraway place.

"The church was packed. There were some hymns and singing, and the preacher said all the necessary words. Then John Snow Boy spoke. Too bad no one could understand what he was saying because I'm sure it was better than the preacher's spiel."

"Was he drunk, too?"

Jack uttered a short laugh. "John Snow Boy doesn't drink, but he speaks English, Inuit and Innu fluently. Trouble is, he mixes them all up into his own language. We call it Innisht. Very colorful but way beyond interpretation. Afterward, there was a pot latch, that's traditional in this neck of the woods, and then we all came here for the wake. Goody made sure all the kids were herded back home by midnight, and to tell the truth, I don't remember much after that."

Senna held the two icy packages of caribou and followed Jack as he left the cabin and headed toward the lake house. "Mr. Granville mentioned he had a sister named Goody."

"Goody Stewart. Kindest soul that ever walked this earth. She lost her husband eight years ago, and then fell in love with your grandfather. Would've married him, if he'd only asked." Jack never slowed as he spoke, just strode along in that big way of his that Senna was beginning to learn.

"Why didn't he?" she asked, struggling to keep up as he climbed the porch stairs and opened the door.

"He said she deserved to be happy," Jack replied, giving her the briefest of glances as he passed through the doorway and headed for the kitchen. He gave the room a quick three-sixty and shook his head. "By God, if Goody ever saw the place like this, she'd skin me alive. Those steaks should thaw quick enough if we put them in cold water. Meanwhile, I'll take you out to the lake where we can begin discussing our new partnership."

He held out his hand for the packages of caribou, sealed them up tightly in a plastic bag, then placed them in a large kettle of water on the countertop. Chilkat watched all of this with his intense wolfish expression but remained plastered to Jack's side.

"There's no partnership to discuss," Senna said. "I'm selling my grandfather's half of the business, and I have two weeks to get everything in order."

"Two weeks," Jack said. "That's not much time, considering what you have to see and do. You'll change your mind about selling the business when you see it. Bug juice." He handed her a can of mosquito repellent as he headed for the door. "Be liberal with it."

"What exactly *is* there to see?" Senna hurried after him, aware that her heart rate was way above normal. Undoubtedly she was stressed about this executor stuff, but she guessed that Jack Hanson's insufferable arrogance might have a little bit to do with it, as well.

"You've met the dogs," Jack narrated over his shoulder as he strode toward the dock, "you've seen the gear, the supplies, the houses. I'll show you the plane, and maybe tomorrow, first thing, I'll fly you out to the river to see the lodge. It's accessible only by float plane or boat." He was stepping onto the weather-bleached boards of the dock, and she was right on his heels.

"You're a licensed pilot?"

"I'm legal, and I have the paperwork to prove it."

"How far away are these places you want to show me?"

"Far enough so's you'll know you're away from it all." His eyes glinted with something akin to daring as he came to a halt and gestured to the plane tethered to the end of the dock. "The plane's good to go, if you are."

Senna teetered beside him as the dock rocked beneath her feet. She stared dubiously at the aircraft. "It looks ancient."

"She's a sweet old girl, a four-passenger Cessna 195. They don't build 'em like this anymore," he said, giving the bright-yellow wing that overhung the dock an affectionate slap, as if it were a favorite work horse.

"What year is it?"

"Nineteen fifty, sporting a Pratt and Whitney 985. Beautiful motor."

"Dear God, that's older than ancient. And my grandfather owns half of it?"

"The half that never breaks down," he said with a grin. "So. What do you think of the view? This lake's four miles across and forty miles long."

Senna looked across the lake to the far shore. "It's a big lake," she said, thinking that this land was lonely and isolated and more than a little forbidding, yet compelling in a way that made her want to see much more of it. "A big land. Are there any towns out there?"

Jack squinted across the distance and nodded.

"Standing on this dock we're looking almost due north. About a thousand miles in that direction there's a village called Kangiqsualuiuaq, on Ungava Bay. Across the Hudson Strait is Baffin Island, and there a few native settlements on that, as well."

"You mean to say that the nearest town to our north is a thousand miles from here?"

"Could be a little closer as the crow flies," Jack admitted. He grinned again at her expression. "Most folks up here follow the waterways, and they seldom run in a straight line. Ever read about the Hubbard expedition?"

Senna shook her head.

"Three men started out on this very same lake, trying to reach the George River and head north to Ungava Bay. Two of them made it back, but Hubbard starved to death."

Senna gazed out across the vast wilderness. "Let me get this straight. We're standing here on the edge of nowhere, but that wasn't wild enough for my grandfather. He had to build a lodge even farther out?"

"For fishing," Jack said, as if that were a reasonable explanation.

Senna gestured impatiently at the lake. "Are you saying there's no fish *here?*"

"Oh, there's damn good fishing here, but Goose Bay's just a hop, skip and a jump away, and where there are towns, there are people. On a busy day you might see four or five boats from this very dock, and float planes droning around carrying sports from away. You know."

Senna shook her head, bewildered. The lake was vast. Four or five hundred boats could have fished all day and never caught sight of each other. "I don't get it. Was my grandfather a recluse?"

Jack rubbed a jaw that was dark with stubble. "Maybe," he shrugged. "Hell, maybe we both were, maybe that's why we got along so well. But first and foremost, he was a fisherman."

"I never thought of him as anything but an admiral," Senna confessed. "I can't even picture him in casual clothing with a fishing pole in his hand." She paused. "So, the lodge was a place my grandfather built so he could be completely isolated from other fishermen?"

"No. We built the lodge to run as a sporting camp for people who wanted a genuine wilderness fishing experience."

Senna shook her head, increasingly baffled. "My *grandfather* wanted to run a sporting camp?"

"What's so strange about that?"

"I happen to work in the hospitality industry," Senna explained, "and I know that to be successful you have to make people feel warm and welcome. The admiral just didn't have the ability to be warm and welcoming. In fact I found him to be quite scary and intimidating."

Jack was studying her with eyes that sparkled with humor. "You might be surprised at how sociable he could be. Gruffly sociable, that is."

"We weren't very close," Senna admitted as she shoved her hands into her jacket pockets. "We didn't get along that well. In fact, I hadn't seen him since my father's funeral. No one in the family even knew where he went after my father's death. He just disappeared. Never wrote, never answered any letters, never showed up for another Christmas."

"That's too bad. You missed out. Both of you did."

Jack turned on his heel and started back toward the house.

"Look, we need to talk about splitting up the business," Senna said, hurrying after him. "Who's going to want to buy half of an old plane?"

"That 'old plane' happens to be a valuable classic," he said over his shoulder. "Don't worry, someone'll pay a good chunk of change for her."

"Maybe, but nobody would want to buy just half of a plane, no matter how valuable a classic it is." Senna hurried after him. "Look, why don't *you* buy out my grandfather's half of the business? It makes perfect sense. You helped to build it. A bank would probably loan you the money, and..."

Jack stopped so abruptly she nearly ran into him. He rounded on her and a broad sweep of his arm took in the entire surrounds. "Lady, I love this place and I'd mortgage my soul to buy out the admiral's share, but no bank would look twice at me." He paused for a moment, his gaze keen, the breeze off the lake tousling his dark hair. "Why don't you just *keep* your grandfather's half of this business? Why are you so damn anxious to sell something he worked so hard to create?"

Senna felt the heat in her face. "I already have a career, Mr. Hanson, and it doesn't involve Labrador."

"No, it involves planning other people's weddings. I got that part. But this place'll grow on you, I guarantee it, and the fishing lodge will generate enough income to make you happy even if you're an absentee business partner living and working in Maine." He towered over her, his eyes intense. "We're only two weeks away from opening. I have most of the help lined up, I just need to find another fishing guide or two. At least think about keeping your grandfather's half. But know this," he added. "If you decide to sell out, I'm not going to make it easy for you. I've worked my ass off to help make this place what it is. This is my future we're talking about, not to mention your grandfather's lifelong dream."

Before Senna could respond, he wheeled and strode away, leaving her standing on the dock and staring after him. He walked the way a mountain lion would, with smoothly controlled grace and power…and a strong hint of sinuous swagger. Her heartbeat was erratic and she was having trouble catching her breath. Her inner voice warned, Watch out. He's dangerous. Wild and unpredictable, just like that mountain lion. Dangerous he might be, and overbearing and conceited, but had a man ever looked so damned sexy in a pair of faded Levi's and a flannel shirt?

Senna's life, up until this very day, had been fairly steady, safe and predictable, but suddenly she found herself smack dab in the middle of a whole bunch of unknowns—and in spite of the dubious circumstances, she found herself looking forward to exploring them, even if it was just for two weeks.

CHAPTER THREE

BY THE TIME THE CARIBOU STEAKS had thawed in their cold-water bath, Senna had done a fairly competent job of cleaning the kitchen, a mandatory task before undertaking supper preparations. While she scrubbed and swept, Jack corralled the trash left behind in the aftermath of her grandfather's wake. He filled four big trash bags with beer cans, bottles and other various and assorted rubbish. Senna regretted not having time to wash the windows, but there were two more weeks of tomorrows to get everything accomplished before she returned to Maine. She stood at the sink gazing out at the lake, the waters sparkling golden at sunset, shimmering like a vast molten ocean of fire. She spotted the dark silhouette of a pair of loons just beyond the dock and was watching them, hands submerged in hot soapy dish water, when Jack's voice startled her from behind.

"Charles and Diana," he said, looking over her shoulder. "They nest on an island not far from here, and every year they raise two or three chicks. Just about every night of the summer, the admiral would walk out on the dock, smoke his pipe, and listen to the two of them call back and forth."

He was standing so near that when she turned her head to speak she almost hit her chin on his shoulder.

Her heart thumped as she looked up at him. "Are we talking about the same man?"

"The one and only Admiral Stuart Anderson McCallum."

"Charles and Diana?"

"You're the wedding planner. You should get that part pretty easy." He continued to stand so close that she could smell the warm scent of his skin, which was one-hundred-percent masculine. No aftershave or cologne for this down-to-earth woodsman.

"As I recall," Senna commented, her hands still submerged in the dishpan, "Charles and Diana were divorced."

"But the early days were like a fairy tale. C'mon, admit it. Every girl dreams of a royal courtship like that."

"How would you know?" Senna said.

"My ex-wife was a big fan of Princess Diana."

"Is that why you named the loons after the royal couple?"

"Your grandfather named them. He said the pair had a formal look to them, a kind of pomp and circumstance that befit a royal family. And the way those two talk to each other sometimes, it's like they know all the tragedies the future holds for them."

Senna looked back out the window, flustered by his nearness. "Maybe they do," she said softly.

"Think I have time for a quick shower before supper?" Jack asked, leaning over the sink for a closer look at the loons and brushing his shoulder against hers. Accident? She doubted it. John Hanson possessed enough arrogance to keep ten men puffed up and strutting around like roosters.

"Yes, plenty," Senna said, focusing on scrubbing a plate and breathing, two mundane tasks that had suddenly become extremely difficult. She wished he wouldn't stand so close, and when she felt him move away and heard his footsteps climbing the stairs she glanced over her shoulder with a frown. Was he planning on making a pass at her tonight? After all, they'd be sleeping under the same roof and sharing the same living spaces for the next two weeks. He probably thought if he seduced her, he could change her mind about selling her half of the business...as if she'd ever allow that to happen!

Senna rinsed the plate and put it in the dish rack with a sudden twinge of guilt. She'd forgotten to call her mother. She'd promised to let her know the moment she arrived and now it was almost eight o'clock. She wiped her hands on the dish towel, retrieved her cell phone from the rental car and walked out onto the dock to give herself the best wide-open shot at reception before dialing. Nothing happened. No call went through. The little screen on the cell phone's face said, "No Signal" and the tiny bar codes that indicated the signal strength didn't even begin to register. She tried several more times before giving up.

Damn! She'd have to drive clear into North West River just to call her mother to let her know she was okay. She entered the house at the same time Jack was descending the stairs and they met head-on. "That was a mighty quick shower," she said, taken aback by the suddenness of his appearance. He'd shaved, nicking himself in a couple of spots. His hair was damp and disheveled. He was wearing a reasonably clean set of clothes along the same lines as the original—jeans, undershirt with a flannel shirt pulled over, unbuttoned down the front and sleeves rolled back He looked virile and disturbingly handsome.

"Mighty quick and mighty cold," he agreed amiably. "You used up every last drop of hot water cleaning the kitchen."

"Oh!" Senna felt her cheeks burn. "I'm sorry...."

"Don't be. The kitchen looks great." He glanced at the cell phone she held. "Were you trying to call someone?"

"Yes," Senna said. She kept recalling the heart-stopping sight of that mountain lion she'd seen, that wild, powerful symbol of strength and grace that reminded her so much of Jack Hanson.

"Why not use the house phone?" Jack asked, one eyebrow raised. "You'll get a helluva lot better reception. Cell phones don't work here. No towers."

"I didn't know there was a regular phone."

"In the living room on the end table."

"If there's a phone, where are the phone lines? I saw no telephone poles for the last half mile of road."

"Underground cable. The admiral didn't like the idea of wires strung everywhere. The electric and phone cable was expensive, but considering the wild storms we get up here on the Labrador, it was a good idea."

"I see." Senna stared at him for a moment more, unable to help herself. He possessed an animal magnetism that was stronger than anything she'd ever encountered. "Supper will be a little late. I'll get started right after this phone call."

He nodded, brushing past her on his way to the kitchen. He smelled faintly of soap, and the residual scents of wood smoke and mosquito repellent that clung to his clothing. He smelled good.

Senna wandered into the living room, the next room on her cleaning agenda. It was a masculine room whose focal point was a big stone fireplace flanked by deep bookshelves. The wall of large windows overlooked the lake, and the comfortable rustic furnishings were well suited to the lake house's character. She located the phone and sank down on the couch, tucking her legs beneath her as she lifted the receiver. Moments later she was speaking to her mother, who was anxious to hear about everything. Senna heard the screen door bang and craned to look out the window. She spied Jack walking out toward the dock, Chilkat by his side. Good. He wouldn't overhear.

She abruptly interrupted their staid conversation about legal matters and as quickly as she could she filled her mother in on the true state of her grandfather's Labrador affairs. "This is going to be much more complicated than I expected, given the fact that everything was co-owned in a full business partnership," Senna concluded. "Tomorrow Jack's flying me out to see the lodge. I only hope it's in good repair and won't take too long to sell."

"What's he like?" her mother asked.

"Jack? Oh, he's okay, I guess, a little younger than I expected...."

"Why doesn't he just buy out your grandfather's half of the business?"

"He told me the banks wouldn't look twice at him."

"You hardly know this man, Senna. Do you think he's safe to fly with?"

"Mom, don't worry. I have a feeling he's a very good

pilot. I'll call you tomorrow night. Right now I have to get supper started. I promised I'd cook if he showed me how to tend the sled dogs."

"Sled dogs?"

"Huskies. The real thing. Twenty of them."

"Goodness. Senna, Tim called. He tried to reach you at your apartment and got worried when he couldn't. I told him about your grandfather dying and that you had to go to Labrador. He sounds pretty down."

"I'll call him. Bye, Mom. Love you." Senna sat for a moment after hanging up and then dialed Tim's number, peering out the window once again while the call went through. Jack was doing something with the airplane. The door was open and he was inside. Good, twice over. She especially didn't want him to hear this conversation.

Tim answered on the third ring. "I'm sorry I bothered your mother, but I was worried," he said. "Are you all right?"

"Fine. My grandfather's death was unexpected and he named me as his executor. I'll probably be here for two weeks settling his estate. It's very beautiful and remote country."

"I can imagine," he commented. "They probably still travel by dog team there." After an awkward pause, he said, "How's everything going?"

"As well as can be expected. My grandfather owned half shares in a business that includes a lake house, a fishing lodge and an airplane, which complicates things. Somehow I have to find a buyer for his shares. How are things with you?"

"Okay. I landed that big account I've been working

on. Ameri-Dyne. You know, the huge dental practice off
Forest Ave."

"Wow, that's great news, Tim," she said. "Congratulations. I know how hard you've been working for that."
Senna caught a flash of movement outside the window
and saw Jack and Chilkat walking toward the house.
"Tim? I have to go. I have a meeting with my grandfather's business partner."

"I miss you, Senna. Let me know if you need anything at all," he said, sounding forlorn.

"I will," she promised.

Senna was sick with guilt as she attacked supper
preparations in the kitchen. Sooner or later Tim would
realize that their relationship was over. But that didn't
ease the pain he was feeling now, and she was the cause
of it. He adored her. Was she wrong to break things off?
Why couldn't she love him the way he loved her? Senna
gave herself a mental shake. This was no time to be
dwelling on her relationship with Tim. She had a meal
to prepare. Caribou steaks, russet potatoes scrounged
from a musty sack of sprouting spuds she found in a
lower cupboard, and canned corn. In the refrigerator she
unearthed two sticks of butter, several fist-sized chunks
of mold that might once have been vegetables, endless
half-empty jars of condiments and a container of very
sour milk. This wouldn't pass for a gourmet meal by any
standards, but Senna realized as she slipped the
scrubbed potatoes into the oven that such standards no
longer mattered. She hadn't eaten since breakfast and
was ravenous.

By the time Jack wandered into the house, carrying
what looked like a shapeless snarl of nylon webbing,
things were reasonably under control. "It'll be another

forty-five minutes," she called out as he dropped into a chair in the living room, the webbing in his lap, and began threading a large curved needle from a spool of dental floss. "I hope you can wait that long."

"That's just about right," he replied, concentrating as he drew the floss through the needle. "Mending these harnesses will probably take that long or better." He picked up a piece of webbing that had been chewed in half and lit a match to melt the ragged ends before beginning to stitch the harness back together. "So," he said, jabbing the needle into the thick webbing. "Have you given any thought to keeping your share of the business?"

Senna moved toward the living room, crossed her arms in front of her and leaned against the door frame. "No. I mean, yes, I have, but no, I don't want to own half of a fishing lodge, thank you very much. Don't you have a friend or relative who might be interested in buying my grandfather's share?"

"Nope." He drew the floss through the harness, pulled the thread tight and cast a brief glance in her direction. "There aren't that many people out there as crazy as the admiral and me. What about your brothers? You have two of them, don't you?"

"Yes. Billy's a computer programmer for a large engineering firm in Boston, and Bryce is a market analyst living in New York City."

"Do they fish?"

"No, nor are they or their wives particularly outdoorsy."

His shoulders slumped. "That explains it, then."

"Explains what?"

"Why the admiral named you as his executor. You were his last great hope."

Senna felt a flush of anger heat her blood. "Are you certain the banks won't loan you the money?"

"I've already looked into it. Even if the bank appraisal came in high enough, there's no surety there. I don't have a steady job, and the fishing lodge hasn't generated any income yet. I'd have to have a co-signor to get any sort of mortgage, and I can't think of a soul on earth who'd be crazy enough to co-sign a loan for me." He paused for a moment, needle poised in mid-air, eyes fixed on a point somewhere between Senna and Baffin Island, then shook his head in a gesture of defeat and returned his attention to mending the harness.

"Why did my grandfather keep sled dogs?" Senna asked, abruptly changing the subject to avoid further jabs from Hanson.

"He liked them. He met a trapper from a village near Mud Lake who was selling his team. The admiral bought the dogs, the komatik and a bunch of traps. He decided he was going to make some money on furs."

Senna felt a twist of revulsion as she pictured the pained and frightened creatures caught in the steel leghold traps. "I think trapping's cruel and awful and ought to be outlawed."

Jack uttered a short laugh. "So did he, after about a month of it. It was brutal work. The snow here is so damn deep and unpackable that the dogs had to swim through it hauling that heavy sled. The admiral would try to break the trail on snowshoes, but he couldn't keep ahead of the team. The leaders would run up on the tails of his shoes and he'd pitch head first into the snow. So he recruited me as his trail breaker, but my trapping career spanned less than a day. I tell you what, it's not easy getting out of deep snow when you fall facefirst into it. A couple of times I was sure I was going to suffocate."

"Did my grandfather ever catch anything?"

"Pneumonia, after one particularly grueling night out. Then he ran into some folks who were touring on snowmobiles. They asked if they could have a ride on the dogsled, so the admiral gave them a ride. They gave him a couple of hundred bucks for his efforts, and that was the end of his trapping adventures. He sold the traps, advertised dogsled rides at the airport and in some local stores at Goose Bay and pretty soon the phone began to ring. That's why he kept the dogs." Jack paused with a faint grin. "Well, that's not the entire reason. He kept them because he came to love them, and believe it or not, that brutish pack felt the same way about him."

Senna tried to picture the admiral mushing a team of huskies down an arctic trail, clad in mukluks and a fur parka, but she couldn't. Nor could she imagine him stroking the head of a dog with genuine affection. It was as if Jack were talking about a complete stranger. She was beginning to realize just how little she knew about her own grandfather. "Are there any pictures?"

Jack paused. "Goody has some, I think, and I have a few. Mostly fishing pictures, a few winter shots of the dog teams. The pictures your grandfather took were of wildlife. Wolves, in particular. He was fascinated by them. But if you want mushing pictures, you'll have to dig through his papers. The admiral must have stashed some here, somewhere, probably in his desk. That's where he kept all the important stuff. He did his writing there, too."

"Writing?" Yet another surprise.

"He kept a journal," Jack said, concentrating on his

stitching. "He wrote in long hand into a spiral notebook every night."

Senna imagined that the entries would be terse and to the point. *Rained today. Worked on chimney. Beans for supper.* That sort of thing. Still, maybe she'd get lucky. Maybe he'd bared his soul and explained why the heck he'd named her as his executor. She would read his journal when she found it, every last word. But what was she supposed to do with all his personal belongings, his clothes, the pictures on the walls. Have a yard sale? That seemed so callous, so unfeeling. Maybe an open house would be a better idea, inviting all the admiral's friends to choose what they might want after Jack had taken what he wanted. She should, after all, give her grandfather's business partner and closest friend first dibs.

Odd that the admiral hadn't left anything to Jack. He could have given him his half of the business and made Senna's job much easier, but all he'd written in his will, in neat, black ink, were two sentences. The first sentence stated, To my granddaughter, Senna McCallum, I leave all my worldly goods for her to dispose of as she sees fit. And the second; To my business partner and friend, John William Hanson, I bequeath memories of many good times shared, and hopes for even better times in the future.

How odd that he would trust her to dispose of his worldly goods as she saw fit. The admiral hadn't thought anything she'd done to be "fit" in her entire life. As Senna pondered the relative whose blood ran through her veins, a bitter memory surfaced, one that illustrated the relationship she and her grandfather had shared. Tim had accompanied her to her father's funeral. They'd only just begun dating and he was sweet to be so supportive during that terrible time, but her grandfather hadn't missed the opportunity to take her aside during the family gathering held afterward at her mother's house. "I certainly hope you're not planning to marry *that* one," he'd said in his stern and judgmental way.

"He was kind of religious about it," Jack said, startling her back to the present.

"About what?" Senna asked.

"Writing in his journal. He'd spend an hour or so at that desk every night." Jack had stopped stitching the harness as he spoke and was gazing across the room at the admiral's desk as if he were seeing the old man sitting there, writing, or pacing in front of the window, smoking his pipe. "He never said much about his life, and I never asked, but I have a feeling it's all there, in that journal."

Senna straightened, glanced over at the massive old desk, and moved toward it. There were three deep drawers on either side and she opened the top left hand one, spying a book, but not a spiral notebook. She lifted the leather-bound ledger, embossed with gold lettering across the front: Wolf River Lodge, with a logo of a howling wolf engraved beneath it. She laid the ledger on the desk and opened it. It was a reservation book for the fishing lodge. She flipped through the empty pages until she reached the month of June and then she paused. From the last week in June on, there were names written into six of the spaces for each and every day.

She turned the pages into July and August, swiftly scanning the names, the phone numbers jotted next to them, the addresses scribbled below. People from all over the United States. People from England and France and Germany. One party from Australia was booked for three weeks solid. The bookings petered out in September, and then from November on there were occasional reservations. She supposed that was for the dogsledding, but she wasn't sure. She closed the book and stood with her hand atop it for a moment, then picked it up and moved to where Jack worked on the harnesses.

"You said the lodge wasn't ready yet?"

He glanced up, saw that she held the reservation book, and shook his head. "Not quite, but the majority of the work is done, there's just a bunch of small stuff left, and about a ton of supplies to be flown in."

"Some of these guests are scheduled to arrive just two weeks from now...."

"I know." A look of pride crossed his face. "We're practically booked for the summer."

"Now that the admiral's dead, how's that going to work, exactly?"

"I'll get the hired help in there right away to get the lodge ready, get the rest of the provisions flown in, find another fishing guide or two, and give 'er hell all summer long. At least, that's the plan."

"What if you're not ready in time?"

"We will be."

"Are all these reservations pretty firm?"

"They've all paid a deposit, and the deadline's past for them to cancel. Don't worry, they'll show."

"How much of a deposit did they pay?" Senna asked.

"Half of their stay. A lot of money." He paused again as if considering his words carefully. "Actually, it's a damn good thing nobody canceled, because we used all of those advance deposits to finish building the lodge."

"I see," she said, standing and cradling the leather reservation book against her chest. "So there is absolutely no buffer in the bank account?"

"No. Matter of fact, the business account is dead empty. The admiral's life insurance will no doubt cover his cremation fees and legal expenses and some of his medical bills, and maybe it'll help a lot more than that, but I had to borrow money for the wake. Goody said I could pay her back at the end of the summer."

"Assuming you go ahead with the start-up, what were you planning to buy the food with, and how are you going to pay the help for the three weeks until the first guests depart and settle up for the balance of what they owe when they do?" Senna asked, steeling herself for the answer.

He hesitated, then jabbed the needle into the webbing again. "I was kind of hoping you'd help out," he said, talking to the harness to avoid meeting her eyes. "I mean, we're business partners now, for better or for worse."

"It's definitely for worse, and very temporary." Senna walked back to the desk, returned the ledger to the top drawer and drew a deep breath. She wondered how she was going to juggle this latest bombshell. Was she going to have to use her entire life savings to bail her grandfather's business out of the red? Might as well beard the giant and find out. "Exactly how much money are we talking about?" she said.

Jack didn't hesitate. He'd obviously already figured things out. "The way I figure it, including the food and provisions, the diesel fuel for the generator, gas for the boats and the plane, insurance, wages for the employees…maybe ten thousand?"

Senna straightened her spine, raised her chin and drew a steadying breath. "Ten thousand dollars. A mere pittance. Well, I suppose I should start cooking those caribou steaks," she said, and marched into the kitchen.

JACK LISTENED TO THE SOUNDS of domestic industry coming from the kitchen and set the mended harness aside, pushing to his feet and pacing to the window with the restlessness of a wolf. Although he'd known her scarcely six hours, he sensed that Senna McCallum had the power to destroy him. She was definitely a strong woman. The way she'd just handled that news about the business needing a financial boost had been admirable. She hadn't batted an eyelash when he told her how much the business needed to get going, and now she was in the kitchen, calmly and considerately cooking supper for him. Clearly she was level-headed and sensible enough to realize that the lodge was worth saving. He only hoped she had enough of a nest egg in the bank to help out.

He returned to his seat and for a few quiet minutes continued stitching up harnesses and then flinched as he heard a series of loud bangs and crashes from the kitchen. The sound of the frying pan hitting the stovetop. The clatter of silverware being flung on the table. Plates hitting the counter hard enough to shatter them. He heard her muttering to herself in angry undertones, and then, very clearly, she said, "You, dog, get out of this kitchen. Go on, I won't have you sitting there drooling while I cook!"

Chilkat skulked into the living room, casting an offended glance over his shoulder as he did. Just as Jack was about to effect his own escape from the lake house,

Senna stalked into the room, brandishing a knife in one hand.

"You really expect me to clean out my savings account to float the start-up of a fishing lodge I have absolutely no interest in?"

"You own a half interest, so the way I see it, you should be at least halfway interested," Jack corrected. "The only other alternative we have is not to open, and that'll set you back a whole lot more because then we'd have to refund the advance deposits."

"Which total exactly how much, dare I ask?"

"Oh, somewhere in the vicinity of thirty thousand dollars, give or take a few thousand."

"I see." She whirled around and stalked back into the kitchen. He heard the loud hiss as the caribou steaks hit the hot frying pan. Jack turned once again toward the door, gesturing silently to the dog, but before he could take two steps, she reappeared.

"I think it's cowardly of you not to have mentioned these financial problems before now," she said, waving the knife around for emphasis. "What if I don't have ten thousand dollars?"

"Then we'd better hope the fishing's good and all of our guests are fish eaters."

"There are a million details in a start-up operation. You quoted ten grand, but it'll probably be closer to twice that amount, though I won't know until I see your set-up. How many guests can you take at a time?"

"The lodge has six guest rooms with two double beds each and can accommodate twelve comfortably, but we'd need more guides to operate at full capacity. By law, there has to be one fishing guide for every two clients."

"How many employees?"

"Four. A housekeeper, a cook and two guides. Three guides, if I can hire another. Four would be even better."

"Plus you. That's seventeen or eighteen people eating three meals a day, seven days a week."

"That's about what I figured," Jack said, nodding.

She spun and returned to the kitchen. More angry noises. Jack gave up on trying to escape. He knew he wouldn't have time. Sure enough, she burst into the room again, eyes flashing. "And just how long do you think one cook is going to last with no helper and all those meals to prepare and no days off?"

"It's a short season, barely two, two and a half months. The cook'll last, and that time will pass in the blink of an eye." Jack snapped his fingers to emphasize just how fast summers flew by in Labrador. "You might even consider staying on yourself and pitching in. Think of it," he continued, forging boldly onward in spite of her ominous expression. "In just twelve weeks time, you could easily double or triple what you'd get for your grandfather's half of the business. You saw the reservation book. We're going to be busy as hell. By summer's end, you won't have any trouble at all getting rid of your shares. It'd be worth your while to wait, and who knows? You might even enjoy spending the summer here and decide not to sell."

Senna regarded him as if he were crazy and shook her head. "I couldn't get the time off even if I wanted to take it, which I can assure you I don't."

"Then I guess you'll just have to trust me enough to open the lodge and run it. We should be able to clear enough money after two months to keep the bank from foreclosing."

Her eyes narrowed. "Why would the bank foreclose? Is there a mortgage?"

"Construction loan. We're four months in arrears of making payments on it. The admiral's medical bills were pretty steep and the insurance payments take forever to come, so we had no choice but to take out a—"

"How big a construction loan?" Her voice was way too quiet.

"Forty thousand," Jack said, tensing for the explosion, "but we have a three-year pay-back period and a good interest rate."

Her expression never changed. She just stood for several moments with her hands on her hips, still as a statue. "Now would probably be a really good time for you to tell me you studied hotel management at Cornell," she said in that same ominously quiet voice, "or graduated top of your class from Johnson and Wales."

Jack glanced over her shoulder toward the kitchen, detecting a whiff of something burning. "Now would probably be an even better time for you to turn those caribou steaks."

SENNA OVERCOOKED THE CARIBOU and the baked potatoes were equally dry, but the canned corn was heated to perfection. Conversation at the table was limited to such requests as "please pass the salt, the pepper or the butter." Cutlery scraped on ironstone. Chewing was conducted with matching scowls of intense concentration. Chilkat appeared to be the only attendee enjoying the supper from his hiding place beneath the kitchen table, where, believing he was unobserved, Jack would slip him the toughest pieces of meat. Senna finished what she could and then laid her silverware across her plate. "I'm sorry about the meal."

"It was great," Jack said, as if he really meant it. At least he had the good manners to pretend.

Senna dabbed her mouth with a paper towel and cleared her throat. "There is another option for us to consider as far as this partnership goes." She crumpled the paper towel in her hand and met his wary gaze. "We could have the entire business appraised right down to its individual components. Airplane, fishing lodge, this house, the trucks, the dogs and gear, the workshop. Then we'd divvy it up in such a way that's fair. That way nothing will be shared jointly, I'll be able to sell my half much faster and easier, and you'll own your portion outright. No partner for you to have to deal with. I'll even give you my half of the plane."

His response was a firm and immediate "No."

"You might at least consider it."

Jack leaned back in his chair with a shake of his head. "Not a happening thing. This place stays just the way the admiral wanted it to be. It doesn't get hacked to pieces just because you want to run back to Maine with a quick chunk of change. I warned you I wouldn't make this easy for you, and I won't. A man's lifelong dream isn't just something you try to dispose of in two weeks, even if he is dead. And you might at least consider seeing what he created before you decide you want to get rid of your half."

"I could petition for partition and force you to divide the property or agree to sell it in its entirety and split the money," she challenged. "The courts would rule in my favor, especially if they could see the mess you made of this place."

"The *mess* you stumbled into was a result of the wake we just held," he said, rocking forward in his chair and leaning toward her. "And as far as bringing this to court, I'll fight you tooth and nail. I might not win. Hell, I probably won't, but I'll fight you to the bitter end."

Senna felt her cheeks flush. "Mr. Hanson, I'm not trying to be heartless or greedy. I'm sorry the admiral's dead, and I'm sorry the two of you didn't get a chance to run the lodge together after all the work you put into it, but that's not my fault. I'm just trying to make this as easy as possible for the both of us. Besides, you have no idea what kind of person might buy my half of the business. Maybe you wouldn't get along. What could be worse than running a fishing lodge you love with someone you hate?" Senna could tell by the look on his face that he wouldn't be swayed. She heaved a sigh of frustration. "What time are you thinking of leaving tomorrow morning?"

He gave her another wary look. "Leaving?"

"Flying me to see this lodge you plan to turn into a gold mine."

His expression cleared. "Sun-up."

"What time does that happen at this latitude?"

"When the sun comes over the eastern end of the lake." His grin was so unexpected and contagious that in spite of her disgruntled mood Senna very nearly returned it. "You'll love the place when you see it, guaranteed. You won't want to sell out, and you won't want to leave. Better pack your overnight bag."

"I'll be ready at sun-up," she said, rising to her feet and gathering up her plate. "But please understand that I have no intentions of spending the night there, or going

into business with you on anything more than an extremely temporary basis."

Jack's expression became stony as he matched her
cool stare with his own. "I guess I shouldn't have expected anything different from a wedding planner," he
replied with a dismissive shrug. He pushed out of his
chair and left the kitchen before Senna could hurl the
plate at him, which was nothing less than his rude and
insulting behavior deserved, but if he had been intending to leave the lake house, his escape was cut off by
another arrival.

The front door opened even as he was reaching for
the door knob and Senna was startled to see a young and
somewhat bedraggled-looking boy in his early teens
with black, shoulder-length hair standing in the darkened doorway. He wore clothing that looked as if were
made of old canvas, and there was a faded red bandana
wrapped around his head.

"Good to see you, Charlie," Jack said. "C'mon in and
meet Senna McCallum, the admiral's granddaughter.
You know. The wedding planner. Senna, this is Charlie
Blake. I forgot to tell you that Charlie almost always eats
supper here. He helps out around the place when he can.
Likes working with the huskies."

"Hello, Charlie," Senna said, still holding her plate
and struggling to control her temper.

The boy gave Senna a brief, inscrutable stare, then
held out a book he was carrying. "Finished," he said.

"Good," Jack said, retrieving it. "How'd you like it?"

"I liked the part when Captain Ahab got tangled up,
and the great white whale dragged him down," the boy
said, solemn-faced.

"Best part of *Moby Dick*," Jack agreed.

"It's nice to meet you, Charlie," Senna managed after this brief interchange. "Sit down and I'll get you some supper."

She began cleaning up the kitchen while Charlie ate and carried on a sporadic conversation with Jack. He began with the book he'd just read, continued with one-sentence subjects she couldn't quite grasp, and peppered his conversation with words she'd never heard before. By the time she'd finished wiping down the counters, Charlie was getting ready to sack out on the couch. This was apparently also the norm, as he knew exactly where to find two blankets and a pillow stashed inside an old sea chest which also served as the coffee table. A small, black fox-like dog had appeared out of the blue arctic twilight to settle down with him, behaving as though it had been born and raised in that very living room.

Senna hung the dishrag and towel behind the wood stove to dry and took Jack aside before heading upstairs for the night. "Just out of curiosity, is there anyone else who might show up to spend the night?"

"Nope. Just Charlie. But unless you want Chilkat on your bed, better keep your door closed. That damn dog takes up most of the mattress. You'd better go up now. I don't know what time morning comes in Maine, but in Labrador it comes really, really early."

"Don't worry," Senna said, turning her back on him and starting up the stairs. "I'm an early riser. You won't be needing to roust *me* out of bed."

"Too bad. That might be kinda fun," he called after her. Senna ignored his parting shot and took asylum in her grandfather's room, closing the door behind her. She leaned against it for a moment, pondering the wisdom of sleeping under the same roof as that brash and arrogant man. His bedroom was just across the hall, and her door didn't have a lock. Well, if he tried anything with her, he'd be sorry. Those three years of karate classes she'd taken in college would come in handy.

As long as the day had been, and as tired as she was, Senna wasn't ready for sleep. She stood in the middle of her grandfather's room, surrounded by his personal belongings, and tried to feel some sort of connection. Strangely, none of his things reflected his lifelong naval career. There were several pieces of vintage carved scrimshaw atop his bureau, a stack of old books, including several regional histories of arctic exploration and the Hudson's Bay Company, a harmonica that looked well used, a beautiful meerschaum pipe, several old buttons that appeared to have been carved out of bone in a pewter salt, a rifle propped behind the door, a box of excellent wildlife photographs, mostly of wolves and caribou, and a pair of well-worn mitts and matching mukluks made out of some kind of fur and hide and decorated with elaborate beadwork. Being surrounded by her grandfather's things was like being in a museum.

She touched each item, pondering the life of a man she hadn't known at all, full of questions that could never be answered, and most of all, full of regrets. She was disappointed that she hadn't yet stumbled across his journal. When she did, she hoped she would learn more about the enigma who was her grandfather, and why he had named her as his executor. At length she went to the window and looked out at the lake, its silken black waters reflecting the pale sliver of a new moon in a sky that wouldn't know true darkness again until the far side of summer. The cove was as still as a mirror. She leaned her elbows on the windowsill and contemplated the vastness of the wilderness beyond the panes of glass, feeling a sudden pang of nostalgia for the two brief years she'd spent in the field as a wildlife biologist, fresh out of college and full of enthusiasm, truly believing she could make a difference.

A day didn't go by that she didn't miss tramping through the Maine woods with a pair of binoculars and a notebook. She'd particularly enjoyed the time spent checking on the radio-collared female bears in their winter dens, gathering data and counting cubs. Bears and coyotes had become her favorite animals to observe, and ravens her favorite birds. The difference she had hoped to make in educating the public about the coyotes' place in the ecosystem never came to pass. The deer-hunters' hatred for that little brother of the wolf was far too deep-seated. If wolves kill a moose in Alaska, or coyotes kill a deer in Maine, these were sins committed by predators that humans had little tolerance for. They shot the wolves from airplanes and wanted to snare the coyotes. That these predators helped the moose and deer population remain healthy by culling out the weak, old and the sick was a foreign and unwelcome concept. The only difference Senna had made in the department was purely statistical. For a brief period of time, she was their token woman field biologist.

Working for her aunt at the inn gave her an income far higher than that of her entry-level biologist's wage at the state, but it didn't come close to fulfilling her passion for wildlife and wild places. Here in Labrador she was sensing ever more acutely everything that she'd missed for the past five years.

Senna heard a faint rustling sound outside her door

and opened it to see Chilkat waiting there expectantly. He stood and nosed his way into the room. Senna hesitated for a moment, listening to the murmur of voices from below. She closed her door again, quietly, then braced the chair beneath the door knob, just in case Hanson got any funny ideas in the middle of the night.

Meanwhile, the big husky leapt onto the bed with the grace of an athlete, curled up dead center, heaved a big sigh of contentment, and closed his eyes.

"Very well, then," Senna relented with a sigh of her own, opening her bag and rummaging within for her pajamas, "but you're going to have to share."

CHAPTER FOUR

EARLY MORNING, AND THE KITCHEN was cold enough to warrant kindling a fire in the woodstove. Jack wished there were bacon. He had a hankering to slice it into the frying pan, smell the fragrant hickory smoke and hear the fat sizzle. He searched the refrigerator twice before giving up. Yawning, he emptied the last of the stale coffee from the can into the pot and thought about all the mornings when the admiral had come down the stairs into the kitchen tamping tobacco into his pipe, reaching for his chipped mug and filling it to the rim. "Lots to do today," he'd growl. "Long row to hoe."

The admiral was used to being first man up. The fact that Jack had him beat every morning had been a bone of contention at first, but eventually the old man had come to enjoy the luxury of coming down to the smell of freshly brewed coffee. Always said the same thing. "Lots to do today. Long row to hoe." Then he'd drink his coffee and smoke his pipe and plan the day.

Jack missed the old man. He wondered if anyone would miss him half as much if he dropped dead. Doubted it. Well, maybe Charlie, and the huskies out in the dog yard. For a little while, anyway. Time was a river that washed a person away. Memories faded, became dilute. The day would come when he wouldn't be able to picture the admiral's face or the way he'd smoked his pipe or paddled a canoe. Made him wonder about Senna. Why had the two of them been at such odds? Damn shame. They could've shared a lot, but it was too late now.

The coffee smelled good. Boiling now, perking along smartly and picking up speed. Let 'er rip. Charlie snored softly on the couch, the crackie stretched out alongside him, awake and watching. Always watching, that dog was. Her eyes never closed. Jack shut off the propane burner under the coffeepot and poured himself a cup, carrying it with him out onto the porch. He stood in his stocking feet, breath pluming into the frigid air. June, and the thermometer stood at thirty-two degrees. Not exactly gardening weather, but crisp and wonderful and completely free of mosquitoes. He stood in silence, watching smoke rise from the surface of the lake, watching the sky pale to the east and the stars slowly fade as he drank his first cup of the morning. He heard a noise behind him and turned, seeing movement through the open door.

Senna was coming down the stairs. She was barefoot, clad in a white knee-length nightshirt with a green cardigan pulled over for warmth. Her slender, pretty legs flashed pale in the gloaming. She rounded the newel post at the bottom of the stairs, not seeing him on the porch, and went into the kitchen, where the fresh coffee waited and the woodstove gave off a strong, welcome warmth. She was pouring herself a cup when he entered the room, and she regarded him steadily as she blew over the top to cool the scalding brew.

"Morning," she said.

Jack stared appreciatively. It had been a long time

since he'd had the chance to admire such feminine beauty this early in the morning. "Guess I didn't have to roust you after all," he said.

"Nope. I've been awake most of the night. I heard you get up and then I smelled the coffee." She nodded to a book she'd apparently set on the kitchen table. "I found some books in my grandfather's room. I thought maybe Charlie would like that one. I sure did, back when I was in grade school."

Jack glanced at the title. *Twenty Thousand Leagues Under the Sea.* "Charlie will, too. Don't think he's read that one yet. The admiral must've been building him up to it. He's read a slew of others. One by one the admiral doled them out, and one by one Charlie read them. Then they'd have their book discussion, usually over supper."

"Does Charlie live here full-time?"

"He showed up one day while we were building the place. He was just one in a crowd of curious locals wanting to know what we were up to, but he kept coming back and doing little things, like picking up the nails we'd dropped, cleaning up our work sites, handing things to us when we were up on ladders. One night he didn't leave. Just slept under the porch with that damn crackie. The admiral told him his parents would worry, and that's when he told us he didn't have any, and his uncle couldn't afford to feed him anymore. That was two years ago. He was just ten years old." Jack took another swallow of coffee and then crossed the room to feed another stick of firewood into the stove and damper it down.

"Truth is, the kid didn't have anywhere to go and nobody who wanted him, so he always landed here, on the

admiral's step. Liked working for the old man, being
told what to do, given daily chores and little jobs that
never quite ended, one chore running into the next, day
after day until months passed, sometimes, before Charlie would remember that shack in North West River
where his uncle's family lived. Then he'd go off for a
day or two with his dog. We always wondered if he'd
come back again, but he always did, and each time he
stayed a bit longer."

Senna took a small sip of coffee and made a face.
"Mud," she said.

"Cowboy coffee. Only kind worth drinking," Jack
said with a faint grin. "You can cut it with water if you
want." She wasn't wearing any makeup. Didn't need
any. First thing in the morning after a night of little
sleep, and she possessed the immortal beauty of a goddess.

"So Charlie liked being around my grandfather,"
Senna marveled aloud as she added water to her cup at
the kitchen tap. She had elegant, fine-boned hands, and
the way they cradled the coffee mug was almost poetic.

"And your grandfather liked having Charlie around,"
Jack said. "Spent a lot of time with the boy, mentoring
him. Schoolteacher came by one day to lay down the
law. Said Charlie was truant and had better start attending, or else. The admiral set her down in the kitchen,
made her a cup of tea, and while she sat there sipping
it, he had Charlie read aloud to her from Homer's *Od-
yssey*. He said, 'Lady, the boy's ten years old, but he
couldn't read one damn word when he came here. Why?
Because you hadn't been able to teach him one damn
thing in four years of trying. Now he can read Homer
and understand it, and you're telling me he has to go

back to your school? Tell me, have your teaching skills improved so greatly that attending your institution would benefit this boy in any possible way?'

"Schoolteacher jumped up and left without finishing her tea, back stiff as a ramrod. The admiral half expected the Mounties to arrive on our doorstep by nightfall, but nothing ever came of it. That teacher never came back, either. We heard she left North West River to take a clerking job in Gander. New teacher was hired. Good one, too, so Charlie went back to school. He's smarter than most of the kids in his class."

"But what about Charlie's uncle? Isn't he the boy's legal guardian? How does he fit into this picture?"

"Charlie's uncle inherited the boy when his parents went through the ice and drowned three years back. He was glad when Charlie took up with us. Has six kids of his own and didn't have to feed the boy anymore. When the admiral asked him a couple of months ago if Charlie could spend the summer as a chore boy at the lodge, the uncle asked if he'd get the boy's earnings. Admiral answered, 'Only if he chooses to give them to you.' So uncle dug his heels in and tells the admiral his nephew can't go to the lodge unless he gets Charlie's pay. 'Fine then,' the admiral says to him as if he could give a damn, 'go ahead and keep the boy for the summer. Charlie's in another growing spurt, and he's eating us out of house and home.' Next day Charlie shows up with his dog and a note from uncle that says, 'Charlie go to lodge for summer.'"

Jack poured another dollop of coffee into his mug and set the pot on the woodstove, nudging it to the side where it wouldn't boil up again. He glanced through the hall into the living room. The boy still slept, watched over by his loyal dog. "The day the admiral died, Charlie vanished. He didn't go to the service, and I never saw him at the wake. I was damn glad he showed up here last night. The last thing I need to worry about right now is where that kid is, and if he's all right."

Senna was watching him over the rim of her cup with all the wariness of a hunted deer. "What will become of him, now that the admiral is dead?"

Jack shrugged. "He's survived this long. The kid's tough. But don't worry, I won't let him starve. They can always hang with me, him and his dog."

"That dog is a strange-looking animal, nothing like your huskies."

"She's an old native breed they called a crackie. The Montagnais Indians of Quebec and the North Shore used 'em for hunting, way back when. They're smarter'n hell. Used to be that a good crackie cost top dollar, and could mean the difference between living good or starving to death come winter. Grocery stores and government welfare put the crackies out of business. They're a dying breed now, don't hardly see any around. Charlie rescued that one from the lake. She was just a four-, five-week-old pup, no bigger'n a minute, and somehow she'd crippled up a leg. The boy happened to be fishing nearby when the Montagnais tossed her overboard. Charlie fished her out of the water and kept her."

"How does he manage to feed her?"

"When he's here with us, that dog eats good. Before he came to live here, he fished. He trapped. The crackie helped him hunt. She could probably survive on her own, but he divides everything with her. He loves that little dog. Calls her Ula. I think that means sister in Athapascan, but I'm not sure."

Senna gazed into the living room at the blanketed form on the couch, guarded by the dog he'd rescued. Her expression softened. Pity? Sympathy? She looked back at him and the wariness returned. "What about you? Where will you go when the business is sold?"

"Unless I'm mistaken, you can only sell your half as long as I want to keep mine. I'm staying put." He finished his first cup of coffee and set it on the counter. "C'mon, wedding planner. Get dressed, and wear your warmest, grubbiest clothes. We have some hungry sled dogs to feed before we fire up that ancient plane and see if she makes it to the Wolf River."

"And if it doesn't?"

Jack retrieved his jacket from the back of a kitchen chair. "Then we might crash and you might never get to see your grandfather's lodge, and that'd be real shame because it's a beautiful place. But don't worry about that Cessna. She's not like a woman. She's never let me down, and she never will."

SENNA HELPED JACK CHOP up chunks of frozen fish for the sled dogs' breakfast, hoping to hurry the process along so they could fly out to see the lodge. As she worked, she thought about the statement he'd made about a woman letting him down and wondered what had caused all that bitterness and cynicism.

She was using an ax for the first time in her life, kneeling as she worked because Jack had instructed her that a person kneeling would never cut themselves. She brought it down on the big stump, the way he'd showed her, chopping each fish into four parts. She tossed the parts into a bucket while he pumped water into two other five-gallon buckets and fussed about the feed shed waiting for her to finish. It seemed to take a long time, and her arm was tired long before she was finished. "Wouldn't feeding kibble be easier?" she asked, setting the ax down and peeling off the leather gloves he'd loaned her.

"Sure. And having no sled dogs would be the easiest of all. C'mon. The dogs are waiting."

He lugged the water, she lugged the fish, donning the gloves again in her own self-defense. This certainly was grubby work, but in an odd way she relished the physical exertion and the reconnection to the mystical circle of life. The Inuit dogs were whirling around at the ends of their tethers, eyes bright and teeth flashing. More than a few were actually foaming at the mouth. Senna was quite happy to let Jack be the one to dole out the fish, which he did with smooth rapidity, quickly making the rounds and emptying the bucket. He followed this routine by watering each dog, and then grabbed a shovel and cleaned the entire dog yard. In jig time he was finished, and Senna realized that she'd done very little except stand on the sidelines and watch.

"I'll feed them all by myself tonight," she promised. "If I'm half owner, that's the least I can do. Now that they've eaten, I think it's time we did the same. I'll fix us some breakfast."

"That's real nice of you to offer," he said, picking up the empty buckets, "but there's nothing in the house to fix. I'll fly you out to the lodge, and after the grand tour we'll catch and fry up a mess of fish for lunch."

"Lunch? But that's hours away. Aren't you hungry now?"

Jack was a big man, tall and broad of shoulder, and lean the way a man who worked hard physically was lean. Surely he needed three square meals a day, and the supper she'd fixed the night before hardly qualified as a square meal. "Nah. Coffee'll hold me over just fine," he said, heading back down the path to the house. "That's why I make it good and thick."

"But...what about Charlie?" Senna protested, hurrying after him with her empty fish bucket. "He's a growing boy. He needs to eat." And I'm *starving,* she pleaded silently. "Maybe we should drive into town for some groceries."

"Nah," he repeated over his shoulder. "Charlie's used to going for days without eating. C'mon, shake a leg. We've got a long row to hoe today."

Senna bit her lower lip and followed after his big strides. She could eat a whole pound of bacon and a dozen eggs all by herself, but if he wasn't complaining about being hungry, neither would she. It felt good to get back into the warm kitchen, where she hovered over the wood stove, rubbing her chilled hands together. "There was ice in the dogs' water buckets," she said.

"June in Labrador can be a little nippier than it is in Maine." Jack poured them each another cup of coffee and ducked briefly into the living room. "Charlie? Time to get up. Rise and shine, boy. We're burning daylight."

Senna took the cup he extended toward her. "My father used to say that," she said, remembering a long-ago time.

"Maybe that's where I picked up the expression." He tossed another stick of firewood into the woodstove.

Senna drew a sharp breath. "My father's been dead for five years. He was killed in a plane crash. There's no way you could have known him."

"Your father was my commanding officer."

Senna felt another jolt of surprise. "You were in the Navy?"

"That's how I met your grandfather. The three of us went on a fishing trip together."

"To Labrador," Senna guessed, her thoughts all awhirl with this sudden overload of information.

"When I was in college, a friend of mine told me about this place," Jack explained. "Said it was the best fishing ever. So, being as I liked to fish, it seemed natural for us to plan a trip. We ended up spending the entire summer working at a fly-in lodge near the mouth of the Eagle River. I started out washing dishes and progressed to being a chore boy, then a maintenance man. Came back the next summer to work at the same lodge, and did some guiding. Anyhow, when I found out your father liked to fly-fish, I told him about Labrador. He asked me to plan a trip for him and his father, so I did. Then he asked me to come along, so I did. The rest is history."

Senna paced to the kitchen window and stared out at the lake, which was hidden beneath a blanket of fog. Wraiths of smoke lifted from the surface and caught fire in the sun's first rays. She felt a sudden, aching sense of loss. "You knew them both better than I did," she said. "My father and my grandfather belonged to the military. We only knew them as men in uniform who were always gone." She drew a painful breath. "*Strangers* in uniforms."

"I'm sorry you feel that way. The military can be a demanding lifestyle...."

"Tell me about it," Senna said, spinning around, her stomach churning with bitter resentment. "Tell my mother about the demands of raising three kids while her husband was flying fighters off a boat cruising an ocean halfway around the world. Tell me about all the lonely nights spent wondering and worrying. Tell me about how my mother coped when her own parents died, and my father couldn't make it to either funeral because the fleet was on some kind of high alert."

Jack's expression was solemn. "I'm sorry."

"Me, too." Senna glared at him, then turned away as the heat of her anger swept up into her cheeks. "Military men should never marry."

"I couldn't agree with you more."

At that moment Charlie came into the kitchen, blinking sleep from his eyes. The small, black fox-like dog skirted about his heels. She was a pretty thing. Fine-boned, almost dainty, with a sharp, intelligent expression. Both were looking, no doubt, for something to eat. But to Senna's surprise, Charlie made a beeline for the kitchen table and picked up the book she had laid there earlier. The boy read the title aloud, then looked at Jack. It was hard to read his expression.

"For me?"

Jack nodded. "For you to read *later.* Right now we're flying out to show Senna the lodge. I'll go prep the plane, and then we're out of here. Leave Ula in the shed. Put some water and kibble down for her. We'll be gone for half the day, at least."

Charlie nodded, reluctantly put the book on the table and turned toward the door. The little black dog followed.

"Can't Ula come with us?" Senna said. "She won't take up much space in the plane."

Charlie paused, hand on the door knob, and glanced back hopefully. "No," Jack said. "Go on, now, and meet us at the plane." After the boy had gone, Jack dampered down the woodstove and moved to the door. "Don't look so huffy," he said to Senna before heading out to ready the plane. "If that crackie ran off after some wild beast while we're at the lodge, we might have to spend the rest of the summer searching for her. She's safer here."

Senna's stomach growled loud enough to perk up Chilkat's ears. "Maybe so," she admitted, "but I was kind of hoping she could hunt us up some breakfast."

"What's the matter, don't you like brook trout?" Jack said.

"I don't like fish, period."

THE FLIGHT TO WOLF RIVER LODGE took longer than Senna thought it would. She hadn't seen a map until she climbed into the plane and looked over Jack's air charts. He traced out their route with his forefinger while Senna strapped herself into the copilot's seat and Charlie settled into the seat directly behind her.

"The Wolf's about a hundred miles north-northeast of us. She empties into White Bear Bay and she's about the best salmon river in Labrador. Everyone thinks that distinction belongs to the Eagle River, and that's fine by me. Let 'em stay down there and crowd the shores. Our lodge is the only human habitation on the Wolf. There's a little settlement at White Bear Bay—four houses, all fishermen. The mail boat stops there once a week." Jack glanced into the back. "You all buckled up, Charlie?"

Jack ran through his preflight checklist and then started the engines. Senna knew nothing of airplanes, but the motor sounded strong and smooth and the propeller spun, and if the man piloting the plane had served under her father, then he was no doubt a competent enough aviator. They were taxiing away from the dock and just starting to pick up speed when suddenly Jack throttled the plane down with a heated curse. "Dammit-all, Charlie," he yelled over the rumble of the engine. "I thought I told you to lock that dog of yours in the shed!"

Senna followed his line of sight and spied a V-shaped ripple of movement in the water just off shore and to the right of the dock. Hard to see, but that movement was the little black dog, swimming swiftly toward the plane.

"I did," Charlie said, staring out his window.

Jack idled the plane and shook his head in disgust, watching the dog's approach. "Well, what are you waiting for? Open the door and drag her in here."

The boy scrambled to unbuckle his seat belt. By the time he got the side door open, Ula had nearly reached the plane. Charlie climbed out onto the pontoon, lifted her out of the water by her collar and deposited her in the cabin, where she shook off a great shower of spray that drenched the interior along with the pilot. Senna couldn't help but laugh in spite of Jack's dark expression. She was glad the crackie was aboard and reunited with Charlie.

Five minutes later they were airborne, heading for the Wolf River and the lodge her grandfather had dreamt into life. Senna watched the landscape unroll beneath the plane. Landscape? More like a waterscape. Endless streams, rivers, ponds, lakes. Water everywhere. In fact, from the air, what little land there was seemed to be dividing one body of water from another. No habitations anywhere. No roads. Just endless and untracked wilderness. Senna found herself entranced by the beauty of it, and searched the open spaces and eskers for signs of wolves.

She cast a covert glance at Jack, wondering at his solitary ways. He seemed like a good enough person, and there was no denying his physical attributes, yet he remained curiously unattached. He'd made reference to a woman who would let him sleep at her house, so no doubt he had alliances with the opposite sex, but his life for the most part seemed almost monastic. Was fishing enough of an addiction that a man could forsake all the comforts of life and not even miss them?

Another half hour droned by. No conversation was possible over the throaty roar of the engine. Every once in a while Jack would point down at something and shout to make himself heard, but though she stared where he pointed and struggled to make sense of his words, she failed to see or hear anything. Finally the plane began to descend. She peered anxiously downward, trying to keep from anticipating something so grand that she'd only be disappointed. A broad dark river twisted through the black spruce, bigger than any of the others they'd flown over. The plane banked around, dropping more swiftly. Still she saw nothing. Was the lodge so small it couldn't be seen from the air?

Her hands clenched together in her lap and she realized she was tense with anticipation as Jack side-slipped the plane, dropped altitude quickly, lined up on a long straight section of river, and touched down so smoothly she barely felt the transition. Rather than stop the plane and cut the motor, he taxied it up the river heading for the bend.

Rounding the corner the river widened out, and on the left-hand shore Senna spied a long dock with a ramp ascending to a porch-like structure above. Above and beyond, perched on the very edge of a promontory overlooking the river, was the lodge, much larger than she had dared to hope. It was V-shaped, each wing at least sixty feet long and paralleling the river. The front of the lodge was the somewhat rounded point of the V, and was floor-to-ceiling glass. The lodge was constructed of honey-colored cedar logs that hadn't yet begun to age and silver. The roof was metal, dark green, and evidently hard to see from the air. A massive stone chimney reared up dead center of the V and a covered porch ran along each wing facing the river, with yet another ramp descending to the lower porch above the dock. There were several matching log outbuildings, one right at the water's edge that she assumed was a boat house, two up behind the lodge itself, and another off the far side.

Jack taxied the plane up to the dock and Charlie jumped out, dog at heel, to tether it to the big posts. The engine cut out and the prop feathered to a stop. Senna sat for a moment, taken aback by the unexpected grandeur of the log structure and the way it so gracefully blended into the landscape. "It's much bigger than I imagined it would be," she said, staring out the plane's bug-spattered windscreen. "And much better-looking."

"The admiral designed it," Jack said. "He picked the place out, too. He spotted this knoll from the air, signaled for me to put down, and said, 'There she'll set, right up there on that point of land with a river view outside every window. We'll call her the Wolf River Lodge.'

"Situated on that high point of land with the river on three sides, there's a steady breeze that keeps the bugs away 24/7," Jack said. "Priceless, that spot. There isn't another like it along the whole stretch of river. You can sit on that great long porch without wearing any insect repellent at all and never be bothered by Labrador's legendary mosquitoes."

Senna shook her head, trying to comprehend the magnitude of the project. "How on earth did you get everything out here?"

"Freighter brought it up the coast to White Bear Bay, which is about twenty-five miles due east of here. The locals rigged up a pretty ingenious barge with a shallow draw to haul the bulk of it up the river. When the river froze up, we flew the rest of the stuff in, or dragged it by snow machine. We did whatever we had to do to get the building supplies in here."

"How long did it take to build once all the supplies were in?"

"Forever, it seemed like. We hired some men from Goose Bay. Good workers. Great carpenters. And an old Scandinavian log joiner from St. John's supervised the raising of the lodge. Fifty years in the business, a real artisan. Spent time with some of the best log-cabin builders in the world, teaching them the finer points." Jack shook his head, his eyes faraway. "We worked like slaves, all of us did. Looking at the whole of it all at once, building the damn thing seemed like an impossible task, but the admiral never got discouraged. Somehow he knew just how to get the job done, step by steady step."

"All those years of military discipline, no doubt," Senna remarked, unbuckling her safety harness.

"No doubt," Jack amiably agreed, his thoughts returning to the present. He grinned at her as he unbuckled his own harness. "C'mon. I think you'll like the lodge even better close up."

As JACK STARTED UP THE RAMP toward the lodge he heard Senna's light footsteps following close behind. "Where's Charlie?" she asked.

"Dunno, but this is the first time we've been back here since the admiral died. I think maybe he just needs a little time to adjust." He glanced back at Senna. "The admiral was the closest thing to real family Charlie had. The two of them were pretty close."

Her forehead furrowed in a frown. "That just seems so unbelievable. The admiral was so aloof with us. With *me*. So distant. So judgmental and so damn unyielding. Nothing I said or did was good enough for him. The fact that Charlie liked him...*loved* him, even, just seems so...so incredible."

Jack stopped in his tracks and turned just in time to grab Senna before she rammed into him, striding up the ramp with her head down, absorbed in her memories. He caught her by her upper arms and brought her to an abrupt halt. Her head snapped up.

"We all change," he said, his voice harder than he wanted it to be, but Charlie was up in the lodge searching for something he'd lost and would never find again and the boy's pain keened on Jack and made him angry with this granddaughter who didn't seem to understand much about anything. "All of us, every day. We adapt to our environment. We change because we have to, in order to survive. Sometimes that means we have to hide the very best parts of ourselves. Your grandfather was a man who held a position of great importance. Great power. He had to make decisions every single day that could have nothing to do with his emotions, his true feelings. He had to make decisions that sometimes caused other people to die."

"I know that," Senna said, her chin lifting slightly but her voice subdued. Her eyes were riveted to his, irises wide, and he could feel the trembling tension of her body.

"He kept the soft side of himself hidden because he had to in order to survive in the world he lived in. You show a weakness in that world, any weakness at all, and you're doomed, and everyone else who depends on you is doomed." Jack felt himself falling into the dark windows of turbulent emotions that stared back up at him. "Don't hold that against him," he said. "He loved you, he just didn't know how to show it after all those years of having to be tough. He didn't know how to love anything anymore. It took that homeless boy to bring your grandfather back to life. It took Charlie to reconnect him to his gentler side, to the part of him that could be emotional, that could care about people, that could love again."

He eased his grip. "The admiral was a good man, and that's all I have to say about that." He released her and she took a step back, her eyes still wide, still drawing him into that dangerous place. He turned away and climbed the steep ramp toward the lodge.

CHAPTER FIVE

SENNA WAS STILL REELING from the vehemence of Jack's rebuke when he led her through the front door of the lodge, which opened into the spacious living room. The dominant feature was the huge fieldstone chimney, measuring at least six feet deep by ten feet wide, with two fireplaces, one facing the living room, the other facing the dining area, the chimney itself serving as the room divider between the two. The living room was stacked with cardboard boxes and wooden crates, some of which had been opened to reveal their contents. Couches, chairs, framed pictures, tables, lamps, bed frames…everything that was needed to furnish a fishing lodge. The floors, what little she could glimpse of them, were of polished pine, and the windows were large and looked out over the river and the black spruce forest below. The building smelled of pine shavings, cedar, varnish and sawdust, all things fresh and new.

Jack led her through the maze of boxes, past the fieldstone chimney. "This is the dining room. We assembled that damn table three weeks ago. Took forever. Custom made, seats twenty-four comfortably. We decided on one big table rather than a bunch of little ones. Telling fishing stories at suppertime is mandatory, and it's easier if the audience is all at the same table."

Senna ran her fingers over the satiny wood. "Cherry?"

"Two pieces of two-hundred-year-old wood, hand-planed and rubbed. Finding chairs that went with it was hard. The Shaker ladder-backs were the closest thing to what the admiral wanted, but they were costly."

"I'm impressed," Senna said. In fact, she was awed. The dining room was elegant in its rustic simplicity. Above the table hung a hammered-copper chandelier with a collage of hand-forged fish leaping around its five-foot circumference. It was a magnificent work of art.

"Let's go into the kitchen. Goody hasn't seen it all put together yet, though she's heard all the stories." Jack tugged her along as he spoke, through the swinging doors at the end of the dining room and into a bright and sparkling space filled with professional equipment any gourmet chef would have coveted. The stove was a big commercial Garland gas range with a griddle, two big ovens, an overhead broiler and eight burners. "Big stove. Big job getting it in here. Four men. Lots of cussing. Look at this." He strode over to one of three stainless-steel refrigerators and pulled the door open. "Big refrigerators, propane and electric combo. Could fit a whole cow in here. See the dent in the side panel? We dropped this one halfway up the ramp. Lots more cussing."

Senna laughed. He was already moving toward a pine-paneled door, opening it. She peeked inside. It was a large pantry, lined with ample shelves. Everything within would be in easy reach and visible, though it was empty now. Jack showed her the baking station, with stainless bins built under the counter that tipped out for access and could hold hundreds of pounds of flour and

sugar. The big piece of marble inlaid into the countertop for rolling out pie dough. The deep, stainless dou-
ble-bay sink with a wide window looking out at river.
He pointed at the skylights overhead that allowed better light and ventilation. Work island. Pot racks, hooks
empty. No utensils anywhere. Everything was still
boxed up in the living room, as yet unpacked.

He guided her back out into the dining room, through
the living room, onto the porch that fronted the guest
rooms. Three on either end of each porch, bare of all furnishings. "There'll be two double beds in each, table between, bureau, chair, writing desk," he said. There were
tiny closets and large picture windows in each room.
Every room had water views because of how the river
curved sharply around the knoll. He showed her the
small but cute bathrooms in each room. Shower, toilet
and sink were all installed. "No room for tubs in these
little bathrooms, but wait'll you see the sunken hot tub
on the lower porch."

The hot tub held six people, and the view of the river
was magnificent from this lower private deck, looking
out over a short set of rapids that filled the air with the
soothing sound of water over rocks. "Good place to
soak away all your aches and pains at the end of the day
with a close friend and a glass of wine," he said.

Then it was down the ramp again to the building off
the dock. "Generator building," he said, opening the
door to expose a large industrial-sized generator. "It
burns propane and the building's insulated, so you don't
even hear it running."

"How do you refuel it?" Senna asked.

"In the spring we can bring fuel in on barges from
White Bear Bay. In September, you'd run aground if you

tried to freight up the rapids, so we put enough tanks in to last the summer and then some, and planned to fill them up every spring. Everything in the lodge runs on propane, too. The good thing is, we don't need to run the generator except for pumping water up into the big storage tank. Once the tank is full, gravity feeds the water into the lodge's systems, but we also have a water pump for when guests want to take showers."

"What's that other building down behind the lodge, the one you haven't shown me yet?"

"Guides' quarters. That's where your grandfather, Charlie and I were going to hang out. There's another little cabin for Goody and her niece, and next to her digs is a shed and fenced area for her coopies."

"Coopies?"

"Chickens. Laying hens. She says she won't leave home without them, so we built her a shed and figured the fresh eggs would be a bonus." He was leading her back to the lodge as he spoke, and though it seemed overly familiar, Senna liked very much the way he took her hand to help her up the steep ramp. She attributed his friendliness to his boyish enthusiasm over the lodge. Now, as they regained the porch and she stood looking about the property, her self-consciousness grew and she pulled out of his grasp. "There's still quite a bit left to do."

He shoved his hands deep into his jeans pockets and slouched against a log porch post. "You should've seen the place a year ago," he said.

Senna studied him, measuring his character against the results of his labors. "I have to admit, the lodge is nothing at all like what I expected. I'm..." She hesitated, not sure how to finish the sentence without sounding as if she'd doubted Jack and her grandfather could pull something on this grand a scale together and make it work.

"...thinking about spending the summer here and helping out?" Jack supplied with a hopeful look.

Senna laughed in spite of herself. "I'm impressed," she corrected, effectively dodging the subject, at least for the moment. "I'm also starving. Let's go find Charlie and catch some fish. I'm hungry enough now to eat anything."

Charlie was in the guides' cabin, sitting on the bottom bunk and thumbing through a leather-bound notebook. He glanced up and laid the book aside when Jack entered, Senna right behind him. Jack picked up the book and glanced at it. His expression darkened as he handed it to Senna. "It's the admiral's journal. I have no idea how it got here." Then to the boy he said, "A journal isn't like a regular book, Charlie. It's personal, and you shouldn't read it unless the person who wrote it invites you to. How'd you happen to find it?"

"It was on the admiral's desk the morning he died."

"And you took it without asking? Why?"

"I wanted to know if I was in it," Charlie said.

Senna felt a pang at the boy's stoic yet vulnerable expression and touched Jack's arm. "It's all right," she said. "There's no harm done."

"Where's Ula?" Jack said, his voice not quite as hard.

Charlie pushed off the bed, eyes inscrutable. "She swam after a duck down on the river."

"When?"

"Right after we landed."

Jack swore softly. "That's it, then. We probably won't see her for hours or days. Maybe months and years.

Damn dog!" He noted Charlie's stricken expression and to Senna's relief he clasped the boy's shoulder. "Don't worry. She'll turn up. Let's catch a mess of fish. Maybe the smell of trout frying in the pan'll bring her on home." Jack reached for the box of hand-tied salmon flies on the little table by the window, handed it to Senna, who still held the journal. "You fish?"

She took the box of flies and shook her head. "My brothers did when they were young, but I never took to it. I didn't like putting the worms on the hook and I don't like eating fish so I couldn't see the point in pursuing the sport."

"Worms? Woman, perish the very thought. We're fly-fishing on this river, not bait-casting. There's a world of difference." He put a can of bug repellent in his jacket and stuffed his other pocket with hard candy from a bowl on the table. "We'll take the skiff," he said to Charlie. "Water's pretty high to be poling the canoe through the riffs. Don't want to get the wedding planner wet. That is, if she wants to come along."

"I certainly do, and I wish you'd stop calling me that," Senna said, as they exited the guides' cabin.

"That's what you are, isn't it?"

"That's what I *do,* not who I am."

"The admiral was right," Jack said, striding toward the lodge at a pace that had Senna half running to keep up. "I've only known you for a day, but I think you could have been much more."

"I'm good at what I do, good enough that I make a damn decent salary, and there's nothing wrong with that!" Senna realized how foolish it was to be defending herself to a virtual stranger who had no business making such a disparaging remark about her job but nonetheless her words were delivered in a rush of anger. Jack kept walking. He gained the lodge's deck and crossed the long porch to the ramp that descended to the dock. "Is there?" she prodded, maddened by his indifference.

"No, not at all," Jack said over his shoulder, not slowing his stride. "You reminded the admiral of himself, that's all, and he thought you should have followed the same path he did."

"And just what path might that be? Sailing the high and mighty oceans searching for enemy to kill?"

"Not exactly. He thought you should have kept on as a wildlife biologist. He thought you should have championed your causes to the bitter end. He admired the way you fought for the coyotes and the bear and was disappointed when you gave up the fight. The admiral took up a similar fight here, on behalf of the wolves. I guess he hoped you'd follow in his footsteps."

"Was that his idea of love, insinuating his own dreams into my life and expecting me to live up to them?" she said, wishing he would slow down and wishing she could just ignore his infuriating words.

"I don't know," Jack said. He reached the bottom of the ramp and stopped, glancing up at her. Senna paused a few steps above him, arrested by the intensity of his gaze. "Maybe it was his idea of immortality." He shrugged. "Hell, I didn't say he was perfect."

"Why didn't he have these dreams for my brothers?"

Another shrug. "He told me they were city boys and you were the one who was wild at heart. Come on, shake a leg. You said you were hungry."

But Senna remained where she was, simmering with latent anger and frustration toward a grandfather she couldn't please and a business partner she didn't want. She gestured back at the lodge. "You'll never get this place ready to go in two weeks time."

"Wanna bet?" Jack stared up at her, his expression borderline arrogant. She heard Charlie's footsteps right behind her and Jack's glance shifted over her shoulder. The boy was burdened with fly rods and life jackets. "Charlie, hand that gear to the wedding planner and help me drag the skiff out," he said.

The skiff was an old sixteen-foot Lund, dented aluminum, stashed out of sight behind the propane shed. While Senna watched, the two of them slid the craft into the water and secured it to the dock. The motor was stored inside the shed, a much newer-looking four-stroke Honda. "This is a good fishing boat for this river. Shallow draw, broad enough beam to stand up to the rugged riffs, rapids, and wind. She'll hold four people easily and six in a pinch, throttled down and riding gentle. You sure you want to come along?" Jack asked as he stood in the stern and bolted the motor onto the rear of the skiff.

"I'm not the type that waits at the gate," Senna said, aware that her cheeks were still burning.

Jack's cocky grin didn't make her feel better. "Charlie, help her in."

"I don't need help," Senna said, handing the fly rods to Charlie, tossing the life jackets aboard and scrambling unassisted into the skiff.

"Guess not," Jack said, eyeing her appraisingly.

Minutes later they were moving upriver. Senna sat in the bow, wind in her face. Charlie was silent behind her, scanning the shorelines for any sign of his missing dog. Jack sat in the stern, navigating up through a series of shallow rapids and into a span of calm water out of sight of the lodge. "Good fishing hole over on this shore," he said, making a slow gentle curve toward a smooth ledge that dropped into the water on the far shore. "Don't need to go very far this time of year. I'll just drop anchor and catch us some lunch."

Jack hadn't been exaggerating. Before Senna even had time to properly study the surrounding riverbanks for flora and fauna, he'd landed four good-sized trout and they were heading back to the lodge. "Don't really need much but a frying pan to turn these beauties into a damn fine meal," he said over the purr of the small outboard motor, "but we always kept a few luxuries at the guides' cabin for times like this."

The luxuries he spoke of turned out to be stashed in an old army-surplus ammunition box that was tucked beneath a bunk. Corn meal, salt, an unopened can of coffee, a plastic jug of corn oil were all quickly retrieved. Charlie kindled a fire on the riverbank as Jack squatted on the gravel bar and cleaned the fish. Soon the smell of frying trout and boiling coffee flavored the cool clean air. While Jack tended the cook fire, Senna heard the boy whistle several times down along the river's edge.

"What if Ula doesn't come back?" she asked.

"She will, eventually. Trouble is, those crackies don't know when to give up the hunt. If she was chasing a diver duck, she could be miles down river by now, still swimming after it." He used the blade of his knife to shift the fish in the pan as he spoke. "If she's not back by the time we leave, she'll be one lonely dog for a while."

Senna watched Charlie pace along the shore. "We can't just leave her way out here."

"She'll be fine. Charlie'll leave something behind that has his smell on it, his hat or his jacket, and she'll be lying right beside it when we come back, whether that's tomorrow or a month from tomorrow. This isn't the first time she's run off."

"But he's so upset…."

"He should've tied her up when he had the chance. There are some plates and forks in that ammo box," he said, glancing at her across the cook fire. "Don't forget the coffee cups."

Senna went to get them from the cabin and held each plate while he dished up the meal. Jack called to Charlie and gave him a plate. They ate silently, listening to the river rushing past while staring into the dwindling flames of the little fire or scanning the shoreline for the missing crackie. Senna forgot all about the fact that she didn't like fish. The flesh of the trout was firm, pink and delicious and she devoured every bite. While she and Jack finished off the pot of coffee, Charlie returned to the riverbank and searched for his dog. The sound of his whistles made Senna feel terrible.

"It's only an hour back to the lake house," she said.

Jack rose to his feet and slatted the dregs of his coffee into the dying embers of the fire. "Your point being…?"

"You could fly back and feed the sled dogs while Charlie and I wait here."

"For the crackie to show up? You could be waiting one hell of a long time."

"On the other hand, she could return five minutes after we leave." Senna collected the plates and cups. "We can't just leave Ula behind," she repeated. "It wouldn't be humane."

Jack grinned. "It wouldn't be humane if I crashed on the way back and you and Charlie starved to death."

"We have a river full of fish, a frying pan, an excellent hunting dog, and a few luxuries stashed in an old army ammo box. We'd be fine. But please don't crash my grandfather's half of the plane."

"*Your* half, now," he corrected, "and don't worry. I wouldn't dream of it." He studied her for a moment. "You sure you want me to leave you here?"

Senna glanced at her watch. "Those huskies need to be fed pretty soon, don't they? You'd better get going. I'll clean up here and then help Charlie look for his crackie. Don't worry, we'll stay right on the river." When he hesitated again she added, "And if by chance you should pass a store, we could really use some bacon and eggs—just in case she doesn't come back tonight."

SENNA HADN'T EVEN FINISHED washing the dishes at the river's edge when the crackie returned. She heard Charlie's shout and glanced up, gladdened by the sight of the little black dog picking her way along the opposite riverbank, something large, floppy and dark dangling from her jaws. Ula didn't hesitate when she spotted Charlie, but leapt immediately into the water and swam diagonally across the strong current. By sheer perseverance she managed to gain the shallows before being carried out of sight around the river bend and then trotted up the gravel shoreline to where Charlie waited. Senna found herself smiling at the heartfelt reunion between the two.

"Maybe you'd better tie her up," she said as boy and dog approached.

"She won't run off again today. She got what she

was after," he said, proudly holding up a black duck by its legs.

Senna was amazed that the small dog had caught and killed such a big duck. "I'm afraid I don't know how to clean it," she admitted.

"I do," Charlie said. "Can I give the crackie the last fish?"

"She's earned it, I guess, and if Jack doesn't come back tonight, we'll eat Ula's duck for supper."

Waiting for Jack to return gave Senna time to explore the lodge again at her own leisurely pace. She poked into all the boxes and crates in the living room, examining the contents, trying to decide where she would hang each of the prints, which room would get which set of furniture, and how the couches and easy chairs would be arranged in front of the fireplace. The urge to see the lodge as it would look when the buyers came to view it was too strong to ignore. Before she knew it she was carrying boxes into the kitchen, unpacking pots and pans, cooking utensils and silverware, plates and bowls, cups and wineglasses. With Charlie's help, she carried the bed frames into each of the six guest rooms. The tools she needed were all at hand, stashed in a box Charlie carried up from the guides' cabin. By the time the sun was nearing the horizon, they'd finished assembling the bed frames and were dragging twelve double box springs and mattresses down the hallway.

By 9:00 p.m. Senna was exhausted. She was also worried. Jack should have been back before now. He'd been gone for almost four hours. She walked out onto the porch, sat on the top step, and gazed out across the river, the rapids gleaming white in the gathering dusk. It was the sound of the river that masked the plane's engine. She heard Ula bark, just one short yap, and followed the little dog's intense stare. Over the black spruce she spotted the flashing red tail light as the plane approached, banked around, and dropped closer to the river. The plane disappeared from sight before landing, but soon she heard the sound of it taxiing toward the bend in the river.

Charlie and Ula went down to the dock to meet Jack, but Senna remained where she was, infused with a combination of weariness and relief that conspired to cement her limbs to the porch. She watched Jack jump out of the plane and reach back in to retrieve a big cardboard box, which he handed to Charlie. He grabbed a second box out of the plane and followed Charlie and the dog back up the steep ramp. "I brought bacon and eggs and a few other luxuries," he said when he was close enough to be heard. "Just in case."

"We also have a nice fat duck," Senna said.

"Charlie told me." Jack climbed the porch steps and set the box down. "Damn crackie. She makes me mad when she runs off like that, but she knows her stuff. We'd never starve with her around, we'd just get arrested for killing black ducks out of season." He rummaged around in the box and pulled out a bottle of wine, sitting down beside her on the step. "Charlie also told me you've been busy."

Senna drew her knees up and wrapped her arms around them, wishing he'd sit a little bit farther away. He was definitely invading her space. "Well, I couldn't see just sitting around and waiting for both you and the dog. There's a lot to do around here to get this place in shape, so I made a start."

"Think we'll be ready in time for the first guests?"

he asked, taking his jackknife out of his pocket, unfolding the corkscrew, and applying it to the top of the wine
bottle.

Senna watched him with a flicker of apprehension.
The idea of a relaxing glass of wine was wonderful
after such a long and demanding day, and she didn't
have the strength to spar with him about the business
partnership. Nonetheless, she couldn't let him believe
he'd won her over to his way of thinking so easily.
"We'll be ready in time for the first prospective buyers
to be flown in," she said.

Jack levered the cork out of the bottle. "I picked out
an Australian Shiraz. It'll go well with the crackie's
duck. I'll get a couple of glasses, if I can find them.
They're in one of the boxes in the living room...."

"No, they're not. They're in the kitchen. I unpacked
a few things while you were gone."

He returned momentarily and sat back down on the
step beside her. Too close again, but his nearness wasn't
really all that unpleasant. She was beginning to get used
to it. "You unpacked a lot more than a few things. The
kitchen looks like it's ready to tackle a major wedding
reception. Just how good of a cook are you?"

"Probably not nearly as accomplished as your
Goody."

He grinned, poured a glass of wine and handed it to
her. "Goody's a fine cook, I guess, but she cooks the
kind of stuff your grandfather liked. Codfish pie, squid
stew, boiled bangbelly. He thought the guests would
like that authentic Newfoundlander fare." He shook his
head, pouring a second glass for himself. "I dunno. Give
me steak and potatoes any day. Cheers."

Senna reluctantly touched her wineglass to his. "Is it safe for you fly after drinking a glass of wine?"

Jack took a sip. "Nope. Strictly forbidden. We'll have to spend the night."

"What about the sled dogs?"

"All taken care of. The next-door neighbor's going to feed them until we get back."

"Your nearest neighbor lives miles away."

"Not really. There's an Inuit family, relatives of Charlie's, in fact. They live less than a quarter mile up the lake, beyond the house."

"No road?"

"That's what the lake's for. Try the wine."

Senna raised her glass for a taste. "Very nice. So enlighten me. What's boiled bangbelly?"

"Pretty lady," Jack said, holding his glass of wine up to the colors of the sunset in a salute to the beautiful wilderness, "even if I knew, I'm not sure I'd tell you."

SENNA COOKED SUPPER in the lodge's kitchen. According to Jack, it was the first trial run of the commercial stove, the generator, the water pump, the water heater, the refrigerator and the lights. Everything worked just fine. She roasted Ula's duck beneath a cape of bacon, baked six big russet potatoes, then broiled a thick steak because the duck wasn't really big enough to feed three people, let alone a growing boy and a man as hardworking as Jack. The groceries Jack had brought were enough to last for a week, and so Senna, knowing they were only going to be there overnight, prepared a feast.

Jack set up a table on the porch, lit by two candles procured from a packing crate and between the three of them they devoured everything. Ula got only the smallest taste of her forbidden duck, snuck to her beneath the table by Charlie, and had to settle for a bowl of kibble to sate her own hunger. Senna drank a second glass of wine and was still sipping it while Jack cleared the table and voluntarily did the dishes, a gesture Senna suspected was meant to soften her up as a prelude to his trying to convince her to remain his business partner indefinitely. She heard the generator switch off when he was done, and then his footsteps coming back out onto the porch.

"Charlie and I'll sack out in the guides' cabin tonight," he said, dropping back into his chair and pulling his wineglass close. "He's already headed down there with the crackie, both of them draggin' their heels, they're so tired. I brought a sleeping bag along for you. It's clean and warm. You can pick whichever guest room you like the best and try out one of those new mattresses."

Senna took another sip of wine. "That sounds wonderful. It's not every day a woman gets an entire fishing lodge all to herself."

"It's not every woman who'd want one," he said. He leaned his elbows on the table. "Just listen to that."

Senna listened. "What?"

"The complete and total absence of a single manmade sound."

"Wild."

"Wild," he echoed with obvious satisfaction.

"This has to be about as far as it gets from living on an aircraft carrier with thousands of other people," Senna commented. "Did you fly, like my father?"

"Yes."

Senna shook her head. "I have to admit, I never understood his love of flying. In fact, I resented it. I hated the planes he flew, the angry, shrieking noise they made, the way the ground shook when they flew at low levels. Those planes were the reason he was always gone…and the reason he died." She lifted her glass for another sip. "I asked him once why he did it, and he said it was because it was a great responsibility to protect his country's freedom. He certainly took that responsibility more seriously than he did being a husband and a father." Jack made no response to her bitter statement, and the silence between them was amplified by the sound of the river rushing past. "So, what made you want to fly, John Hanson?"

Jack kicked back in his chair, cradled his wineglass on his stomach, and looked out across the river, gleaming in the mysterious arctic twilight. He drew a deep breath and blew it out in a philosophical whoosh.

"Sex," he said. "I knew from watching that movie, *Top Gun,* that all the most beautiful young women went wild over aviators wearing leather jackets and dark mirrored sunglasses, and since I was equally wild about beautiful young women, I decided to learn how to fly. I took lessons in junior high and got my private pilot's license when I was sixteen. Got pretty good grades in school, too. A Wyoming senator I met at the state science fair sponsored my application to M.I.T., and I was accepted. It was my ticket off the farm and into the air."

Senna watched him as he spoke. Jack had a handsome profile, strong and masculine, and the way his head was tilted back against the chair's headrest as he gazed back through the years allowed her to admire it openly. "Somehow I doubt you needed a leather jacket and dark mirrored glasses to get all the sex you wanted," she commented. "I think there might have been a little more to it than that."

He tipped his head just enough to briefly catch her eye. "Kinda," he admitted. "I grew up on a Wyoming farm, the firstborn son of a dry-land farmer. I watched the rainless clouds taunt the burning sky, and watched my parents grow prematurely old, struggling to make a living off the land. I couldn't wait to escape all those endless hours sitting on the seat of the big tractor, going up and down the rows of wheat, up and down the rows of corn, dawn 'til dusk, day after day, all summer long, ever since I'd been old enough to handle the controls, while the hawks soared and stooped over the freshly mown fields hunting for mice. They were free. I was a slave to the earth.

"I guess you could say it was the hawks that lured me away from that damn place, but it was a kind of miracle, getting that envelope in the mail and reading the words I'd never thought to read: 'Congratulations, you have been accepted to the Massachusetts Institute of Technology's School of Aeronautical Engineering...' That was the most exciting moment of my life. I kept the letter hidden in my pocket for a week before telling my parents.

"They'd been counting on me taking over the farm. They never understood my fascination with flight. They disapproved when I spent all of my summer money on flying lessons with Joe Robey, the local crop duster. They'd thought it was frivolous, irresponsible.

"My mother cried when I told her. My father just nodded his head and went back to work. Then I packed my things, climbed into my old Chevy truck, headed for the east coast and never looked back." Jack drained the last of his wine and stared out across the river.

"So you graduated M.I.T., and then you joined the Navy," Senna prompted after a long silence.

"Yup. I flew some of the most sophisticated flying machines ever built, and I got to wear the leather jacket and the dark mirrored sunglasses, and sure enough, the ladies were wild about me. Life was good."

Senna studied him as he spoke, and decided that if all he'd ever aspired to was to sweep floors as a janitor, the ladies would be no less wild about him.

"The flying was great," he continued. "Then I got married. I didn't want to give up flying, especially when I made Navy flight test, and for a while everything was okay. But then things started to go wrong with my marriage, or maybe things had been going wrong for a long time and I just didn't realize it. I guess you were right about that. Military men should never marry. My wife filed for divorce. Shortly after that, your father was killed in a plane crash. A couple of years later I got this call from the admiral, asking me to come to Labrador."

Senna wished the sky were a little brighter. She wanted to read his expression, but his eyes were dark hollows, gazing out across the distance. "Do you have any children?"

"None. Lisa wanted to wait until I got out of the service. I think that's one of the major reasons she divorced me. She wanted kids and a normal home life, and I kept reenlisting. Three months after our divorce was finalized, she married this accountant from her home town. A month later she was pregnant. She has two kids now, and you can be sure they won't grow up like you did. Their father will be there for them, whether they like it or not."

"Was your father in the Navy, too, before he became a farmer?"

"Nope. Drafted into the army, spent two tours over in 'Nam. Couldn't wait to get back to the farm. He died of a heart attack several years ago. I never had a chance to say goodbye. They buried him before I could get back home."

Senna reached out and laid her hand on his arm. "I'm sorry," she said. "I know how hard it is to lose your father."

CHAPTER SIX

JACK LOOKED AT SENNA and straightened in his chair. "Sorry to be so long-winded," he said, pushing to his feet. "I'll get your sleeping bag out of the plane. It's been a long day and tomorrow won't be any shorter." He walked down the steep ramp, the chill air bracing against him, clearing his head. Senna was a beautiful, compelling woman, and he'd been too long a bachelor. He was enjoying her companionship way too much. He picked up the sleeping bag from the passenger compartment and stood for a few moments, wondering if he should jump off the dock and let the icy waters cool his blood. She was, after all, intent on selling the admiral's half of the lodge and killing the old sea wolf's dreams. Somehow he had to convince her otherwise. He'd worked too hard to give up now, and he knew how heartless a woman could be about a man's dreams. His ex-wife had taught him that.

He carried the sleeping bag back up to the lodge. Senna was nowhere to be seen. He followed the small sounds, locating her in the farthest room with the stunning overlook of the rapids. "Trust a wedding planner to pick out the most scenic room," he said, tossing the sleeping bag onto the new mattress. "I'll get you a pillow."

"Got one already," she said, turning from the window, which she'd opened to the sound of the river. He saw that she was holding a pillow to her as if she were cradling a baby.

"Flashlight?" he said, extending his arm.

"Love one, thanks," she replied, taking it from him.

"See you in the morning, then."

"You know," she said when he was almost to the door, "there are five empty bedrooms up here. I don't see why you and Charlie shouldn't take advantage of these wonderful new mattresses."

"Charlie feels closer to the admiral when he's in the guides' camp. It was where your grandfather stayed," Jack explained as a strong gust of wind blew out of the north and pushed against the window panes, making a lonesome sound. He saw Senna's arms close more tightly around the pillow. "Of course, if you're afraid to stay up here by yourself..."

"Don't be ridiculous. I'm not afraid of being alone, and it isn't even really dark."

"Well, if you should change your mind, there are four bunks in the guides' cabin." He made the offer reluctantly, because the last thing he wanted was to toss and turn all night while she lay within arm's reach of him. "But I'll warn you in advance, the bunk mattresses aren't nearly as comfortable as these, and I've been told that I snore like a lumberjack."

Senna moved so suddenly that she startled the darkness, plucking the sleeping bag off the bed, ducking past him and marching out the door. "So do I, for all I know," she said over her shoulder, "but I'd feel guilty sleeping on one of those brand-new mattresses while the two of you suffered and I doubt anything could keep either one of us awake tonight."

SENNA COULDN'T HAVE BEEN more wrong. As exhausted as she was, sleep eluded her, and she couldn't blame her sleeplessness on loud snoring or the hard mattress. She lay awake on the bunk directly above Jack, intensely aware of how close he was. She could hear his breathing. It was deep and steady. Not snoring. Not yet, anyway. But he was definitely asleep, as were Charlie and his little crackie. All of them were breathing the measured, even breaths of deep slumber while she lay wide awake, staring up into the darkness, listening to all the sounds of the night and the rapid beating of her heart.

Her thoughts whirled in confusion. She'd been so sure this morning of what the proper course of action would be. Wrap up everything as soon as possible and return home. Now, she wondered if selling the lodge immediately was wise. Maybe Jack was right....

No, he *was* right, no maybe about it. Operating the lodge for a mere three months would increase the property's value tenfold. Jack was right and she was wrong. Furthermore, the longer she knew him, the more she realized that although he had no experience in the hospitality industry, he was perfectly capable of running the place. In the morning she'd tell him of her decision. She would return to Maine for the summer, and he would run the lodge. In the fall, she'd put her share of the business on the market, and who knows, maybe with one successful season on the books Jack could then convince a bank to loan him the money to buy her out.

He loved the place. No doubt about it. He'd invested so much of himself in it, not just his money, but his time and his labors and his dreams of the future. For Jack to lose the lodge now would be a terrible thing.

Senna rolled over with a sigh. This was all the admiral's fault. If he hadn't died, this wouldn't be happening. Why hadn't he just left everything to Jack? That would have made much more sense. It was obvious that the two of them had been great friends. She and the admiral had no such history, yet he'd left her his entire half interest in the business.

Why?

She rolled over again. Tomorrow she'd call Granville in Goose Bay and tell him about her decision to open the lodge for the summer. She'd call her mother to keep her apprised and call work to check on how things were going in the sales department.

Senna twisted restlessly within the confines of the sleeping bag. She heard the wind moan along the cabin's eaves, a mournful sound that made her shiver. There was movement in the bunk below her. Jack turning onto his side? She held her breath, listening. It sounded like he was still asleep. Good. She didn't want to disturb him with all her thrashing. Her thoughts tangled in a confused web and Jack Hanson was monopolizing more and more of them. She was lying here, wide awake, when she would have been better off arranging the living-room furniture up in the lodge or reading her grandfather's journal in the hopes of finding the answers to why she was here in the first place.

THE SMELL OF FRYING BACON awoke Senna from what she believed had been a completely sleepless night. She lay in her bunk, cocooned within the warmth of the sleeping bag, and peeked down at the woodstove and the man who stood over it, forking strips of bacon out onto a folded-up paper bag. Charlie and Ula were gone. Morning sunlight streamed through the window and she could see a patch of the river, smoke rising from the water. The morning air must be chilly. She sat up, brushing her hair out of her face. She'd slept in her clothing, so getting dressed was not the issue it might have been in front of a man she'd known for less than two days. She unzipped the bag, sat up and dangled her stockinged feet over the edge. "Good morning."

He glanced over his shoulder. "Morning. How many eggs do you want?"

"Two, please, and do I smell coffee?"

They ate at the little table by the window, not waiting for Charlie. "He and the crackie took the boat up-river," Jack explained, buttering another slice of toast. "There's a place he likes to fish a bit beyond where we went yesterday."

"Is it safe, him going off alone like that?"

"That kid has more common sense than most of the human population on this planet and he can survive in the wilderness, a skill not many have these days."

"Does he have a life jacket?"

"Yes, Mother McCallum. More coffee?"

"Please." Senna nudged her cup toward him. "I've been thinking about the lodge."

Jack set the pot back on the stove, an easy reach for him. His expression was guarded. "What about it?"

"I think we should open in two weeks just as you had originally planned and run the lodge for the summer. My half will sell quicker and for a lot more money if we do, and the fact is, I can't afford the alternative of refunding all those advance deposits on top of the overdue bills."

He lifted his cup and narrowed his eyes through wraiths of steam, regarding her silently over the brim. Senna was surprised at his reticence. She'd expected a much more enthusiastic reaction to her announcement. She finished the last of her breakfast and took another sip of coffee, wondering at his sudden reserve. "I thought you'd be pleased."

"Oh, I am," he said. "Three months is better than nothing. But I guess I'd be more pleased if you told me you'd decided to keep your half and honor your grandfather's dream. You might just discover that he was a man of great vision."

Senna flushed. "Unfortunately that's not an option. When had you planned on moving Goody and her niece out here?"

"Goody was making up the list of provisions when the admiral died. We were going to bring her out right about now to help with the start-up."

"Then perhaps you should go see her as soon as possible and make sure that the two of them can still come. I'll set up charge accounts at the various businesses to pay for what we'll need, and then you could start flying the supplies in. I'm assuming there's going to be a lot more stuff."

"Yep."

"And Goody's coopies have to be flown in, too?"

"Yep."

"What about the sled dogs?"

"We were going to set up a dog yard out behind this cabin."

Senna frowned. "Won't they howl?"

"Like a pack of wolves," Jack said. "The sound will add to the wilderness atmosphere."

"What about communications?"

"There's a satellite phone up in the lodge, behind the reception area. I'll show you where it is and how to operate it."

"They're expensive, aren't they?"

"Hugely, but you can't run a business like this without a reliable form of communication."

"We have less than two weeks to get the place ready and the clock is ticking," Senna said, pushing out of her chair. "We'd better get started."

"Wait a minute." Jack stood, instantly dwarfing the small cabin. His expression was guarded. "We need to talk about where you'll be staying. Goody's cabin is smaller than this one, and it only has two bunks. I hope the rooms up at the lodge will be fully booked all summer. We could build an addition onto the back of Goody's cabin, or set you up with a cabin of your own, but that'll take some time. I'm thinking you should take this cabin. It doesn't have running water, but it's comfortable, and Charlie and I can set up tents for the guides."

Senna held up her hand to silence him. "Not to worry. I'll only be staying for as long as I had originally planned, and then I'm heading back to Maine and the rest of the summer will be up to you." She picked the plates up off the table on her way to the little sink. "And you needn't worry about my cramping your bachelor lifestyle for the next two weeks," she said over her shoulder. "I'll move my things into a room up at the lodge just as soon as I've cleaned up here. You were right about the bunk mattress. I didn't get a wink of sleep last night."

JACK PACED UP TO THE LODGE, head down, shoulders rounded, hands shoved into his jacket pockets. He should be feeling good about things. The admiral's granddaughter was going to help get the lodge ready for business and wait until summer's end before putting her half of it on the market. This was what he'd hoped she would decide when she saw the place, and yet when she'd made the announcement he'd felt as if the earth had suddenly tipped on its axis and thrown him off balance.

Maybe it was the way she'd been sitting there at the table, hair mussed from the pillow, eyes drowsy with sleep, cheeks flushed from the heat of the woodstove, looking about as real as a woman ever looked first thing in the morning, and as beautiful as the morning itself. Maybe it was the way her slender hands cradled the coffee mug, or the graceful way she raised a forkful of eggs to her mouth, or the way she gazed out the window, contemplating the river while she sipped her coffee. Maybe it was the way she'd tossed and turned all night long, sighing her restless dilemmas into the silence. Maybe it was the way she'd listened to him talking about his farm-boy upbringing the night before, as if she was really interested, as if she really cared.

Whatever the reason, when she'd said she was only staying until the lodge was ready to open, he should have felt glad that she was at least volunteering to pitch in and help with the start-up, then trusting him to run the lodge by himself. But instead he'd felt even more unsettled. Eleven more days of sharing this place with her, of rubbing shoulders with the admiral's granddaughter. The idea hadn't seemed that dangerous a couple of days ago, but now, for some reason, it was disturbing as hell.

Still, it would give him more time to convince her that she shouldn't sell out. Jack trotted up the porch steps, entered the lodge and immediately began ripping into the unopened crates. He had to get this stuff unpacked, move everything into the guest rooms and arrange the living room properly before flying out, because when they returned they'd be bringing more stuff and still more stuff after that. Every flight would be jammed to the guppers until opening day, and then he'd be ferrying guests back and forth and guiding clients on the river and the nearby lakes. So much to do. No time to wonder about this uneasy churn of feelings in his gut.

By the time Senna arrived, carrying her sleeping bag, pillow and flashlight, Jack had moved all the bureaus and chairs into the rooms and was assembling the little pine bedside tables. She deposited her things in the room she'd chosen the night before and began hanging the stacks of framed prints, tapping picture hangers into the logs, hanging the picture, then stepping back to critically appraise the placement.

"I'd put that one over the mantelpiece," Jack suggested, glancing up in time to see her leveling the print.

"Oh? I think it looks fine right where it is. I like these Audubons, but what on earth do they have to do with Labrador?"

"Labrador has ducks," Jack pointed out. "We ate one last night."

"Yes, and out of season, too. Good thing there were no wardens lurking about. I think the lodge should have original artwork appropriate to the place."

"I'll be sure and pick you up some paintbrushes and canvases while I'm getting the provisions," Jack commented, tightening a table leg.

"I was thinking more along the lines of getting my grandfather's photographs enlarged and framed." Senna held up another print, eyeing it critically. "Some aboriginal touches would be nice, too."

"Yeah. We could cover the couches with caribou and wolf skins. I'll pick us up a few hunting rifles while I'm at it. Charlie knows how to tan hides. I thought that one would look good in the dining room," he added, referring to the picture she held.

"Really?" She looked at the print. "It seems to go with the one I just hung. I think they should stay in the same room, don't you?"

An hour later they were arguing over the arrangement of the living-room furniture. "The seating works much better this way," Senna insisted. "You come through the main door and you can bear right into the dining room, or straight ahead to the reception area for registration, or left into the living room. See what I mean?"

"The couches work better turned the other way," Jack said.

"Better for what?"

"Sitting and looking at the fireplace. Isn't that what couches are for?"

She glared at him for a moment, and then stalked toward the kitchen, reemerging with two cans of juice from the refrigerator. She handed him one, opened the other, and took a long drink. "You really think this place'll be ready in time?" she said.

"Only if you quit being so bossy and argumentative."

She looked around at the stacks of boxes as yet unpacked, pressed her hand into the small of her back, and sighed. "You'd better round up Goody and her niece. We're going to need all the help we can get. There's tons of cleaning yet to be done, and every single window has to have those awful manufacturer's labels scraped off before they can be washed. Where's Charlie, anyway? Shouldn't he be back by now?"

Jack opened his can of juice and downed half of it in two big swallows. "You keep unpacking and I'll find Charlie. Then we'd better saddle up and fly out of here. You're right. We need help, and lots of it."

BY MIDAFTERNOON THEY WERE back at the lake house, where Jack let Senna and Charlie off on the end of the dock before continuing to Goose Bay. "Think you can handle the dog chores by yourself?" Jack asked.

"Of course."

"Charlie'll help, won't you, Charlie?" he said, catching the boy's eye. "I laid some groceries in yesterday, so you won't starve tonight, and you can always drive into Goose Bay for a wild night in the big city, it's not that far. We'll fly back to the lodge first thing in the morning."

"We'll be fine," Senna said, kneeling to hug Chilkat who had come to greet them. "Will you be spending the night in town?"

"Probably. A little bit of socializing from time to time helps keeps me civilized," he explained. "Charlie, better keep Ula tied up. Keep an eye on things for me, would you?" That said, he taxied a short ways from the dock before opening the throttle and taking off. Senna watched the plane climb and then bank around, heading for Goose Bay, waiting until it was out of sight before turning for the lake house, Chilkat at her side. Already, Charlie was nowhere to be seen, and already, she felt Jack's absence in a way that was too acute to be ignored. She tried to squelch the churn of jealousy she felt when she wondered where he'd be spending the night. It was really none of her business if he had a bountiful array of pretty girls in every port…and she was fairly certain he did.

She tossed her day pack on the kitchen table and thought about the admiral's journal. If she did nothing else tonight, she would read through it, and try to understand the man he'd been. It was still early. She had plenty of time to meet with the lawyer and discuss her grandfather's estate. Goose Bay wasn't that far, and she could have supper there before returning to the lake house. She rang her mother's house, getting no answer, then phoned Granville, who answered on the first ring.

"Of course I have time to see you this afternoon, m'dear," he said, sounding tickled pink to have gotten a phone call from her, or from anyone, for that matter. "Come right along on."

Senna left a note for Charlie on the kitchen table, informing him that she'd fed the sled dogs, promising to be home by 9:00 p.m. and telling him that there were cold cuts in the refrigerator, bread in the bread box atop the counter. She felt guilty leaving him, yet for all she knew he was in North West River by now, visiting his uncle. "I'll be home by dark," she promised Chilkat, who walked her out to her car and watched her leave with those solemn, wolf-like eyes.

How strange the world looked to her now, after just two days of being out of touch with the hustle and bustle of humanity. Of course, one could hardly classify Goose Bay as being a hustle-and-bustle kind of place, but compared to the lodge on the Wolf River it felt like New York City. Mr. Granville ushered her immediately into his office, sat her down and poured her a cup of strong black tea.

"So, you've seen the properties, then. The lake house, the fishing lodge?"

Senna nodded. "Jack Hanson flew me out to the Wolf River yesterday."

"Ah. Good." Mr. Granville opened the file on his desk and adjusted his glasses as he sifted through the papers inside the folder. "Now where did I put that letter…"

"Letter?"

"Yes," Granville said, rustling through the file. "A letter your grandfather wrote just before he died. He asked me to wait until you'd seen the lodge and met John Hanson before I gave it to you."

Senna sat up straighter. "Why?"

"I don't know, m'dear. I'm sure the letter will explain that, if I could just find it…."

Senna fidgeted impatiently while he searched. "It must be in there. That's his file, isn't it?"

"Yes, yes…" Granville scanned the file's tab and cover page, nodding affirmation, "but for some reason it's not in here." He pushed his glasses onto the bridge of his nose and looked across the desk at her. "Oh, don't worry, m'dear. It's here somewhere. Maybe I misfiled it…it was an emotional meeting, the last time your grandfather came here. He knew he didn't have long to live. It was just a matter of days, y'see. We shared a few glasses of screech and talked about all the good times, walked down to the pub in the rain…" Granville sighed, removed his glasses, rubbed his closed eyes. "Good times we had together, your grandfather and I. He was a great man, but I'm sure you knew that."

Senna leaned forward in her chair. "Mr. Granville, I've changed my mind about putting the property on the market right away. Jack's going to open the lodge and run it for the summer, like he and my grandfather had originally planned. He's going to bring your sister Goody Stewart and her niece out there as soon as possible. He's fetching them tonight, as a matter of fact."

Granville donned his glasses and stared in owlish surprise. "Does Goody know about this?"

"I would assume so. Jack told me it was all prearranged. Why?" Senna felt the beginnings of a tension headache gathering in her temples.

"Well, when the admiral died, Goody figured the lodge wouldn't open. She took a job over on the Island working for a friend who owns some kind of a restaurant in Black Tickle."

"Has she left yet?"

"I believe she took the mail boat just yesterday. Her grand-niece is still at the house. Lives there, see. Wavey wouldn't leave Goose Bay for all the tea in China. She's stuck on Jack, that one is." Granville shook his head.

"*Grand*-niece?" Senna's image of a seventy-year-old woman accompanied by her fifty-odd-year-old niece, two solid and reliable employees to anchor the cooking and cleaning chores at the lodge, vanished in the aftermath of Granville's dismaying news.

"Wavey's my granddaughter, my daughter's only child."

Senna's headache was becoming more of a reality. She took a sip of the tea. It was without a doubt as strong as it looked, but a little caffeine might be just what she needed about now. "That's not good news,

Mr. Granville. We were counting on Goody to cook for us. Can Wavey cook?"

"Wavey could do anything she set her mind to, if she would just set her mind to something. She's a beautiful girl, but…" Granville took his glasses off again, pressed the bridge of his nose between thumb and forefinger, and shook his head.

"Mr. Granville, my grandfather's letter. It's very important that I read it. Could you please call the lake house or the lodge just as soon as you find it?" Senna rose to her feet as she spoke, as did Granville.

"Of course, m'dear. I have both numbers and I'll ring you up just as soon as I put my hands on it, I promise." Before she left his office, he told her about a good place to eat close by. "Everyone at the base eats there, see," he said.

Senna was surprised to find that it was raining when she stepped outside and began walking down the street, and even more surprised to see an occasional snowflake pelting down out of the leaden sky. At 5:00 p.m. the little pub was nearly empty. Senna was shown to a table by the only window, where she searched the menu for boiled bangbellies and was relieved when she didn't find any such fare listed. It was probably something Jack had made up. She ordered a burger and fries and drank a Molson ale while she waited, watching rivulets of rain zig and zag down the windowpanes. What if Granville couldn't find the letter? Judging from the general state of disarray his office was in, that was a very real possibility, especially if the two of them had been drinking screech at the time her grandfather handed it over.

Even more troubling, where were they going to find

a cook willing to spend an entire summer at a remote fishing lodge on such short notice? Her burger arrived and Senna devoured it, recalling that she hadn't eaten since breakfast. She was finishing off the last French fry when she saw two people walking down the street toward the pub, both bare-headed in the cold rain. The young woman had long dark hair, a pale English complexion and was laughing up at something the man had just said. The handsome man was none other than Jack Hanson. Even as she stared, Senna realized that the young woman could only be Wavey, Goody's grandniece—and she also knew that this peaches-and-cream girl was never going to slave over a hot stove or scrub a dirty toilet.

Just one look at the way Wavey was gazing adoringly at Jack and Senna knew they were going to need to hire both a cook and a housekeeper if the lodge were to operate for the summer. Charlie was supposedly the chore boy, but he was young, and like all youngsters had shown little desire to help with any chores whatsoever. Dear God. If the situation weren't so desperate, it would be funny.

Jack and Wavey entered the pub and Senna hid behind a menu as they made their way to the bar. As soon as she'd paid her bill, she gathered her things and stood. No fear of being seen by those two as she walked out the door. They were way too interested in each other to pay any attention to the other pub patrons. Senna pulled her coat on while she walked down the street, filled with anger and frustration. She was angry with herself for feeling so frustrated, and frustrated for feeling so angry.

As she drove back toward North West River, she tried

to put the image of that beautiful girl clinging to Jack's arm out of her mind, but she couldn't. Was Wavey one of Jack's girlfriends? Granville had said she was stuck on Jack. And why was she, Senna McCallum, a successful career woman with a job in Maine, even thinking about such things? Charlie was still nowhere to be found when she arrived at the lake house, but Chilkat welcomed her back with a glad little "woof," flattening his ears and fanning his tail as she climbed out of the car.

"Hello to you, too, old boy. Let's go check on the rest of the team, shall we?" He accompanied her down the short path to the dog yard, where she counted heads and actually dared to pat a few of them before returning to the house. She took a long, hot shower and afterward fixed herself a cup of tea, which she carried upstairs to her grandfather's room along with his journal. She climbed into the bed as Chilkat sprawled across the foot of it and switched on the bedside lamp. If Granville never located the letter, at least she had the journal. She only hoped the reading wouldn't be too dry and dull. She drew up her knees, propped the leather-bound volume against them, and opened the cover. She'd call her mother in a little while, just as soon as she couldn't force herself to read another word.

CHAPTER SEVEN

JACK TOOK THE NEWS of Goody Stewart's departure with all the grace of a poleaxed prizefighter, slumping in Goody's doorway while Wavey tried ineffectually to pull him inside. He rubbed his face, dazed and unbelieving. How could Goody run off like this? What were they going to do without her? Who was going to prepare all those authentic Newfoundlander meals?

"Come on, Jack. Don't look so glum. Goody needed to get away from here when the admiral died," Wavey was saying, still tugging at his arm. "Don't just stand there looking lost. You still have me, don't forget, and I'll never let you down."

He stared at Wavey's pale face and those dark expressive eyes. Hope stirred within. "Can you cook?"

"I can read a cookbook," she said. "That's a start, isn't it? How tough can cooking be?"

"Oh, God," Jack groaned. "Did Goody leave behind a list of supplies, by any chance? She started working on one a couple weeks ago…."

A frown puckered Wavey's smooth brow. "What kind of supplies?"

"You know, like flour and sugar and…" Jack gave up. "Wavey, can you think of anyone, any of your friends, any of Goody's friends, who can cook, who can clean and who can work like a dog under less-than-perfect conditions?"

The frown deepened and her lips pursed. "I know a girl named Chloe," she offered slowly. "She used to work on the base, cleaning, but she got pregnant. I think she can still mop floors and stuff like that, but she probably shouldn't bend over too much. She's only six months along but she's pretty big. Everyone thinks she's going to have twins because twins run in her mother's side of the family, but I think she's just really big, and she's put on weight, too. A lot of weight. Some do, you know, when they're pregnant. I can ask her, though, 'cause I know she really needs money…."

Jack groaned again and collapsed against the door frame.

Wavey's face suddenly brightened. "Gordina Hutchinson! She works at the pub. We could walk down there and talk to her, she's probably working tonight, but we can't let Harley overhear. He'd kill you if you ever stole Gordina from him. He says she's the only cook he's ever found who can fix a runny omelet for a customer while suffering from a bad hangover."

"Queasy."

"C'mon Jack," Wavey said, tugging him in the opposite direction now. "Let's go down there. It won't hurt to ask her, and she does make a really good runny omelet."

By 10:00 p.m. they'd visited every pub, restaurant and tavern in Goose Bay and exhausted all possibilities. Wavey was leading the way back to Goody's house. She kept hauling Jack up against her when he veered off on another tangent. "Well, here we are," she said as they reached Goody's plain little house looking out over the Sea of Labrador. "I still think Gordina's the best bet, and she said she'd come."

"She smokes," Jack said, wondering what Senna had fixed for supper, if she'd found the steaks he'd stashed in the refrigerator and the exorbitantly expensive asparagus he'd placed beside it on the top shelf. He felt a twinge of envy that Charlie was sharing her company at the lake house while he'd floundered through every eatery and drinking hole in Goose Bay trying to scare up a good cook at the last minute.

"Yes, but she's the only one who said she'd come."

"She smokes while she cooks. I saw her." Jack felt as old as the universe as he stood on Goody's threshold. "Look, I appreciate all your help tonight, Wavey. If you still want to work at the lodge, be ready at dawn."

"I'll be ready," Wavey said, and Jack was startled when she reached out and seized two fistfuls of his jacket just below his throat. "You don't have to go, Jack," she pleaded. "Stay here tonight. Stay with me. We'd have the whole house to ourselves. You don't have to be alone anymore, I know how lonely being alone can be…."

Jack closed his hands over hers, pried them off his jacket, and held them securely in his own. "Wavey, you're a good girl, and I'm flattered, believe me, I am, but I've always thought of you as a baby sister and I always will. If you want to work at the lodge, come out to the plane at dawn. I won't blame you if you don't show up. The job is about as unglamorous as it gets. Good night," he said, closing the door firmly in her face and beating a hasty retreat.

Gordina was still working at the pub and Harley was nowhere to be seen. "If you want the job, be at the plane docked in front of Goody's house at dawn," he told her, and she nodded grimly, cigarette clenched in one corner of her thin mouth, blue smoke wreathing her face.

Jack returned to his plane, relieved to see that Goody's house was dark. Wavey must have gone to bed. He could have slept on the couch in the living room, but decided that would be unwise. The wind gusted and the plane was rocking on its pontoons. He climbed into the cockpit and settled himself in his seat with a sigh of pure exhaustion. He wanted the lodge to be a success more than he'd wanted anything in his entire life. But he was almost positive that neither Gordina nor Wavey would show in the morning, Gordina because she wanted more money than he could promise her, and Wavey because he wouldn't sleep with her. Without skilled help, the lodge wouldn't fly.

It was cold and raw inside the plane. Sleet skittered off the windshield and the rough harbor chop splashed up against the undercarriage and rocked the plane on its pontoons. By morning there might be an inch or two of snow on the ground. Jack huddled deeper into his jacket, reached for a blanket out of the back and draped it over himself. He was bone-tired. It was time to let go of all life's troubles for a little while, and let the universe sort things out.

From the Journal of Admiral Stewart Anderson McCallum:
February 23

Forty-two below zero. Too sick to run dogs today. John took both teams out and did all chores. He's cutting firewood now, I can hear the chainsaw.

Clients coming next week, day-trippers. He'll
have to deal with them, too. Take them out on the
lake if the weather allows, or use the Naskaupi
Trail if it doesn't. Every day now I feel more useless, though he takes up the slack without com-
plaint. Without his help I wouldn't be able to stay
out here. I doubt I'll see another winter. I only
hope I live long enough to see the lodge completed.

With my own death so near at hand, I feel the
weight of countless other deaths on my conscience. Many times I've looked up at the stars in
the night sky and wondered why I'm still alive
when so many good men are dead. Our existence
on this planet seems no more than a series of cha-
otic events, randomly strung together. If logic and
reason had any place at all in this universe, and if
there really were a godly hand behind the sun rising and setting, day after day, year after year, millennium after millennium—would any of us be
standing here at the end of our lives, wondering
why?

Senna closed her grandfather's journal, leaned her
head back against the headboard and closed her eyes.
Dear God. Not every entry had been as dark, as troubling, or as profound, but toward the end his writing had
become more and more melancholy and introspective.
Reading this journal had proven to be a far different experience than she had anticipated. There were very few
entries describing meals cooked, and very little of the
trivia that cluttered the average day. Some entries were
delightful, enthusiastic descriptions of the animal and

plant life. He would describe in beautiful detail the various plants growing along the edge of the lake, how the ducks and geese migrating through in early fall would come ashore to eat the ripe berries, how the bakeapples would ripen in August and the locals would harvest them for incomparable pies and preserves and how the black bears would sit on their haunches stripping raspberries from the thickets near the lake house.

But clearly the wolves were his love. His observations were keen and astute, and he even knew individual animals by sight, especially around Wolf River. There was a big black female wolf he saw frequently. He called her Raven, and noted that she was the alpha female of the Naskaupi pack. Senna found his entries about the wolves fascinating enough to keep her riveted to the pages of the journal.

Had there been time, she might have called her mother, but now it was past midnight, and she still had a ways to go 'til she reached the last journal entry. Thus far, she'd encountered no mention of herself in her grandfather's writings, though Charlie was mentioned frequently. Charlie had come back an hour ago, creeping into the lake house with Ula and settling onto the sofa for the night, both of them startled by her presence at the foot of the stairs.

"Is that you, Charlie?" she'd spoken into the dark room, knowing what the answer would be but needing to hear it, just the same.

"Yes," came the somber reply.

"Did you have supper?"

"Yes."

"Is Ula with you?"

"Yes."

"All right, then. Good night."

No reply. The jury was still out where Charlie was concerned. He certainly wasn't very communicative. Where had he gone? What had he eaten for supper? She'd never know because he'd never tell her. He lived in a different world. They all did. She, Jack and Charlie, all flung together haphazardly, first by her grandfather's life, and then by his death, the three of them sharing the same spaces but worlds apart within them.

Senna set the journal on the bedside table, pushed the quilt aside and stood. She wondered where Jack had gone when he'd left the pub with that girl, but there was really no mystery there. He was spending the night with her. Jack was with Wavey. And why, exactly, should that bother her so much? Why should she be standing at the window in her grandfather's room at the lake house, looking out at the dark waters where rain and sleet and snow kept the loons, Charles and Diana, from haunting the twilight with mournful predictions of a sorrowful future? Why should she be thinking of Jack when she should be counting the days before she returned to Maine?

No reason, really, but she was....

THE LOONS WOKE HER in the quiet dawn. The rain had stopped in the night and lying in bed Senna could see a few faint stars lingering in the westward sky before the pale light strengthening in the eastern sky erased them. It was going to be a fine, shining day. She stretched beneath the covers, glad for the wool blanket in the chill morning air. The journal lay on the bedside table and she reached out her hand, brushing the cover with her fingertips. She'd read the whole thing last night, learning oh, so much about a man she'd previously considered a stranger. There had only been one brief entry about her, and that was to document that he'd named her as his executor and Granville had made it official. No further explanation. Her disappointment had been intense, but that was the only thing about the journal that had disappointed. The rest of it could be published as his wilderness memoirs just as it stood.

She'd call her mother this morning, right after making a pot of coffee. Too bad Charlie didn't know how to make a pot of coffee. It would be nice just to lie here and smell coffee perking and the tang of wood smoke flavoring the air as he started the morning fire. He should be up to speed with things like that if he intended to pull his weight at the lodge. Ha! Chore boy, indeed!

Chilkat snored at her feet, but not so loudly she didn't hear Charles and Diana commiserating just off-shore. And then she heard something else. The deep, throaty roar, distant at first and then growing ever stronger, of Jack's plane returning. Sleep was forgotten as she flung aside the bedding and leapt to her feet. She looked out the window in disbelief. Sure enough, there was the plane, dropping down and landing with a brief spray of water, then taxiing toward the dock. What on earth was he doing back from town so early? Senna fumbled to get dressed and had just reached the foot of the stairs when he came into the house, bursting through the door with a rush of cold air.

"Morning," he said as if it was the most natural thing in the world to meet her this way. "Coffee ready?"

"Actually, I was waiting for you to get here and fix it for me," Senna replied, following him into the kitchen.

"Sorry, can't stay that long." He opened the refrigerator and grabbed the gallon jug of milk. "Gotta bring this along, Wavey has a kitten and there's no milk at the lodge." He shut the refrigerator door, straightened, looked at her square in the eye for the first time. "Goody isn't coming. She's taken a job on the Island working for a friend at some restaurant in Black Tickle, so I had to hire someone else. Her name's Gordina Hutchinson and she's very experienced. Cooked at a restaurant in Goose Bay."

"I know about Goody. Granville told me. And as I understand it, Wavey is Goody's *grand*-niece."

"Grand-niece, second cousin twice removed, whatever," Jack said with an impatient wave of his hand. "Gordina can't cook boiled bangbelly, but I'm told she fixes a mean runny omelet. We're damn lucky to have her, and Wavey, too. I didn't think either of them would show up this morning."

"That's good news. Wonderful." Senna combed her fingers through her hair, wishing she'd had time to brush it. "Wavey has a kitten?"

"Yes, and Goody couldn't take her coopies with her to the Island so they're crated in the plane, squawking and flapping and creating more organic matter by the moment. Twelve of 'em. It's pretty queasy. Hope the smell goes away. I'll take this load to the lodge and come back for you and Charlie."

"Fine," Senna replied.

"Maybe you could have the coffee ready by then?"

"I'll do my Girl-Scout best."

Jack grinned at her. He looked tired and a little frazzled, as if he hadn't gotten much sleep, but of course, spending the night with Wavey would almost guarantee any red-blooded man a complete lack of sleep. He glanced at his watch. "I'll be back in two hours. Six o'clock sharp."

"We'll be ready."

He nodded and left, taking the jug of milk with him. It figured Wavey would have a kitten. Something fuzzy and adorable, something that cuddled and purred. Senna watched him stride down the dock, untie the cleat ropes, and climb into the plane. She felt Chilkat nudge her hand as she watched the plane take off and dropped her fingers to stroke the top of the old dog's head. "A kitten," she said, disgusted, then returned to the kitchen to kindle a fire in the woodstove and start a pot of coffee.

The kitchen warmed up in jig time and she carried the first cup of coffee with her into the living room. Charlie was bundled in his sleeping bag on the couch sound asleep with Ula curled beside him, eyes open, watching her. She sat down at the admiral's desk and sipped her coffee, sorting through lodge construction invoices, unpaid electric and gas bills, charge slips from a lumber company in St. John's, an overdraft charge from the bank and a ledger that tracked hours worked but didn't specify who had worked them. Great.

She knew it was her savings account that was going to pay Wavey and Gordina, as well as all these outstanding bills…and there were a lot of them. She'd have to keep careful track of her expenses so that Jack could refund her what he owed. In the meantime, there was a pack of hungry sled dogs waiting to be fed. She'd pay these bills when she finished the dog chores, and, she hoped, everything would be in order by the time Jack returned.

Chilkat once again supervised her trip to the dog yard

and stood guard while she scooped out their morning meal. She was so preoccupied with a million and one lodge start-up conundrums that she forgot to be nervous about the huskies that jumped and whirled with excitement as she dished up breakfast. She even scolded one for trying to stuff its head in the bucket as she walked through its circle. Feeding done, she cleaned the entire dog yard, then made sure all the water buckets were topped off. She wasn't surprised that she had to break a skim of ice on many of them. Last night's rain had turned to snow before it tapered off, and this morning the black spruce were quite beautiful in the dawn, standing at attention like frosted soldiers in the early light.

Back at the lake house Senna called her mother and told her everything that had happened. "Your grandfather's business partner sounds like he has a lot of energy for an old man," her mother commented when she'd related their activities of the past two days.

"Jack's probably somewhere in his mid-thirties."

"My goodness. When you told me he was younger than you thought he'd be, I didn't realize he was *that* young. How did he and the admiral happen to go into business together?"

"Dad was his commanding officer. He accompanied Dad and the admiral on a fishing trip to Labrador, and, strange as it may seem, they struck up a friendship."

"Will wonders never cease. So you're planning to help open the lodge?"

"Showing that it's a potentially profitable concern is the only way I'll ever be able to sell my half of the business. Anyway, I thought you'd want an update. We're flying back to the lodge this morning with our two new hires. God only knows how they'll work out."

Her mother laughed. "All you can do is hope for the best and prepare for the worst."

"Amen to that. Wish me luck, Mom. Love you."

As soon as she'd hung up the phone, it surprised her by ringing. When she answered she was surprised even further to hear Tim's voice on the other end of the line. "I'm just calling to make sure you're okay," he said as if in apology.

"I'm fine, Tim. Very busy," Senna said with a pang of guilt. She hadn't thought about him at all in the past day, though he was still obviously upset about their recent separation.

"Listen, I know it might have been presumptuous of me, but I have some contacts in the insurance field and I sort of put out the word that you were trying to sell a fishing lodge in Labrador. Turns out one of my coworkers has an acquaintance who works in the real-estate division of Sotheby's in New York City. He wondered if you could take some digital pictures of the lodge and e-mail them back. There's a good chance he could find a buyer for your half of the business before the end of the summer."

Senna was momentarily taken aback. "Wow. That's fast work."

"I want to help. You know that. No matter what becomes of us, I'll always be your friend."

"Thanks. I appreciate that. I'll try and get some pictures to you and a description of the property."

There was a pause, then Tim spoke. "I know I shouldn't say this, but I really miss you."

"Tim…"

"I know. I'm hanging up now. Just take care of yourself, okay?"

Senna hung up the phone and dropped her head into her hands with a moan.

JACK STAYED AT THE LODGE just long enough to unload the two women, their bags, Wavey's frightened kitten and the jug of milk onto the dock, and then carry the heavy crate holding Goody's coopies up the steep ramp to the chicken shed behind the cook's cabin. He invited Wavey and Gordina to explore the lodge in his absence, instructed them to start doing the things that needed doing, which he thought should be obvious, and then immediately got the plane back into the air. Senna would have the coffee ready, and he was craving a hot, strong mug. He'd spent a sleepless night trying to forget all his problems, and in the end he'd wished he'd flown back to the lake house, just so he could worry in his own bed. Not that Senna would have appreciated his company. She'd been glad to get rid of him, no doubt, and had enjoyed a nice peaceful evening at the lake house, though he'd noticed when he got the milk out of the refrigerator that she hadn't eaten the steak and asparagus.

An hour later, Senna was pouring him a mug of coffee while Charlie loaded gear into the plane. He glanced into the living room. The admiral's desk was open and a considerable stack of envelopes was piled dead center. "Doing some paperwork?"

"Paying bills, some of which are way overdue."

Jack avoided her accusing stare. "It seemed like everything came in over-budget...."

"That's usually how it is with new construction. I paid all the ones with the late notices. How does the mail work around here? You don't exactly have a mailbox I can drop these into, and it's important that they go out as soon as possible, before we have a collection agency breathing down our necks."

"We can post them where I gas the plane up." He finished the last of the coffee. "I'll go feed the dogs."

"Done," Senna said. "Fed, watered, and cleaned."

"Charlie…?"

She laughed. "Guess again. If he shows nearly as much ambition as a chore boy at the lodge, then you'll be doing his job, too."

"Oh, Charlie's okay. He pulls his weight, you just have to know how to motivate him."

"I'll just have to take your word for that. Are we ready to go?"

"Ready."

"When do you plan to move the sled dogs to the lodge?"

"Chilkat can come with us now. I'll set the dog yard up today and ferry the rest of them in tomorrow. Should be able to do it in two trips."

"Two trips?" Senna looked at him in disbelief. "All those big huskies in just two trips?"

"Sure. We can pack 'em in like sardines. They don't weigh much. They look big, but they're mostly just fur and fangs. Let's go, wedding planner. We're burning daylight."

THE MARINA IN NORTH WEST RIVER carried aviation fuel, as most did in this neck of the woods. There was also a store that sold everything from chewing gum to pine tar and oakum, and they had a mail drop there, too.

Jack filled the wing tanks while Senna posted the bills. He hoped she'd take a while, because Gilbert Truvo was standing on the dock rubbing his chin and working himself up to say something bad. Unfortunately Senna arrived just in time to hear every single word.

"Look, this'll have to be the last time, Jack. I know you got a plane to fly, but I got a business to run. You haven't paid down your charges in almost two months now, and aviation fuel is damned expensive. I'm sure you understand. Business is business."

Senna's expression never changed. She walked right up to Truvo, reached into her day pack and drew forth her wallet. "Do you take credit cards?" she asked.

Truvo shifted uncomfortably. "Yes, ma'am, we sure do."

Truvo took the proffered credit card and shuffled off toward the store. Jack finished fueling, looking everywhere but in Senna's direction, and wondered how he was ever going to make this right. Things were already worse than bad and times were going to get even tighter before enough money came in to turn the tide…if the tide ever did turn. He'd been broke so long he'd gotten used to it, but having Senna around had immediately cast a different light on eating fish five times a week and cutting new holes in his leather belt as his waistline shrank.

Truvo returned with the itemized receipt of two months worth of charges, stamped Paid, and hesitated between handing it to Jack or Senna. Senna reached out her hand and he gave it over with an apologetic shrug directed at Jack. "Sorry, Jack, but business is business," he repeated.

"Don't I know it."

"I'll run you up a line of credit, like before, long as I know it'll get paid."

"It will be, Mr. Truvo," Senna said.

When they were both back in the cockpit strapping themselves in, Jack glanced across at her. "I'll pay back every cent," he said.

"I'm not worried," she replied, fiddling with her buckle. "I spoke with a friend this morning who has an acquaintance who works in the real-estate division of Sotheby's in New York. I'm going to take some digital pictures of the lodge and e-mail them back. He said there's a good chance they'll find a buyer for my half before the end of the summer."

"Great," Jack said without enthusiasm, feeling more like a loser by the moment. "What's this friend of yours do?"

"He sells big insurance policies to big companies."

"Makes big bucks, too, no doubt."

"Yes, as a matter of fact." She turned in her seat and handed a brown paper bag to Charlie. "Candy bars and dog biscuits, just in case any of you gets a craving."

Jack taxied the plane away from the marina, hoping she'd expound on this mysterious relationship a little further, but Senna just gazed out the window at the little harbor. "What's his name?" he finally asked, just before the plane lifted into the air.

"Tim Cromwell."

"Tim?" Queasy, Jack thought, a guy named Tim who sold insurance policies. Well, that was probably a perfect match for someone who sold weddings to gullible couples. He shoved the throttle forward with an irrational surge of anger, and he was still in a surly mood when he put the plane down on the Wolf River an hour later. "Tie Ula up," he growled to Charlie as the boy stood in the rear passenger compartment. "We don't need her running off again." He glared at Senna. "You'll need to show Wavey how to clean the guest rooms and run the laundry equipment. I thought maybe she could get the linens on the beds, set up the bathrooms…"

"I do know a little bit about back-of-the-house operations, Jack," Senna returned, equally testy, as she unbuckled herself from the safety harness.

"Wavey's willing, but inexperienced."

"About *some* things, I'm sure." Acid dripped from Senna's words. She pushed out of her seat, grabbing her day pack, and prepared to disembark.

"What's that supposed to mean?"

Senna paused. "I'm just wondering if she's going to make a suitable housekeeper," she said.

"You think I can't hire good help?"

"I think you probably hire what suits you."

"I hired what we needed to get this lodge up and running," he shot back.

"What *you* needed, maybe, but I highly doubt that girl will benefit this lodge in any way, shape or form. Come on, Chilkat." She dropped down onto the dock and climbed the ramp without a backward glance, the old dog at her side.

Jack scrambled out of the plane, tripping over Wavey's empty kitty carrier and stumbling to his knees with a curse. "I know how to hire good help!" he bellowed after her as he struggled to his feet, but she never acknowledged him. He stood watching her stalk up the ramp, her back rigid with anger.

What the hell did she have against Wavey? She hadn't even met the girl yet. Damn, but that woman made him mad!

CHAPTER EIGHT

SENNA WAS FUMING AS SHE CHARGED up the ramp. Did he think she was blind? She knew the real reason Wavey was here.

By the time she reached the lodge she was convinced that the only thing for her to do was throw this whole sorry mess of an estate into Granville's lap and return to Maine. She entered the living room and looked around, boiling with frustration that nothing had changed. Foolishly, on the flight in, she'd imagined that all the stickers would have been scraped from the windows, the glass would be sparkling, the heaps of boxes and crates would have been unpacked, the sawdust and cobwebs swept up and dusted away, the floors scrubbed and buffed. Instead, she was upset to see that everything looked exactly the same as when they'd left yesterday afternoon. Jack's two new hires had been given three whole hours to get a jump on the work, yet nothing whatsoever had been done. Not one thing.

Why was she so surprised? Wavey was nothing more than a very young sex kitten with a crush on Jack, and Gordina was a complete unknown, though it stood to reason that she was probably just as young and gorgeous as Granville's granddaughter. The two of them had no doubt been purring and slinking about while all this work remained to be done. And where was Charlie, the chore boy?

"Wavey! Gordina?"

She got no answer. Then Jack burst into the room, out of breath from having chased her up the ramp. He skidded to a stop and looked around the untouched room the same way she had. "Looks like both of your new hires have been kidnapped," Senna said, planting her hands on her hips.

Before Jack could respond Chilkat uttered a growl deep in his chest and lunged toward a stack of boxes in the center of the room, hitting them squarely with his shoulder and sending them toppling as a very small kitten leapt from the midst of the chaos, let out a terrified yowl, and in one frantic bound managed to ascend the tallest pinnacle in the room, which just happened to be Jack. Senna stared wide-eyed as he reached up and deliberately pried the terrified kitten off his head, dangling it high above a transfixed Chilkat.

"Wavey!" he bellowed at the top of his lungs as several deep scratches on his forehead began to ooze blood.

There was a sound from the direction of the kitchen, and then Wavey rushed out, her hands raised to the sides of her pretty face at the sight of her kitten squirming in Jack's grasp above Chilkat's slavering jaws. "My kitten!" she cried out.

"Where's Gordina?" Jack said, lifting the kitten higher as both Wavey and Chilkat lunged for it.

"Give me my kitten!" Wavey wailed. "You're hurting her!"

"What have the two of you accomplished while I was gone?" Jack thundered.

"We were hungry. We didn't have breakfast, so me and Gordina fixed something to eat…."

"It shouldn't take three hours to eat breakfast."

Senna stepped between them, her fingers curling through Chilkat's collar. "Wavey, take the kitten to your cabin and then come back immediately. There's a lot of work to be done around here and little time left to do it."

Wavey focused on Senna for the first time and blinked startled eyes. "You must be the wedding planner," she said.

"I'm Senna McCallum, the admiral's granddaughter," Senna snapped, sick to death of being referred to as the wedding planner. "Go on and lock that kitten up in a safe place before Chilkat has an early lunch."

After Wavey had departed with the kitten Senna looked at Jack, who was dabbing the blood off his forehead, and shook her head with a short laugh. "I have to hand it to you, Jack. You sure know how to pick 'em."

"If you think you can do better, be my guest," he said, turning on his heel and departing the lodge.

By noon Charlie and Ula had predictably gone missing. Wavey was washing windows in the living room, her every movement the embodiment of graceful lethargy. Had any living human being ever moved so slowly? Jack was down on the dock, still unloading the plane, while Gordina prepared lunch for them. Senna was scraping the dreaded decals off the living-room windows with a razor blade and counting down the moments until she could escape this awful predicament and return to Maine. Chilkat had planted himself in the open doorway, apparently sleeping but not really, for every time Senna glanced at her grandfather's old dog, he was looking right back at her with that steady, fixed gaze as if he was waiting for her to do something.

But what?

Well, she *could* scream in frustration. A long, loud horrible scream would give Chilkat something to sit up and take notice of, and it just might make Senna feel better. She could scream at Wavey to hurry up because at the rate that girl was washing windows, it would take her two weeks just to finish the living room. And then there was Gordina, a woman who could quite easily have wed Count Dracula. A fifty-four-year-old bloodless, gaunt and unsmiling woman with a close-fitting cap of straight, slate-gray hair. Definitely not another sex goddess for Jack to toy with, for which Senna was grateful, but the woman smoked, and when Senna had laid down the law about smoking inside the building, Gordina had given her a malevolent look that made Senna's skin crawl. The woman was definitely frightening, but if she could cook, all would be forgiven...except smoking inside.

Senna paused, eyes narrowing. Even with the windows and doors open in the living room, she was sure she'd just caught a whiff of cigarette smoke. She laid down the razor blade and walked quietly toward the kitchen. She peeked just to make sure, and yes, there Gordina was, standing at the work island, lit cigarette clenched between pursed lips, shredding a head of cabbage as if it had done her severe bodily harm in the past but never would again.

"Gordina." Senna stepped into the kitchen. "I asked you not to smoke inside the building."

Gordina paused, still clutching the big knife and the remains of the head of cabbage. Her eyes narrowed defiantly. Even as Senna stared in anger, a long section of ash fell from the end of her cigarette and landed in the mound of shredded cabbage. Senna spun around and stalked back into the living room and out the front door. She could see Jack down by the plane, going through a tool box on the dock. She was so furious she didn't recall her feet touching the ramp on her way down. "Gordina has got to go," she snapped as she drew up in front of him. "Right now!"

Jack had straightened at the sound of her approach. He was wearing a baseball cap with some flying logo on it and he tugged the brim down over a gathering frown. "You mean, before lunch?"

"Right now," Senna repeated. "I told her not to smoke inside and she's smoking in the kitchen. She's not only smoking while she fixes lunch, but the ashes of her cigarette are falling into the food."

"Queasy."

"*Fire her.* I'd have done it myself but she was holding a very big knife. Fire her, and fly her back to Goose Bay. *Right now.*"

Jack dropped a brass fitting back into the tool box. "Okay." He took off his hat, whipped it against his pant leg a couple of times, pulled it back on and started up the ramp. He paused a few steps beyond her and turned around. "Are you sure about this? What if I can't find us another cook?"

Senna put her hands on her hips and glared. Jack sighed and continued on his mission while Senna returned to the living room and went back to scraping windows that faced the dock so she could have the pleasure of watching Gordina leave. Minutes passed, and there was still no sign of them descending to the plane. Half an hour later Jack walked into the living room. "Wavey, better go check on your kitten," he said to the girl, who was gazing out the window with a rag in her hand as she daydreamed her way slowly through the afternoon.

Senna waited until Wavey had disappeared before challenging Jack. "Well? What's the hold up?"

Jack shoved his hands into his jeans pockets and drew a deep breath, blowing it out with a grimace of pain. "The thing is, yesterday I begged Gordina to quit her job and come to work for us because we needed her desperately. She says her boss won't take her back, and she has this sister who went bonkers when her husband ran out on her, and her sister lives in this special home now because she needs care and is on several medications, all of which costs Gordina a lot of money, and—"

"Did you fire her?" Senna interrupted.

He straightened and squared his shoulders. "She promised she wouldn't smoke inside again."

"*Jack!*"

"She promised." He shrugged helplessly. "Besides, where the hell are we going to find another cook at this late stage of the game?"

SENNA OPENED HER EYES with a moan and lay motionless on the bed, hoping she was wrong, hoping the murky gray light infusing the room didn't really signify the coming of yet another dawn. Hoping the gray mane of the Labrador morning was still hours away because she'd never been quite so sore in all her life. Any movement at all was sheer torture. Even her hair hurt. She counted on her fingers the days that she'd been here. Time had passed so swiftly that she had to count twice to be sure. Seven. Seven days of non-stop work had just about done her in, and she had one more week to go. One more week before the lodge opened and she could head home. Seven more days 'til she could immerse herself in a big bathtub full of hot water for at least twenty-four hours.

The burning question was, would she survive them? Maybe, if she took them one moment at a time. One catastrophe, one set-back, one contingency at a time. Hope for the best and prepare for the worst....

She heard the faint howling of the sled dogs from behind the guides' cabin. Normally she would have thrilled to the sound, so like a pack of wolves, but today she closed her eyes and moaned again. If the dogs were howling, it really was morning.

A laugh came from out of nowhere and cramped her aching stomach muscles as she remembered the trip to fetch the huskies in Jack's plane. It was funny now, but it hadn't been then. To keep to his original plan of making only two trips, he'd crammed ten dogs into the passenger compartment, stuffing them in one after the other, loose. Senna had watched this loading procedure with a dubious frown. "Is it really wise, taking so many all at once?"

"They carry this many dogs all the time in smaller planes during the Iditarod," he'd reassured her. "I've seen pictures."

"Maybe so, but those sled dogs were probably tired after running a thousand miles," Senna pointed out, "whereas your dogs are pretty rested up and lively."

"These guys'll be fine. They're trained to behave, and besides, they've already sorted out their pecking order. There's no reason for them to fight, and if there's so much as a growl I'll push the yoke over and give them a couple of seconds of weightlessness. Guaranteed, that'll settle them down. Quit worrying." Half an hour later they were airborne with ten dogs in back, heading for the lodge. The flight went smoothly for about twenty minutes, when, without any advance warning, all hell broke loose. One moment it was just the throaty roar of the plane's engine droning steadily along, and the next it was combined with the horrific bedlam of ten big sled dogs all at each other's throats.

Senna cast one look over her shoulder and knew they were in deep trouble. All she could see were slashing fangs and flying fur. "Take the yoke!" Jack bellowed after two seconds of weightless flight only served to intensify the fight. He unbuckled his safety harness and hurled himself into the maelstrom. Senna didn't even have a chance to refuse the task of flying the plane because quite suddenly she was the pilot. Fortunately there were no tall mountains in the area because it seemed to take a very long time for Jack to beat the dogs apart, and even then half of them were still going at it when he wormed back into the pilot's seat, reached for the controls and aimed for the nearest landing place, which happened to be a little blip of a pond dead ahead, barely big enough to handle the plane.

The landing was rough, the engine cut out, and the plane drifted of its own momentum toward the shore. Jack jumped out onto the pontoon, hauling dog after dog out of plane and hurling each, one at a time, into the water. "Get out, grab those tethers, wade ashore and tie the bastards up to trees as you catch 'em!" he shouted as he grabbed another dog and tossed it overboard. "If they start to fight again, let 'em kill each other. Don't get between them."

Fifteen minutes later, wet, muddy and covered with blood and gore, mostly belonging to the dogs, she was helping Jack tend his lacerated hand using the plane's first aid kit. His temper was still up and he was swearing like a lumberjack, especially when Senna doused the wounds with hydrogen peroxide. "Goddammit, woman, are you trying to kill me?"

He held up his hand when she was finished and examined the bloodstained bandaging, then glared at the equally bloodied sled dogs tied far apart to spindly black spruce trees along the pond's edge. They stared back, pieces of ear missing here and there, cuts on muzzles oozing, clumps of fur hanging off in saliva-soaked tatters. Their tongues were lolling and they looked absolutely content.

"Well, you were right about those dogs," Senna couldn't resist saying. "They're all fur and fangs." And then she couldn't help but add, "Did any of those Iditarod pictures you saw look like this?"

After the emergency landing they'd divided the dogs into two groups, this time tethering them inside the plane and flying five at a time to the lodge. It took the remainder of the day to transport the rest of the team from the lake house, but there were no more fights. Jack's hand had swelled to twice its normal size by the end of the day but for the past few days he'd functioned at full capacity, stubbornly refusing to go to the hospital in Goose Bay for X-rays and antibiotics, dulling the pain with handfuls of aspirin.

"You could lose that hand if you don't get it cared

for," Senna warned, "and how, exactly, does a devout fly-fisherman fly-fish one handed?"

But the swelling was gradually going down, and in time all that would remain would be the scars. As for the sled dogs, they were hardly the worse for the experience. Two of them required stitching up, and Senna did the honors using dental floss, a curved needle and a pair of forceps, following Jack's instructions as he steadied each dog, one at a time, in his arms. They were surprisingly compliant for such tough, grizzled creatures. "They know you're trying to help them," Jack explained.

"I honestly don't see why you'd want to keep such a savage pack of beasts," Senna said, tying off a knot.

Jack had stroked the head of the dog he held with his bandaged hand, holding no grudge whatsoever. "They're great dogs," he said. "Wait 'til this winter. You'll see what I mean."

There was an awkward silence after that slip of words, Senna holding the forceps, Jack holding the dog, both acutely aware that there would be no sharing of a winter experience. There would be no winter in Labrador, no sled dogs traveling down snowy trails. In fact, in a few more days, there would be no more Labrador at all for Senna. She'd be back in Maine, running the sales department at the Inn on Christmas Cove…

Planning weddings.

Senna shifted tentatively in bed and sighed. So much could happen in the next seven days. So much had happened in the first seven. So much that she hadn't even thought about her job back in Maine for several days. Hadn't even wondered how things were going without her. She'd been too worried about Jack's hand and the multitude of tasks that faced them before opening day. Senna tried another whole-body stretch and then lay still again, analyzing the results.

Seven more days…

JACK KINDLED A FIRE in the guide cabin's woodstove and put the coffee water on to boil. He flexed his injured hand. It still hurt like hell but the swelling had gone down considerably and he was pleased with how quickly it had healed. Everything healed quicker in the clean outdoors. He drank his first cup of coffee sitting at the little table, jotting down the day's duty list; things that must be accomplished come hell or high water. "Charlie, time to get up," he said, pushing to his feet and carrying the mug with him to the door, where he stood in the doorway and looked out on the morning. The dogs saw him and howled again, raising their voices together like a pack of wolves. He wondered if Senna was up yet, and if Gordina and Wavey had survived another night in the "awful scary cabin," which was how Wavey described the remoteness of the entire place: "awful scary."

Senna was right about Wavey. The girl was basically useless. No matter how many times she was shown how to do something, she reverted back to her own techniques the moment she was left alone, and her own techniques involved moving as slowly as she could while looking dreamily beautiful. Senna was right about Gordina, too. She was an awful cook. She might make a killer runny omelet when devastated by a bad hangover, but unfortunately the killer part of that description had been literal. She hadn't yet smoked another cigarette inside the building, but Jack was almost hoping that she would so he could fire her, which he should have done in the first place when Senna had asked him to.

Jack threw the dregs of his coffee onto the ground and reached for his jacket on the wall peg behind him. Time to feed the dogs. "Charlie. Get up. We have a long row to hoe today." He banged the door shut behind him, hoping the noise would roust the boy. Charlie didn't have all that much ambition, but what twelve-year-old did? Truth is, Senna'd been right about him, too. Jack had spent the better part of the past two days cutting wood, and right after breakfast he was going to have to get right back at it. Once the guests arrived he wouldn't have time to be doing chores like that. He'd be on the river, guiding dawn 'til dark, and Senna would be gone, back to her wedding planner job in Maine. Back to Tim Cromwell, the insurance salesman.

One more week and she'd be gone. Having her here had been a tremendous boon. In fact, he had to admit that without her organizational capabilities and her experience in the lodging industry, he'd have been out in left field. She'd already called all the guests in the reservation book to reconfirm their reservations, and by doing this had discovered a cancellation, which left them with an empty room they had to fill for the last week of August. She'd immediately placed a call to the Labrador office of tourism, and to every other fishing lodge in Labrador, informing them of the unexpected vacancy, and by the end of the day she'd gotten a call back from a lodge on Eagle River with a referral to a repeat guest they'd had to turn down due to being fully booked. She immediately called the client, who lived in Great Britain, and just like that they were fully booked for the summer again.

Meanwhile she was a dynamo putting the lodge together, making sure everything worked and everything was in sync. The guest rooms were beginning to look like actual guest rooms with all the amenities, including baskets of soaps and shampoo in the bathrooms which she insisted on. "Little touches make a big difference," she argued when he objected to the additional cost. "Just because we're in the middle of the wilderness doesn't mean we can't have some luxuries."

There were fresh flower arrangements each morning on the dining-room table, there being an abundance of wildflowers blooming on the slope below the main lodge. She organized the registration area, sold him on the idea of turning an extra wardrobe into a dry bar, kitty-cornered into the living room, where guests could mix their own drinks and help themselves to bar snacks. When he brought up the cost she shot him down again.

"The cost should be built into your rates. These folks don't want to be nickeled and dimed as they go. They want an all-inclusive package. They want the experience of a lifetime, and they want to share those experiences, especially their fishing stories, in front of the fireplace with a good glass of scotch. Are you going to be the bartender? I don't think so. You'll be comatose by 8:00 p.m. every night, trying to get enough sleep to make it through the next day. We'll set up a good bar, keep it stocked, and let them help themselves from it."

She tried to enhance Gordina's culinary skills by diplomatically offering to do different tasks in the kitchen, hoping to show by example how to put an excellent meal together, but Gordina was not to be swayed from her belief that she was already an outstanding cook and pointedly ignored Senna's suggestions. Senna organized the laundry room and had Jack string a clothesline in back of the lodge. "No point in using the gas dryer if the sun's shining, especially with that nice breeze. Every little bit of fuel we conserve is a little less we have to barge up the river. Besides, sheets dried in the sunshine smell sweeter than anything on earth."

Jack doubted they would smell sweeter than Senna's hair, which made him want to turn and follow after her every time their paths crossed during the course of the day. And in truth, it wasn't just the smell of her hair. He was beginning to get a little addicted to everything about her. The way she moved, the way she laughed, the way she argued constantly with him, even the way she defended Charlie's crackle when Jack discovered it was Ula who was digging under the fence and eating Goody's coopies. In three days the dozen that had originally been crated in had dwindled to a count of nine. Jack caught the little black dog quite by accident on the fourth night, when, making a trip to the outhouse behind the guides' cabin, he heard a hen squawking.

Flashlight in hand, he burst into the chicken coop and there she was, the bright-eyed black crackie, with one of Goody's coopies dangling in her jaws, about to duck back through the fresh hole she'd dug beneath the fence. He'd let out a roar that brought both Charlie from the cabin and Senna from the lodge at a dead run. In his rage at the dog and at the long, hard and frustrating day he turned on Charlie.

"A hunting dog that kills chickens is worse than useless. You should've kept her tied, like I told you to!"

"She hates being tied," Charlie cried out, his face taut with emotion, fingers curled through the dog's collar. "She wants to be with me."

"Well, she wasn't with you just now, was she? She was in here, killing Goody's coopies!"

Senna grabbed his arm and forced him to look at her. "Jack, calm down."

"A dog that kills chickens is no good," Jack said, shrugging off Senna's grip. "She'll have to go. Leave her with your kin in North West River, Charlie, or get rid of her, if you can find a home for a dog that kills domestic livestock."

"Stop this talk!" Senna demanded, pushing between him and Charlie, her eyes flashing and her body rigid with anger. "If the dog couldn't get into the coop, she wouldn't kill the chickens, would she? You made a poor job of that fencing, John Hanson. That's *your* fault, not Ula's. Are you telling me your sled dogs wouldn't be under that fence and eating those coopies if they got loose? Ha! Feathers would be flying. They'd kill them all for the sheer joy of it in the time it took for you to get out here, but would you get rid of them if they did? A dog is just a dog, but a man should be able to do a job right from the beginning. Fix that fence properly, and there'll be no more problems with Goody's coopies being killed."

Somehow she'd turned the whole massacre into his fault, heaping the deaths of four laying hens on his conscience, and the next morning he'd spent two hours resetting the wire fence a good foot below ground level and stacking rocks around the perimeter. Charlie helped without being prodded, and no more of Goody's precious coopies had disappeared.

What if Senna hadn't been here for that? Jack rubbed the sleep from his face as he walked toward the dog yard carrying a bucket of kibble and then stopped abruptly, blinking with astonishment at the sight of Senna crouched beside his lead dog, Quinn, holding him steady while she checked on the five stitches she'd used to pull that nasty gash in his shoulder back together. He felt a sudden kick of gladness at how his day was starting. She rose to her feet as he approached. "Quinn's healing up nicely," she said, shoving her hands into her jacket pockets. "So are you, judging by the way you're holding that bucket with a hand that not too long ago would have passed for hamburger."

Jack grinned. "Good as new. You're up pretty early for someone who nearly passed out at the supper table last night."

"That was a combination of Gordina's cooking and the heat from the fireplace," she said. "It's amazing what a good night's sleep can do. That, and a handful of aspirin. I'll help feed the dogs, if you want."

"Glad to know I'm not the only one who considers aspirin one of the major food groups. Here, dish this food out and I'll water. I've been thinking about that funny vibration in that hood vent in the kitchen. I should pull it apart and have a look before we open, the noise is pretty obnoxious, we don't want to wake our guests at 5:00 a.m. with the breakfast start-up. I'll probably finish cutting wood today if I get right after it. Charlie said he'd start splitting it and Wavey's supposed to be altering the bed skirts. I don't know how the measurements got that screwed up and to be honest I'm not even sure Wavey can sew but she's Goody's niece and I promised Goody when she agreed to be our cook that Wavey could spend the summer here helping her out, so even though Goody never came, it looks like we're stuck with…"

"Jack?"

He stopped in the act of pouring water into a can attached to a dog house and glanced up questioningly. Senna had finished dishing out kibble and was standing in the middle of the dog yard, holding the empty food bucket with an unfathomable expression on her face. "Are you and Wavey involved? I know it's none of my business, but from a guest's perspective, we have to think about how things might appear. I mean, she's very young."

Jack stood in shocked silence for several long moments, realizing that the morning, which had started out so full of promise, had suddenly turned sour on him. "Did I hear you right?" he said, speaking calmly in spite of the surge of anger that boiled through him. "You think I'm *involved* with Wavey?"

At least Senna had the grace to blush. "I didn't mean to pry, I only asked because… Well, the truth is, I'm just concerned that… It's just that I don't want anyone, any of our guests, that is, to think that… I mean, Wavey's *very* young, and I just think…"

"That your business partner is playing around with a very cute and very young housekeeper," he said, nodding slowly. "You're absolutely right to be concerned, and you're absolutely right that it's none of your business. We may be temporary partners in this enterprise, but my private life is none of your concern."

Senna's color deepened. "I'm sorry if I offended you, but—"

"And you know what?" His voice was hard. "Because I'm such a damned decent guy, I'm going to tell you right here and now that there's nothing going on between Wavey and me. She's here only because she's

Goody's niece. Oh, excuse me, *grand*-niece. But we're not *involved*, as you so delicately put it."

"I said I was sorry," she repeated. "Maybe I was out of line to mention it. But regardless, we have just seven more days to get this lodge up and running, so instead of standing here and bickering, let's just get to work, shall we?"

She dropped the empty kibble bucket at his feet and swept past him without another word, behaving as if he'd been the one who'd started this foolish conversation about Wavey. He watched her go, confounded by how she always managed to turn things around, then lashed out at the bucket with his foot and cursed in such a manner that the sled dogs all watched him with cautious eyes and flattened ears.

SENNA SKIPPED BREAKFAST because she couldn't stand the thought of sitting at that table with Wavey and struggling to eat Gordina's awful fare while Jack fixed her with that cool, sardonic stare of his. So instead she jumped right into the first thing on her agenda, which involved firing up the diesel generator, switching on the computer and entering each and every reservation written into the book, a job that would take most of the morning. She was sitting in the reception area doing this when the satellite phone rang.

"Wolf River Lodge, this is Senna speaking. How may I help you?"

"Senna?"

"Tim?" Senna wondered how long this agony was going to go on. "How on earth did you get this number?"

"Your mother gave it to me. I hope it's all right if I call you there."

"Yes, of course. What's up?"

"I think I've found a buyer for the lodge," Tim said.

Senna's grip on the phone tightened. "That's...good news, Tim."

"His name is Earl Hammel. He'd like to come stay for a bit, see the place."

"That's going to be a problem. We're fully booked for the summer. Six rooms per night, seven nights a week. There aren't any rooms available."

"Senna, this guy seems pretty serious about buying the lodge. It would be nice if he could stay there."

"That's true, but surely the fact that we're full in our start-up season will impress him."

"Actually, he's interested in the lodge for personal and corporate use. Its business history doesn't interest him. He's in Europe right now but should be back soon. Senna, he could very well write a check for the entire property on the spot. He's no lightweight. He's a very wealthy man."

"That may be so, but Jack doesn't want to sell his half of the business."

"He might if the price was right. Can you talk to him about this and get back to me as soon as possible? I promised Earl I'd let him know."

"Okay, I'll run it by him." Senna knew she should be glad that Tim had found a buyer so quickly. If Jack agreed to sell his half of the business, which would be a miracle no matter what Earl Hammel offered for a price, then Gordina and Wavey could return to Goose Bay and she could go home to Maine. But instead of feeling grateful at this sudden turn of events, she was sitting here on the verge of a full-blown panic attack.

There was a pause on the other end. "Look, Senna,

I'm sorry if I'm overstepping my bounds. I thought you'd be happy about this."

"I'm grateful for your help, Tim, I just don't think Jack will go along with it. But I promise I'll talk to him. Thanks for calling."

"Will you call me back with his answer?"

"Yes, of course I will."

"I miss you, Senna."

"Tim…"

"I know. I'm sorry. I'll talk to you later."

Senna massaged her aching temples after hanging up and sat for a few minutes, collecting her thoughts. She heard the old plane's motor start up and pushed out of her chair, moving to the window to stare down toward the river. Jack hadn't mentioned flying anywhere today. He was supposed to be cutting and splitting wood and making sure the kitchen fan in the stove hood was functioning properly. He had a lot on his plate, yet he was taxiing around the river bend, and not long afterward she heard him open the throttle for his take-off run.

Senna turned back to the registration area and then had a sudden thought. Maybe he was taking Wavey back to Goose Bay as a result of their early-morning argument. She went into the kitchen where Gordina was washing up the breakfast dishes. "Gordina, where was Jack going?"

"Didn't say." Gordina still hadn't forgiven her for not allowing her to smoke inside and refused to look her in the eye or even glance in her general direction.

"Where's Wavey?"

"In the laundry room working on the bed skirts."

Senna was torn between disappointment and relief. It would be good to have the girl gone, but who would fill her position? "I think we should work on some sample menus after lunch," she said to Gordina. "We need to firm up the meal planning and make sure we have all the provisions we need."

Gordina made no reply, and Senna bit her lower lip to keep from saying something she might regret. She returned to the registration computer, where she spent the rest of the morning entering data. By the time she heard the plane returning she was more than ready to stretch her legs and make amends with her business partner. She was standing on the dock, Chilkat beside her, when Jack taxied up. Charlie and the crackie were with him. Charlie jumped out and tied off the plane, then he and the small black dog galloped up the ramp toward the lodge. Jack jumped out onto the pontoon, then turned, reached into the plane and picked up a crate. He set it on the dock and retrieved a total of four more. Two of them were wooden and stamped with a vineyard's logo.

"Our start-up liquor supply," he said by way of explanation. "I brought everything that was stored in the cellar at the lake house, along with the rest of the dog food, and everything that was in the freezers. The plane's pretty full."

"You might have told someone where you were going, and that you were taking Charlie with you," Senna said.

"Sorry about that, but you were having a bad morning and I guess I was, too." He looked around, a suspicious frown gathering. "Where the hell's Charlie disappeared to so quick? This stuff's heavy."

Senna couldn't help but laugh. "Good thing I'm strong, isn't it? Let's get started. We have some important things to discuss over lunch."

CHAPTER NINE

BY THE TIME THEY'D LUGGED everything up the steep ramp, most of Senna's pent-up frustration had been worked out of her and she was just plain tired and hungry. Gordina had fixed a lunch of cabbage-and-potato soup. Wavey had already eaten and Charlie was nowhere to be found. Senna and Jack sat at one end of the big dining-room table and dipped into the bowls Gordina set before them. The broth was watery and tasteless, and both the potatoes and shredded cabbage could have used a lot more cooking time to soften them up. As soon as Gordina had left the room, Jack caught Senna's eye.

"Queasy," he admitted.

Senna dropped her spoon with a clatter and pushed her bowl aside. "This soup is hardly fit to feed Goody's coopies. What are we going to do? Gordina's the main event, and nothing she's prepared so far has been remotely edible. She refuses to take any suggestions from me, so tutoring is out. We need to sit down with her and go through a meal-planning session. One week's worth of breakfast, lunch and dinner. We'll write it all down so she knows exactly what she's going to be preparing each day, I'll outline the recipes, and we'll prepare a shopping list. We need to get everything stocked up before the guests arrive...."

"Calm down," Jack soothed as if she were an irrational child.

Senna rocked forward in her chair. "Don't tell me to calm down. This whole thing is shaping up to be a disaster!"

Jack slouched back in his seat, raising his arms in a gesture of surrender. "Okay then, go ahead, get all riled up," he said. "Fly off the handle, if it'll make you feel any better."

"Don't patronize me!"

"Patronize you?" He leaned forward, shoving his bowl aside. "Woman, I adore you for what you've done around here," he said, his words so unexpected that Senna was momentarily speechless. "Everything," he continued with an all-encompassing wave of his arm. "The admiral designed the place and I helped him build it, but it took you to bring this lodge to life. Flying back here today, all I could think of was what if you hadn't come at all? As much as we squabble and disagree about everything, you're definitely the runner carrying the torch to light the Olympic flame. I guess what I'm trying to say is, I'm damned glad you're here, and if you want to get histrionic on me, you're more than deserving of it. I know I'm not that easy to work with."

Senna met his intense gaze and all the barbed words she'd been about to fling in his direction died a sudden death. She sat in silence.

He raised an eyebrow. "You said we had some important things to discuss over lunch," he prompted. "I'm all ears, and not only that, I promise to behave myself."

She drew a sharp breath as she thought about the potential buyer Tim had found for the lodge, and realized that she couldn't possibly initiate such a conversation at this time. That information could wait until later. A few hours wouldn't make any difference. Besides, she knew how he'd feel about it. It was her *own* feelings that were confusing her. She pushed out of her chair. "Right now the most important thing is making sure our meals are palatable to the guests. I'll get Gordina and we'll plan a menu that even a new hire at McDonald's could handle."

Jack rose to his feet before she could leave the room. "The real reason I left here today was to try and get in touch with Goody Stewart, but I couldn't. I left a message with the friend she was supposedly staying with in Black Tickle. I told her what we were doing, that Wavey and Gordina might not work out, and that we were desperate for her help."

Senna nodded. "It was worth a try. Maybe we'll get lucky. Maybe she'll come."

"I took Charlie along so he could visit his relatives and ask if anyone wanted a seasonal job. It was a just a thought. They spend their summers at fish camp. Maybe one of the women would want to cook or clean, make some money, and we need another guide or two...."

"Maybe we'll get lucky there, as well."

"It was just a thought," he repeated.

Senna looked at him, feeling a warmth from deep within that turned the quick, nervous flutter in her stomach into something much more. "It was a good thought," she said.

"I'll take Wavey back to Goose Bay on my next trip," he said. "She's not helping that much."

"She does enough so that if we didn't have her, we might be in even worse shape," Senna admitted. "Until we can find someone to replace her, I think it's best if she stays. And I'm sorry I questioned your integrity earlier. It's just that…well, she's so beautiful, and the way she hovers around you, I was just—"

"I know. You were just jealous." Before she could respond he picked up his bowl, took hers out of her hand and started for the kitchen. "I'll get Gordina."

Senna watched him leave and sat back down. Damn the man for being so arrogant and grinning at her that way, as if he read her very thoughts. Yes, she *was* jealous. The realization made her mad. She had no right to be jealous. John Hanson was his own man. And besides, she would be leaving here soon. She should be thrilled at the thought, yet she hadn't been able to tell Jack that Tim had found a potential buyer. Senna looked around the room, picturing a fire in the fireplace, the table crowded with guests who were laughing, talking, enjoying the meal and each other's company. She thought of the charming guest rooms, with all the little unexpected luxuries awaiting them.

She imagined the long, lovely days the guests would spend here, fishing with Jack or just sitting out on the porch and absorbing the peace of the surroundings, letting all of life's stresses vanish from their fast-paced lives while reconnecting to the sun and the moon, the wind and the stars, and the timeless life-giving force of the river; rising to the spiritual awakening of a pristine dawn and retiring to the breathtaking beauty of an arctic twilight. She'd miss all of that when she went back to Maine. Oh, in a smaller way some of those same things happened there, but this was a place where the wolves and caribou still roamed a vast and roadless wilderness….

Senna shook herself out of her reverie as Jack reappeared, Gordina in reluctant tow. The older woman sat stiffly at the table, bony face rigid, refusing to look in Senna's direction. Jack handed Senna an orange and dropped into a chair, kicking back and balancing on the rear legs.

"So, Gordina," he said, beginning to peel his own orange. "Aside from runny omelets, what exactly *is* your house specialty?"

JACK COULDN'T SLEEP. The moon made the night so bright he thought he might as well just get up and split wood. What the hell. Physical labor sure beat lying in a narrow bunk fantasizing about how Senna was going to change her mind about selling her half of the business. He got up, paced to the door, and opened it to the rush of cool air and the sound of the Wolf River. If he were a smoker, he'd light up a cigarette right about now and contemplate becoming a monk or a drunk. He couldn't stop thinking about her. She was bewitching him, driving him nuts, and the thought of her leaving in a few days was making him even crazier. Four more days and she'd be gone. Four more days...

He should be sleeping. It was 2:00 a.m. and in a few hours he was supposed to fly into Goose Bay to pick up another load of provisions. He hadn't slept the night before, and he wouldn't sleep for the rest of his life, the way he was feeling tonight. Damn the woman for tormenting him, and damn the admiral for leaving his half of the business to her, and damn his commanding officer for creating her in the first place!

Jack pulled on his jeans and stuffed his feet into his boots. Senna wouldn't hear his labors, tucked away in her room at the lodge and no doubt sleeping the peaceful sleep of the untormented. He'd split wood until he was exhausted, then he'd jump in the river. It was a good plan. A productive plan. After breakfast, he'd fire up the old Pratt and Whitney and fly into Goose Bay to flesh out their grocery list. Maybe he'd just keep on flying. Maybe if he flew far enough he could get Senna McCallum out of his blood.

But somehow Jack knew that no matter how far he flew, he couldn't escape her. In ten days Senna had somehow insinuated herself into his soul, become the reason why his heart beat and he drew breath. In spite of his resolve to steer clear of emotional entanglements, she had become part and parcel of his past and future.

Jack buttoned his flannel shirt, pulled on his jacket and stepped out into the twilight. He wrenched the splitting maul out of a stump beside the door and reached for the first piece of firewood. He liked splitting wood. There was a satisfying feel to the heft of the maul, the swift smooth arc through the air, the solid strike into the end grain of the log, and the resulting explosion of one piece into two. He liked the tangy smell of the spruce, the earthy ferment of the woods around him, and the wild restless churn of the river below.

Half an hour later sweat was running down his forehead, trickling between his shoulder blades in spite of the cold night air. He stripped out of his jacket and was lifting another piece of wood when a pale flash of movement caught his eye. He straightened, letting the handle of the maul slide through his fingers. Wavey materialized at the edge of the clearing. She was in her nightgown, barefoot, with a sweater drawn over her shoulders. Warning bells rang in his head as she moved closer. "I heard you out here," she said.

"Go back to bed, Wavey. It'll be light in an hour." He spoke gruffly, angry at her intrusion.

"I can't sleep," she said, stepping even closer, invading his space. "I was lying in the darkness thinking about you, Jack." Wavey's hands were holding the cardigan together at her neck, but as she spoke she let the sweater fall open and ran her hands down over the swell of her breasts. The nightgown she wore was a thin, flimsy thing that did little to hide any part of her. "Thinking about you, and wishing you were lying beside me," she continued in a breathless voice.

"I told you before, I'm not interested in what you're offering. Go on. I'm busy here."

But instead of retreating to her cabin she advanced again, and Jack took another step backward, tripping over a piece of wood. He lost his balance, falling onto the woodpile with an angry bellow. He was struggling to his feet when Wavey fell on top of him, planting her mouth on his and writhing against him like a wild cat, trying to unbutton his shirt and unzip his pants at the same time. Her hands were everywhere all at once. "I want you so much, Jack!" she cried out when he pushed her off him. "I love you and I could make you happy, I know I could. Let me prove it to you…!" She was still pleading with him when he set her on her feet and shoved her in the direction of her cabin.

"Go," he said harshly, pointing his arm. *"Go!"*

She spun and ran through the woods, weeping like a child. He sat down onto the chopping block and dropped his head into his hands with a heartfelt moan. There were no gods in the heavens. If there were, surely Senna would have been the one drawn by the sound of him splitting wood, and one thing was certain and scared the hell out of him.

He never would have sent her away.

SENNA WAS DRINKING HER FIRST cup of coffee on the porch when she saw Jack coming up the path from his cabin. His hair was plastered to his head and his face was freshly shaven. He was dressed in clean chinos and a hunter-green flannel shirt. "I'm going into Goose Bay after breakfast to pick up another load of provisions," he said, climbing the steps and pausing beside her. "Do you need anything?"

"Several dozen cases of frozen dinners might be a wise investment," she said with a smile. "I'm going to work in the kitchen with Gordina today, whether she likes it or not. Tonight we'll serve a meal similar to the ones she'll be preparing for our guests. I think if you bring back everything on that list, we'll be fine."

"Good." He nodded, then started toward the kitchen.

"There is one other thing you could get," she added.

He paused, ran his fingers through his wet hair. "What's that?"

"Some petunias. I think a planter on either side of the base of the porch steps would look pretty. Maybe white, pink and purple, with a little lobelia trailing down. Try to find a purple that's fragrant. Some of them smell very sweet."

"Petunias?" Clearly he didn't think much of that idea.

"Oh, and one more thing. A good bottle of champagne. I think a pre-grand-opening celebration is in order before I leave. We've worked hard. A little treat would be nice."

He appeared startled by her request. "What kind of champagne?"

Senna smiled up at him over the rim of her mug. "Tell you what, I'll give you the money, you surprise me."

"Okay." He was studying her as if she were an extra-terrestrial newly arrived from another planet.

"Why are you staring at me that way?"

"Just wondering how you always manage to look so beautiful first thing in the morning, and why you're being so friendly."

"It helps one's physical and emotional state to get a good night's sleep," Senna said. "People who split wood in the middle of the night can't expect to feel all that chipper in the morning."

His expression instantly changed to one of wary caution. "Sorry if I woke you."

"Oh, you didn't. The moon was so bright and the night was so beautiful that I decided to go for a little walk. I heard you splitting wood, so I thought I'd stop by your cabin and say hello." Senna raised her mug and took a sip, noting that Jack's expression had definitely gotten stonier. She grinned at him. "I guess Wavey couldn't sleep last night, either."

"You spied on me?"

"I was just wondering why you were splitting wood at two in the morning."

"No doubt you got quite an eyeful," he said, running his fingers through his hair again, leaving it tousled in damp disarray. "I hope you're satisfied." He turned and strode down the porch, the kitchen door banging shut behind him.

Senna hadn't meant to anger him, and spying on him had certainly not been the reason she'd walked to his cabin last night, but she wasn't the least bit sorry that she'd seen the interaction between the two. Jack's behavior toward Wavey had erased all suspicions that there was anything between them.

Senna watched the fog rise from the river. The morning was gray and quiet, still too early to know if it would be sunny or overcast. She was contemplating the odds when she heard the kitchen door bang again and Jack reemerged, striding back down the porch with an insulated travel mug in one hand. He passed her without so much as a look, started down the steps, and began descending the steep ramp.

Senna scrambled to her feet and started after him, tripping at the top of the ramp and spilling most of her coffee. She set the cup down and caught up with him as he was beginning his preflight check of the plane. "Jack, honestly, I wasn't spying on you. I didn't know Wavey would be there."

"Forget it." He was wiggling the rudder, the flaps, and checking some fluid in the engine itself. "Doesn't matter."

"Look, I'm sorry," Senna said, frustrated that he wouldn't acknowledge her. Her fists clenched at her sides. "Okay, that's not true. I'm *not* sorry. I'm glad I saw you send Wavey off that way. It made me feel a whole lot better."

He untied the tethers, stepped up onto the pontoon and opened the side door, giving her the briefest of over-the-shoulder glances. "Good," he said. "As long as you feel a whole lot better, that's all that counts."

Senna reached in her pocket and pulled out a wad of crumpled Canadian bills, extending them toward him.

"For the petunias and the champagne," she said. "The rest of it you can put on our charge account."

He ignored the offering, climbed into the plane and slammed the door behind him. Moments later she heard him holler, "Clear!" just before turning the engine over. The prop whirled to life as the engine uttered its throaty rumble. Senna took a few steps back as the prop wash pushed against her and the plane began its downriver taxi. She stood there until it disappeared around the corner and the loud take-off roar faded as the plane climbed into the air and drew away.

Senna shoved the money back into her pocket and sighed, hoping that by the time he returned he'd be over his big mad. She picked her way along the riverbank for a while, enjoying the solitude and reluctant to return to the lodge, where the sour-faced Gordina held dubious rule over a kingdom she should be expelled from, and the sensual Wavey would appear for another day of day-dreaming when she was supposed to be working. A few moments of exploring wouldn't be such a bad thing. She could make up the lost work on the other end of the day.

The edge of the river was hard to follow, choked with the debris of previous high-water floods, but now and then a clear sandy stretch would beckon. Senna made a mental note that Charlie would have to clean up the riverbank on both sides of the lodge to allow guests to fish the deep pools from shore. It would be a good chore for him, one he'd enjoy since he could simply toss all the driftwood back into the river. Then maybe he could trim back some of this brush to establish a walking path and...

Senna stopped abruptly, studying the damp sand at her feet. "My goodness," she breathed. She was looking at a track, a very large canid track, at least seven inches long and four inches wide.

Wolf!

She stepped carefully to avoid marring the perfect imprint and looked for the next one. Easy enough to find. She followed the set of tracks up the shoreline until they veered into the brush, and then she followed them by sheer perseverance and intuition, finding a single paw print here in the mud, another partial track farther along, an indentation in the lichens, a broken patch of fern. The riverbank climbed and flattened out and she found herself on an established game path, winding through the thick forest of black spruce. She picked up her pace, traveling head-down, intent on finding the next clue, wondering if she'd be lucky enough to catch sight of the wary and magnificent creature. She wondered if it was Raven, the black female her grandfather had written of in his journal.

The path eventually dipped down into a wet, boggy area, soft and spongy with moss. She picked her way carefully, aware that soon she should be heading back. There was lots to do, and someone had to keep an eye on the two employees, else they'd spend the morning drinking coffee and gabbing. But just now, with the woods full of birdsong and redolent of clean, earthy smells, this was the place she'd much rather be. As soon as the sun broke through the morning fog, she'd get back to the lodge. She spied another imprint in the moss and felt a gathering thrill. She wished she'd brought her camera along, but then again this had been a spur-of-the-moment adventure.

The bog she was traveling through climbed onto a low esker and she paused for a breather, trying to catch a glimpse of a familiar landmark. She could no longer hear the river, just the increasing whine of mosquitoes, and she had no insect repellent. With a sigh she realized it was time to go back. Just as she started through the bog again, carefully retracing her steps, it began to rain. The rain was cold and steady, but it drove away the mosquitoes, which was a relief. She hurried along, pushing through low undergrowth, swatting at bugs and wishing she'd worn a hat. The going became more difficult and several times she floundered in water up to her knees. She didn't remember the path being this rough or wet on the way through. Could she have somehow veered onto the wrong track?

Senna stopped, listening for the river, but all she could hear was the sound of the rain and the few persistent mosquitoes that pursued her. She realized that without the sun to take her bearings by, she had no idea what direction she was traveling in. She drew a deep breath and let it out slowly. There was no need to panic. It was broad daylight, and would be for many hours yet. In fact, this time of year in Labrador it never got truly dark. All she had to do was find her own footprints and follow them back to the river. She turned around and began to retrace her steps, trying to find where she'd lost the trail.

JACK STOPPED BRIEFLY at the lake house to pick up another of the admiral's books for Charlie to read and while he was there he searched through his room for a set of clothes worthy of sharing a bottle of champagne with a beautiful woman. He'd been too long without the need for anything fancier than blue jeans and work boots, and the one dress shirt he came up with had threadbare cuffs and wouldn't pass muster. In the bottom drawer of his bureau he kept a sock stuffed with an odd assortment of change, and he took the whole sock. Whatever was in it was going to serve as the champagne fund. He hoped it would amount to enough for a fairly decent bottle, with enough left over for some petunias and a respectable dress shirt.

But the champagne was paramount, although Senna probably wouldn't share it with him after his surly departure. The very idea that she'd witnessed Wavey's behavior the night before caused his stomach to churn. By the time he'd flown thirty minutes away from her, he realized that the reason he'd been so upset was that he realized if Wavey hadn't shown up at his cabin, Senna would have. It would have been Senna who came into the clearing to see why he was splitting wood at 2:00 a.m. Damn that Wavey! He should have packed her out of there this morning and dropped her back at Goody's house.

Jack stopped in the living room to check the phone's answering machine. A brief message from Granville, for Senna. "I'm sorry to report I still haven't found your grandfather's letter, m'dear, but I know it'll turn up. I'll have some paperwork for you to sign soon, I expect the courts will be sending it along any day now."

Another one for Senna. "Hi, it's Tim. You haven't called and I'm getting worried. I'll try to get the lodge's number from your mother. Talk to you soon, I hope. Miss you."

Hearing that message sent Jack into an even darker state of mind. He stalked back to the plane, satisfied to see that it had begun to rain. Rain suited his mood. He climbed into the plane and headed for Goose Bay. One of the benefits of spending all those years in the Navy was access to the base commissary. There were good prices there, and a fair selection to choose from. He stocked up on all the necessary items to get them through the first full week of feeding twelve guests, but when it came to choosing the champagne he enlisted the help of one of the employees, who asked the advice of another, until finally four people were actively debating the merits of the different champagnes, not that there were all that many to debate. The more they talked, the more confusing the choice became.

"I don't mean to interrupt, but is this a special occasion?" a middle-aged woman who was perusing the wines inquired.

Jack nodded, relieved by her interest. He needed a mature woman's perspective. "Very special. A great woman and a once-in-a-lifetime event."

"Then you'll want a very special champagne," she said with a knowing smile. "Perrier-Jouet. The one with the pink flower painted on the bottle."

Jack scanned the selection and the woman touched his arm. "Don't bother looking, you won't find it here," she said with a kind smile. Probably the wife of the base commander. She had that look of patient and long-suffering regality about her. "You'll need to go to a first-rate liquor store or wine shop, and even then you might strike out. This is Labrador, after all."

It was handy that Goody had left her car for Wavey and Jack to use. Jack took full advantage, driving to the nearest purveyor of fine wines and cheeses, where he asked for the bottle of champagne with the flower painted on it.

"You're in luck," the shopkeeper said. "I have one

bottle in stock. Pricey stuff, so I don't keep much on hand."

Jack pulled out his sock. "How pricey?"

The shopkeeper watched as the bills and coins spilled out onto the counter. "A hundred bucks," he said.

Jack tried to hide his shock. The other bottles back at the commissary had been in the ten-to-twenty-dollar range. He sorted through the bills, counting what he'd accumulated over the past three years. It came to $114.52, Canadian. No doubt about it, he'd never be a rich man. "How much does caviar cost?" he said.

"Depends on the type. You got the flying fish caviar, that's cheap. You got the beluga caviar, that'll cost you twice your life's savings for four ounces." The shopkeeper paused, watching Jack organize the loose change. "Strawberries go well with champagne," he suggested. "Or a fine cheese, or smoked salmon on petit points."

Jack paid for the champagne and with what was leftover bought a nicely aged cheese and some of the most expensive crackers ever made. The shopkeeper ceremoniously packed this in a very attractive shopping bag that Jack knew Senna would like. He felt better about life in general as he left the shop, bag tucked under his jacket to keep it from getting wet, and carefully loaded the bag into Goody's car. Back at Goody's house he ferried all the groceries down to the plane, and the last thing he tucked in was the shopping bag with the champagne, right beside the pilot's seat. He was doing pretty good. All the errands were done, and it was only eleven o'clock. He'd be back at the lodge in an hour. He hoped Senna wouldn't be too mad at him for not getting the petunias, but at the moment he was dead broke.

"Jack!" a voice called out as he was locking Goody's car up. He saw a man wave from down the street. "Jack, bye! I couldn't believe my luck when they said you just flew into town. I only just arrived myself."

"George?" Jack squinted through the rain. "George Pilgrim. I'll be damned!"

"I was sorry to hear the old admiral had died," George said, pumping Jack's hand as they met beside George's battered pickup. "You knows how much I liked the old warhorse. I just come over from Lab City, y'see. Went to visit my daughter. Bad news there, the iron-ore workers just went on strike. They belong to the steelworkers' union. Bad business going on now, sabotaging ore trains and such. The men are out of work, and it scares 'em and makes 'em ugly."

George Pilgrim was a native of Mud Lake, the son of a Montagnais girl and an Air Force man who had flown through her life one night. He was undoubtedly one of the best outdoorsmen in Labrador, having been a ranger for over forty years, patrolling the better part of Naskaupi and keeping the poachers on their toes, but he was in his seventies now, and starting to slow down. He guided fishermen mostly, to keep food on the table and his hand in the game. He and the admiral had raised a little hell together in the past five years and had formed a good friendship.

"I'll buy you a beer," Jack said.

"I'll buy you a bite, if you'll buy me a beer," George grinned, his ruddy face beaming.

Minutes later they were in the same pub where Gordina had once worked, ordering burgers and drinking beer. "It's good to see you, bye," George said. "You're looking fit. Is the admiral's lodge built, then?"

"It's built. Come out with me and see it. We're opening next week."

George shook his head with regret. "I'd like to, but
I'm having a surgery tomorrow. That's why I'm here.
They found a bit of smut in my innards, y'see, and they
have to cut it out. They say the hospital here is pretty
good."

"How long will you be in?"

"If it goes good, not long. If it goes bad, I might not
come out. That's why I went to see my daughter. Didn't
tell her about it, though. Didn't want to worry her."

"You're too tough to die in a hospital, George. I'll
pick you up when you're ready. Call the lodge, we have
a satellite phone in there, and I'll come get you. You can
hang out there and recuperate. The fishing's pretty good."

"Oh, aye, I'll bet she is. The Wolf's a fine trout and
salmon river. So tell me, bye," George said with a knowing look. "Who's the lucky lady?"

Jack took a swallow of beer as the burgers were slid
in front of them and avoided George's question by glancing up at the man who'd delivered his order. "I see you
have a new cook?"

"Yep. Some high-browed lodge owner stole Gordina
from me a week ago and thought he was really getting
something, that's the joke on him. I got me a real chef
now. Business is already picking up. Gordina couldn't
cook worth a damn, and she was a sour old bitch, to
boot."

Jack leaned toward George after the pub owner had
shuffled off. "Guess which high-browed lodge owner
stole Gordina from this place a week ago?" he said, lowering his voice. "And he's right, she can't cook worth a
damn and she *is* a sour old bitch."

"You're not going to tell me about her, bye, are you?"

"It's the admiral's granddaughter, you old coot. Am I that plain to read?"

"I can read the tracks a woman makes on a man's heart as well as I can read animal tracks in the woods. Pass that ketchup along. It's good to see you like this. You need a good woman, and if she's the admiral's granddaughter, then I'd say you done all right for yourself."

"The lodge is booked for the summer, George. I could use another guide once you're up and about. Hell, I could use two of you, and if you know of anyone who can cook or clean rooms, or do prep work, or anything at all…"

"I'll think about it." George nodded, squeezing ketchup on his burger and fries.

"You can do your thinking at the lodge, while you recuperate. There's a bunk with your name on it in the guides' camp."

"I'd like that, Jack, bye, I truly would," George said. He set down the ketchup and the two men shook hands solemnly over the table before eating their burgers.

CHAPTER TEN

LUNCH WITH GEORGE TOOK over an hour, and by the time Jack got the plane back into the air it was two o'clock. He opened up the throttle, flying into a stiff headwind laden with rain and wondering if Senna would be worried. No doubt she was getting madder by the moment, wondering if he was shirking his work, wondering if the plane had crashed, worrying needlessly about nothing at all. By the time he landed on the Wolf, he was dreading how angry she was going to be and wondering how he was going to explain his tardiness and the lack of petunias. He carried the box of meats up the steep ramp, wanting to get some into the refrigerator and rest into the freezer as soon as possible. Inside the lodge he heard laughter in the kitchen and entered the room to the unlikely sight of Wavey and Gordina playing cards.

"What the hell's going on?" he said, setting the box down on the work island. "For cripe's sake, with all the work that has to get done, you're playing cards?"

"We stopped for a cuppa," Gordina said defensively, nudging the teapot on the table. "We were tired and need a break." Wavey said nothing, just stood and left the room with a hurt, pouting expression on her face.

"Where's Senna?" Jack asked Gordina.

The older woman looked surprised. "We haven't seen her all day. We thought she was with you."

Gordina's response caught Jack completely off guard. For a few moments he stared at her, hoping he hadn't heard her speak those words. And then, all at once, his heart rate surged off the scale as adrenaline flooded through him. He turned and went to Senna's room, banging on the door and bursting in. Empty. Chilkat was snoozing on the rug in front of the living-room fireplace, and looked as if he'd been there all morning. Jack's blood had turned to ice by the time he returned to the kitchen. "Where's Charlie?"

"Down to your cabin, I expect. Not much wood gets cut in a hard rain."

Jack ran to the guides' camp, relieved to find Charlie on his bunk, reading. "Charlie, Senna's missing. She's been gone all day. I need your help. Get the crackie and come with me."

As he spoke he picked up his pack and began cramming things into it. Survival stuff for a cold overnight in bad weather. Compass on a thong around his neck. Map in the front compartment of his pack. Dry clothing. Rain gear. Flashlight. Fire starters. Gorp and jerky. Sleeping bag. Tarp. Everything he could fit in went into the pack, and it was a big pack. He filled his thermos with strong, hot coffee left over from that morning, the pot still on the woodstove. It was as black as tar and would float a teaspoon. He added about a cup of Charlie's instant hot cocoa mix and a generous tablespoon of real vanilla extract. From past experience he knew this particular brew could practically jump-start a dead man. He stuffed the thermos into the pack. His stomach was filled with nameless dread.

"The last time I saw her was early this morning," he said, shouldering the pack and picking up his rifle. "She was standing on the dock when I flew out of here. We'll start the search there. Charlie, for the love of God, get a move on!"

SENNA WAS HUDDLED IN A BALL, knees to her chest, shivering, when she heard Jack's plane fly over. It took a few moments before the distinctive roar of the engine insinuated itself into her dazed mind. She leapt to her feet, ducked out of her shelter and raced out onto the open esker, hoping to catch sight of the old plane, hoping she could orient herself to its direction, hoping she could use it to navigate her way back to the river. But the gray, murky overcast, the thick veils of mist that shrouded the dark forest, and the steady rain all conspired to obscure it from her sight. She strained her ears trying to hear some change in the engine's pitch, but she couldn't really tell which direction the noise was coming from.

Tears filled her eyes as the sound faded into the vast silence of the wilderness, which closed back around her in a thick, suffocating blanket and smothered the last glimmer of hope. She was cold and wet and plagued by the mosquitoes but none of that mattered a damn compared to the depth of fear she felt. She was scared, and that was the most frightening sensation of all. She was really, truly scared. She'd never been scared of anything, ever, but she'd never been this lost before. It had taken every ounce of her self-control to stop the frantic search for the game trail she'd followed. It had taken all of her will power to realize that she was running in circles, exhausting herself, becoming colder and more panicked by the moment.

That very terror she was experiencing had overwhelmed and killed others who had been lost in far less wild circumstances, and it was her knowledge of that deadly panic that had undoubtedly saved her from the same blind, hopeless fate. This was the stuff wardens had talked of, when hunting season rolled around. Stories of men getting disoriented in the woods, running until they dropped from exhaustion and perished of hypothermia. One man even threw his rifle away and was found two days later after a massive search, dead from exposure, but the real cause of his death had been his succumbing to panic. She'd read the little orange survival book that all hunters were encouraged to carry and tucked away all those nuggets of knowledge, never realizing that she would one day need them desperately

This was the day.

When she'd realized how fast and how furious she was using up all her reserves and getting nowhere at all, she'd stopped, gasping for breath, and then stock of her situation. She had no compass. She had no matches with which to kindle a fire. She had no hat. Her jacket was water resistant but that didn't do much good after such a long, steady exposure to the rain. She had no emergency food, no signal whistle, no knife. In short, she had none of the items that the little orange survival book recommended all people carry with them when they went into the woods, but she did remember the gist of what the book had preached. "When you realize you're lost, stop and make camp. Prepare to spend the night out. You might be uncomfortable, but if you put enough effort into the shelter you build, you can be reasonably protected from the elements."

Shelter was the first order of business. If she were going to survive this experience, she'd have to create some sort of cover from the elements, without the benefit of an axe or saw, and in a land where two-hundred-year-old trees stood barely twenty feet tall. Once Senna knew what she had to do, she focused on the project and her sense of panic abated. She scouted the adjacent woods until she found a spruce that had been uprooted by the strong winds, laying the trunk over at a forty-five-degree angle before the tip became caught up in a thick tangle of other trees. Since black spruce was the abundant tree, she began breaking the longest boughs she could from the biggest trees she could find, until she had amassed a huge stack. Then she layered them thickly, beginning at the base of the uprooted tree, until she had created a tiny lean-to just big enough for her to sit under. She then gathered more boughs and laid them inside the lean-to to keep her off the wet ground and crawled inside. While not completely waterproof, the majority of rain was turned by the thick thatching, and if she could have kindled a fire at the lean-to's opening she might even have been comfortable.

She'd sat there for what seemed like hours, leaving the shelter periodically when the cold became so intense that she was shivering uncontrollably. She would crawl out and run in circles to get her circulation going, and when she became too tired to keep moving she'd crawl back into the shelter. The rain kept on, the dreariness contributing to her growing sense of despair. When she'd heard the plane approaching she had scrambled out of the lean-to, craning skyward and calling out Jack's name as if he would hear her, and when the plane passed over unseen and the sound faded, she fought back the tears as she crawled back inside. Jack would soon know she was missing, he'd figure out she was lost, and he would find her. All she had to do was wait inside her lean-to, stay calm, and he would find her.

JACK CURSED THE RAIN. He cursed it loudly, savagely, repeatedly. He cursed the cold. He cursed the wild land and the dark woods and Charlie's crackie, who was moving forward ever so slowly, stopping to delicately sniff every dripping branch, every wet rock, and he wondered if the little dog was really trying to pick up Senna's scent or if Ula was just reading all the stories of the forest. The rain had washed away all but the deepest of tracks. He'd found the blurred paw print of a big wolf at the river's edge, and Senna's boot track beside it, but those were the only two defined tracks they'd seen. The rest of the search had been based on the crackie's painstakingly slow progress away from the river and into the woods.

Charlie had taken Ula to the one imprint of Senna's boot track, held out Senna's crumpled nightshirt for her to sniff, which Jack had thought would be the best item of clothing to use, and that was all. For the past hour they'd been following her along this old game trail while she acted as if she were on a relaxing Sunday jaunt.

Who the hell knew what the crackie was smelling. Wolf? Caribou? It could be any of the dozens of animals that called this land home. The crackie was nothing more than an Indian hunting dog. Sure, she had a keen nose, but no training in search and rescue. Jack had never felt so hopeless as he did following that useless little chicken killer. He was already hoarse from shouting Senna's name into the unforgiving wilderness. Damn the crackie for moving so slowly. Damn the rain for making so much noise. Damn his heart for beating so loudly in his ears! And damn Charlie for his stoic expression. The boy never displayed any emotion whatsoever.

It was cold, and the rain was like ice water. Senna had been out in it since 6:00 a.m. and here it was, nearly twelve hours later. Search and rescue statistics had shown that for every hour that passed, the search area expanded by countless square miles. There were only two of them; they couldn't possibly walk a grid that would cover the amount of territory that twelve hours of being lost could encompass. If they hadn't found her by 10:00 p.m., he'd send Charlie back to the lodge and have him call for the rangers to come in. Jack would stay out and keep looking. He'd look forever if he had to. He'd look until he found her.

"Hanson," Charlie said.

Jack stopped and turned back. Charlie had picked something out of a spruce branch and he held it out to Jack. It was a long piece of dark hair. Four pieces, actually, a tiny lock of what had to be Senna's hair. Jack looked ahead to where the little black crackie moved slowly and purposefully along, sniffing this and sniffing that. *Find Senna,* he willed the dog silently. *Find her, and you can eat all of Goody's laying hens and I'll buy you more when you're done with them.* He tucked the lock of hair into his jacket pocket, took a fresh grip on his rifle, and walked forward into the chilly rain.

WITHOUT A WATCH IT WAS DIFFICULT to say what time it was, but Senna became aware that the gray gloom was deepening. That meant it had to be past 11:00 p.m. She was exhausted from running to keep warm and spent longer periods of time sitting in the little shelter, clenched up with shivers. The hunger pains she'd felt hours ago had long since passed, but the cold had intensified. Jack was out there somewhere, looking for her. She had shouted his name a few times, knowing it was futile but feeling comforted by the sound of his name. She knew he was out there and she knew he would find her.

She dozed off at one point, in spite of her misery, and had a strange dream. She dreamt that a black wolf came through the forest of black spruce, walking on silent feet, in the deep moss, and stood in front of her lean-to. She felt that the wolf was Raven, and that she was trying to tell her something, and she wondered if maybe the animal was carrying a message from her grandfather. What was he trying to tell her? It was so hard to read the expression in those intense yellow eyes. The wolf was tall at the shoulder with long gangly legs and thick fur dripping with rain. Big paws splayed strongly upon the wet earth, as if the animal knew just where it belonged.

"Hello, Raven," she murmured aloud in the midst of her dream. "Tell the admiral I wish I could read his letter. Maybe you could tell me what was in it…."

And then she woke and blinked her eyes and the black wolf was gone. It was dark, but the cold was easing. She felt her shivers beginning to ease as a curious, sleepy warmth soothed through her. Jack would find her soon. All she had to do was stay awake….

THE CRACKIE LOST THE TRAIL where it went into the bog and the water closed over any scent that might have remained. Jack couldn't believe it. He and Charlie kept walking wider circles, looking for some sign, any sign at all. Jack was hoping that Senna would have come out on one of the higher eskers but they'd been thrashing around for over an hour and the damn dog was clueless. He thought about firing his rifle to let Senna know where they were, but he was afraid she'd try to come to them, and hurt herself in the dark.

"Too wet here," Charlie said, stopping on one of their passes and shaking his head.

"Senna came out of this bog somewhere, dammit!" Jack responded savagely, unable to suppress his emotional outburst. "We'll keep walking bigger circles until Ula smells something."

He knew he should send Charlie back to the lodge as he had originally planned, but if Charlie went, so would the crackie, and he'd lose any chance of picking up Senna's trail. It was after midnight now, and hard to make out the shapes of things in the raw, wet gloom. He stumbled into knee-deep water and cursed, then heard a sound that made the hair on the back of his neck prickle; the long, low drawn-out howl of a wolf. The crackie froze, lifting her small, finely shaped head, sharp pointy nose tasting the air. And then, without warning, she bounded off through the muskeg, throwing up plumes of water.

Charlie called after her but she paid him no heed. Jack cursed the day he'd ever set eyes on that creature, but for lack of anything else to do, he plunged after her, holding his rifle and the flashlight up as he waded through bog water that sometimes reached mid-thigh. He could hear Charlie thrashing close on his heels as he kept his eyes fixed on the dark little dog that was steadily drawing away from them. The crackie's bearing was true. Sure enough, she was going after the wolf. In his helpless rage, Jack hoped the wolf ate the useless beast.

The crackie gained higher ground and quickly disappeared from view. By the time they reached the place where she had vanished a good five minutes had passed. Chances were they'd never see her again because if she had gone after that wolf, she was done for. Jack bent over his knees and struggled to catch his breath while Charlie called the dog over and over again, unable to believe that she was truly gone.

"You're wasting your time," Jack said, straightening. And then he heard another sound. Very faint. Almost imagined. He held up his hand to silence Charlie's calls. "Did you hear that?" he said. And then without waiting for an answer he bellowed Senna's name as loudly as he could.

He waited, hardly daring to hope. But there! Over there! The sound came again, very faint but unmistakably human.

"Which direction do you make that?" he said, knowing the boy's senses were keener, and Charlie pointed. The boy knew the wilderness the way city kids knew city streets. Jack immediately set off in the direction Charlie had indicated, stopping every few hundred feet to holler again and wait for a response. The faint sound became gradually louder, until he could hear that she was calling out his name every time he called out hers. By now he was half running, his forearm shielding his eyes from any unseen branches in the murky light. He fell twice on the rough ground and forced himself to slow down. Wouldn't do if he busted a leg now.

It took forever to reach her, and when he did he stopped so abruptly that Charlie rammed into him from behind. Senna was kneeling with her arms around the little black crackie in front of what looked like a pile of brush. "Jack!" she cried when she spotted him, and suddenly she was in his arms, plastered against him, holding him tightly. "I knew you'd come. I knew you would!"

"Are you all right?" Jack handed his rifle to Charlie and held Senna as tightly as she was holding him, weak with relief that she was alive, that she was in his arms. She was soaking wet and after a few moments he felt her begin to shake. "We'll get you warmed up," he said. "Are you hurt?" Her face gleamed up at him, as pale as the moon and laced with scratches from her journey through the woods.

"I knew you'd come, Jack," she repeated. "I knew you'd find me."

Charlie, unbidden, was already building a fire. He used the dried moss hanging on the dead black spruce limbs for kindling, and a few wax scrapings from a candle stuffed in his pocket to ignite it. While Jack swiftly rigged the rope and tarp between two trees, Charlie fed bigger and bigger pieces of kindling into the flames until the wetness of the wood no longer mattered and the fire leapt high, reflecting its light and warmth.

"I brought dry clothes," Jack said, pushing Senna under the tarp and uncapping the thermos. "I want you to change into them, but drink this first." She took the cup with trembling hands and sipped. "Drink all of it," he ordered, pulling the clothing out of the pack.

"I thought I heard a wolf," she said. "And when I slept, I dreamt about one standing right outside my shelter, looking in."

"Keep drinking."

She obediently sipped, and then her whole body was gripped by convulsive shivers. "Oh, God, I'm so cold."

"Keep shivering, that's a good sign. You're more than a little hypothermic. Okay, hand over that cup and strip out of those wet things while Charlie and I get more wood for the fire. The clothes I brought'll be huge on you, but they're dry."

Beyond the light cast from the fire Jack stood in the rain, his knees weak. He was shaking as badly as she was. He caught sight of the crackie hovering on the edge of the firelight and called her to him, dropping to the ground to embrace her. "All the laying hens you can eat, girl, and steak once a week," he muttered gratefully into the little dog's ear, his voice hoarse with emotion.

SENNA DIDN'T REMEMBER MUCH at all about their trip out of the woods four hours later in the predawn light. She had no sense of how long it took, only that her legs wouldn't work right and Jack ended up carrying her most of the way through that wretched bog while she kept repeating, over and over, "Put me down. I can walk."

She was still saying it as he carried her along the narrow game path to the river, down the brush-choked shore, and up the steep ramp to the lodge one slow step at a time. Still mumbling it when he bypassed the dark lodge and kicked open the door to the guides' cabin, hollering to Charlie to fire up the woodstove while he lowered her gently onto the bottom bunk. He lit the lamp, and Senna gazed at his rugged, handsome profile in the golden light. "I could have walked," she said.

"Charlie, get that stove as hot as you can while I get

the plane ready. I'll fly her into Goose Bay, there's a good hospital there."

"I'm fine," Senna insisted. "I was fine the moment you found me. Being lost isn't a fatal disease."

What on earth was the matter with him? Jack acted as if she were dying. There was so much to do at the lodge but she'd wasted an entire day and her feet hurt and nothing had been accomplished except she'd gotten big blisters on her heels. Her legs ached. Cold. It was so cold in here…. She heard the cabin door open and close.

"Jack?"

"I'm right here." Good to have him moving close, bending near. His hand brushed the hair back from her forehead. Hand rough with callouses. Strong hand. Tender gesture. Sweet. She closed her own hand around his wrist, relishing the warmth.

"I knew you'd come, Jack."

"You're safe now, Senna. It's over."

"Did you see the wolf?"

"No, but we heard it howl."

"I'm not sure I really saw it. I think I must have dreamt it."

His hand brushed her forehead again. "Charlie showed me the tracks. That wolf looked right into the shelter you built, and if it hadn't howled when it did, Ula might not have found you, though she brought us damn close. Now sit up for me and drink another cup of my special brew while I get the plane ready." He helped to prop her against some pillows, pressed a hot mug into her hand, then turned to leave.

"Jack?" Senna said as he opened the cabin door. He paused and looked back, questioningly. "I'm not going anywhere," she said. "I'm cold and tired, but I'll be fine just as soon as the cabin warms up. If you'll just let me stay here for a little while, I'll be fine…."

Fifteen minutes later the cabin's temperature was at least a hundred degrees, Senna had finished the mug of his special brew, and she was lying on her side as the warmth worked its way through her, inside and out, watching Jack boil up a pot of oatmeal. He was talking about the benefits of oatmeal with honey and raisins, narrating as he cooked. His voice soothed and comforted and lulled her toward sleep. She closed her eyes, intending to continue listening until the oatmeal was done, but when she opened them again sunlight was streaming through the cabin window. She lay very still for a moment, relishing both the warmth of her bed and the feeling of safety that she felt in this little cabin. Gradually her gaze focused on Jack, who was slumped at the table, head cradled in the curve of his arm, asleep.

Charlie was in his bunk, the crackie curled at his feet, but the bunk above her was empty. Jack could have slept there, but he obviously hadn't made it that far. Senna moved her legs and felt the weariness in her muscles. She could only imagine what Jack would feel like when he wakened, after the extreme exertion he'd made hours earlier. He looked so vulnerable, sleeping like that. So much like a boy, yet there was nothing boyish about him, except maybe that brash grin of his, and his naive enthusiasm when it came to this place.

She pushed the blankets back, noting that he'd added another while she slept. Four blankets, all wool. No way had he taken any chances on her getting cold again. She swung her legs over the edge of the bunk and stretched. The crackie lifted her head and gazed at her with those sharp black eyes. "Hey, little girl," Senna said softly. "You have my undying gratitude."

Ula studied her a moment longer and then dropped her head back onto her paws and heaved a weary sigh. Senna stood, and stared down at the clothes she was wearing; they hung off her like dish rags off pot hooks. Jack's clothes. Huge. Long johns, ragg-wool socks, stiff wool shirt and matching thick wool Swedish army pants. She bent down and rolled the pant cuffs up enough so that she could walk, and then moved to the stove. A deep bed of embers still glowed within, and she fed a few sticks into the firebox, filled the coffeepot with fresh water, and measured coffee into the basket.

Within minutes the water was boiling and the smell of coffee permeated the cabin. Senna put a frying pan onto the stovetop and rummaged through the icebox for anything to eat. Gordina's horrific cooking had inspired Jack to keep his own stash of food on hand, and Senna found everything she needed to make a fine breakfast in his cooler. Soon the smell of hickory smoked bacon joined the fragrant plumes of coffee steaming out of the pot, and Jack awoke. He did so with a jerk, lifting his head off his arms and sitting up suddenly. For a moment he stared at her without reaction, but then he slumped forward onto his elbows and rubbed his hand over his face. "You should be in bed," he said, pushing away from the table to rise. "I'll fix you something to eat and then feed the dogs."

Senna dropped her hand onto his shoulder and pressed him back down into the chair. "I'm perfectly fine, and it's my turn to cook."

Senna filled two mugs with coffee and handed one to Jack, who was studying her in that maddening way of his. "Don't take this the wrong way, because without a doubt you're the toughest, smartest, and most beautiful business partner I could ever hope for," he said as he accepted the mug of coffee, "but the next time you decide to follow a set of fresh wolf tracks, at least take a map, a compass and waterproof matches. Better yet, take me."

Senna lifted her hand. "Say no more. I learned that lesson the hard way."

Jack blew the steam off the top of his mug, eyes narrowing. "You did good, building that shelter the way you did and staying put. That was smart. Most people who get lost in a big wilderness get so scared they start running and can't stop."

"Believe me, my little adventure started out that way."

He slouched back in his chair, hair tousled and unshaven face still showing deep weariness. "Just please don't go running off like that again. That escapade took ten years off my life."

"I'm sorry. You shouldn't have carried me the whole way."

"You don't weigh much more than a minute."

"I could have walked."

"If the going had been easier, maybe, but it was pretty dark and getting through that damn bog was nasty. Believe me. *Nasty.*"

"Believe *me,* I know. I went through it many times myself, over and over like a human eggbeater trying to thrash my way out," Senna said.

"Maybe I should have let you walk, but you were rambling on about all this stuff that didn't make any sense at all and I knew I had to get you back here and warmed up as fast as possible."

"Well, thank you." Senna dropped her eyes to hide her feelings, because suddenly, embarrassingly, unbearably, what she wanted to do at that moment, even with Charlie asleep on his bed, was lean over and kiss him. "I promise I won't go chasing after wolves again any time soon."

"Chase after them all you want, just promise to take me with you." He shook his head, studying her again. "It's not every woman who has a wolf come to her door."

"I'm still not sure that wasn't a dream," she said.

"Dreams don't leave tracks." He scraped his chair back and stood, stretching. He moved to the stove and fed another stick into it. Even after all he'd been through, he still moved in that confident, athletic way. The man was enormously strong to have carried her so far. Senna wished she could remember more of that awful journey but it was all a blur. She'd have to get Ula some special treat, and Jack…what could she ever do to repay him? She was wise enough to realize that if he and Charlie's crackie hadn't found her, she would have been in serious trouble.

"How many eggs?" she asked, holding the carton in her hand.

"Between the two of us we can take care of a dozen, easy," he replied. "Throw 'em all in the bacon fat, woman. I'm going to wash up and shave and dish the dogs up some breakfast. Poor bastards were neglected yesterday. Didn't get their supper."

He returned just as she was taking the bacon out of the pan. His hair was still dripping and his freshly shaven jaw was razor-burned from his brisk scrub-up in the river. "I met an old friend of your grandfather's in Goose Bay yesterday. George Pilgrim," he said, pouring himself another mug of coffee. "Retired ranger, and the best guide and outdoorsman I've ever known." Jack dropped back into his chair. "Fact is, he's the reason I was late getting back here. We had lunch together. He was having surgery today for some intestinal thing, and I told him he could come here to recuperate. I hope that's okay with you."

Senna glanced at him over her shoulder, spatula in hand. "Of course it is. You'll need to find out from his doctors exactly what he needs, because out here, you better have what's important when you need it."

Jack nodded. "I'll make sure."

"Maybe you'd better call tonight, to check on him."

Jack nodded again. "I will." He took another sip of coffee, and as Senna was dishing out the eggs, bacon and toast, he said, "Speaking of recuperating, you should go back to bed right after breakfast. The cabin's nice and warm and you'll have it to yourself all day."

Senna whirled around, eyebrows raised. "I can't just lie in bed, any more than you can. There's way too much to do. Besides, I'm fully recovered."

"You sure?"

"Of course I'm sure."

"That's too bad. You looked so damn cute all cuddled up in the blankets that I was hoping you'd stay a little longer," he said, giving her a grin that wasn't the least bit boyish.

CHAPTER ELEVEN

WAVEY AND GORDINA HAD DONE little to justify their existence in the time between Senna getting lost and breakfast the following morning. They'd carried a few things up from the plane, but Jack still had to unload most of the provisions he'd picked up in Goose Bay the day before. By the time the last of it was hauled up to the lodge, unpacked and stored away, his legs were like rubber. He collapsed on the porch step and might have passed out there except for a gentle touch on his shoulder. Senna sat down beside him and offered him a cup of strong hot tea and a ham sandwich. She'd showered and changed into her own clothes, and her energy levels had rebounded the way he wished his own would. She looked beautiful, as always.

"I just got off the phone with my aunt who owns the inn where I work," she said. "She's FedExing all the amenities we'll need, including the turn-down chocolates and two dozen bathrobes for the rooms."

"Turn-down chocolates and bathrobes?" Jack said. To him the concept was ludicrous. This was, after all, a wilderness lodge where the fishing was of paramount importance and nothing else really mattered.

"Of course. Nice, thick luxurious ones that our guests can wear to and from the hot tub. She's giving us a great price on the amenities and the robes. Speaking of hot tubs, we should fire ours up and give it test run after supper. You could definitely use a long hot soak after yesterday, and so could I."

Jack contemplated this unexpected but promising suggestion while taking a swallow of the strong tea. He thought about the bottle of champagne he'd purchased with the last of his life's savings and a light bulb went off. "I'm game if you are."

"You're on. I'm helping Gordina in the kitchen tonight, whether she wants my help or not. She has two more days to learn how to cook a meal that can be eaten by humans. And another thing. I've unpacked all the liquors into the bar area, but I've been thinking about the logistics of it. What if a guest over-indulges and falls off the porch steps? Are we liable? Does our insurance cover that?"

"Good question. Better call the insurance company, and ask Granville. Oh, by the way, he left a message for you at the lake house. He hasn't found a certain important letter yet, and you may need to sign some papers soon."

"Granville is a dear, sweet man, but I think he was a better friend to my grandfather than he is a lawyer to me. As far as the legal documents go, if they haven't arrived before tomorrow, he'll have to forward them to Maine."

Jack felt a painful twist in his gut at her words and looked away from her, across the river to where the dark spruce hid all the mysteries of the wildest places. "Think of all the adventures you'll be missing while you're back there planning other people's weddings."

Senna gave a rueful laugh as she pushed to her feet

and stretched. "I think I've had enough adventures in the past two weeks to last me a lifetime, thank you very much."

SENNA SPENT THE EARLY AFTERNOON unpacking crates of her grandfather's expansive collection of books and arranging them by category into the bookshelves that spanned one entire wall, perusing some of them briefly and wishing she had more time to spend reading. Wishing she had more time *here*. The thought was not new to her, even after the horrendous experience of being lost the day before. She wanted to stay here with Jack and Charlie and shepherd the opening of the lodge for business. She wanted to make sure that the meals were prepared correctly, that the flowers were picked fresh daily, that tea was served each afternoon promptly at 4:00 p.m. and that the guest rooms and public areas and kitchen were kept spotlessly clean. She wanted to stay for all those reasons, but most of all she wanted to stay because of how she felt about Jack, who still didn't know about the prospective buyer Tim had found because she still hadn't found the right moment to tell him.

Senna sighed, thumbing through a wildlife encyclopedia. A photograph slipped out of the book and fell to the floor. She picked it up and turned it over. A black wolf stared back at her, its eyes just as yellow and vivid as those of the wolf she'd seen yesterday. Her grandfather must have taken this picture. She looked at the back and sure enough there was a date penned in the upper left-hand corner, and written beside it in his neat hand, "Raven, Naskaupi wolf near the Wolf River."

"I bet it's the same one I saw yesterday," Senna murmured, feeling an eerie tingle through her body. She knew the picture had probably been taken from a great distance because she'd seen several telescopic lenses among her grandfather's photographic equipment, yet it appeared that he'd been eye to eye with the great wolf.

She heard a man's tread coming across the porch and looked up as Jack entered the lodge. He had a wrench in one hand and a greasy rag in the other. Senna rose to her feet and showed him the photograph. He turned it over and read the back.

"If he'd lived, the admiral would have championed the Naskaupi wolf pack," Jack said, handing the picture back. "He hated the fact that they're persecuted because they follow the caribou herds, culling out the weak. He knew the wolves kept the herd healthy, but the locals shoot them on sight, thinking they're decimating the caribou. That's why it was so unusual for that wolf to come so close you. Usually the mere whiff of human scent sends them off in the opposite direction at thirty miles an hour."

Senna tucked the photograph into the book and sighed. "Why is it that any predator other than human is regarded as pure evil and labeled a varmint? I sure don't miss the politics at my old job, or the mindless hatred and persecution of the coyotes, but I do miss the field work, and all those days spent in the woods."

"Even after yesterday?"

Senna laughed. "Even after yesterday."

"The admiral was right about you," Jack said. "If you can still crave being in the woods after yesterday, you're wild at heart. I'll go fire up the hot tub and get the water heating, then feed the dogs."

"I'll hunt up our cook," Senna said. "With any luck she's already prepping the meal."

GORDINA HAD LITTLE REGARD for the idea of an early supper, and even less for Senna's plan to help her prepare it. "I can manage on my own," she said with a huffy attitude.

"Yes, I'm sure you can, but many hands make light work. Believe me, you'll have a whole summer of cooking by yourself and wishing you had help."

Senna had spent a great deal of time in the banquet kitchen at the Inn on Christmas Cove and was familiar with prep work, hot-line protocol and basic culinary techniques. While not a chef in any sense of the word, she recognized a good one when she watched one in action and could tell a great one just by the way his or her staff worked together. She could easily step in during a crisis and perform nearly all the jobs in the busy kitchen, whether it be creating apps, cooking entrées or washing dishes. She tried to instill some of this knowledge to Gordina as the two of them prepped for the evening meal, but Gordina wasn't the least bit receptive. Wavey appeared halfway through the process and volunteered to plate up the salad, which was a simple spinach and strawberry presentation with a sprinkling of pistachios and a honey balsamic dressing.

One and a half stressful hours later the meal was as ready as it would ever be and Senna was at her wits' end. There was no way Gordina was going work out, and Wavey, in her slow, dreamy way, had dropped half of the very expensive pistachios onto the kitchen floor while plating and garnishing the simple salads, a task that took her a good five minutes.

Senna left the kitchen long enough to light the fire in the dining-room fireplace and make sure the glassware and silver were polished at each place setting. The flames were licking up into the kindling and curling around the log when the satellite phone rang in the reception area. She answered it on the third ring. "Wolf River Lodge, Senna speaking. How may I help you?"

"Senna, it's Tim. I'm sorry to bother you, but I need to get an answer from you about your partner's thoughts about selling the lodge. Hammel's flying back from Europe tonight and he's going to be calling me in the morning."

Her heart plummeted at the sound of Tim's somber voice. "I'm sorry I didn't call you last night, Tim, but I..." She almost told him about being lost but caught herself in the nick of time. "I'm really sorry."

"Do you have any information yet? What should I tell him?"

"I haven't told Jack yet, but I know he won't sell his half," she said, her grip tightening on the receiver. "You'll have to tell Mr. Hammel that."

She heard his sigh. "That's too bad. It'll be difficult for you to sell half of a business that doesn't have a history of making money. What if I brought this guy out to the lodge so Jack could meet him? They could talk things over, discuss different options. Do you think that might change his mind?"

"I doubt it. He loves this place."

"Hammel really wants to see it. He can fly to Labrador on July second. Could you run that by Jack? It wouldn't hurt for the two of them to meet."

"Okay. I'll tell him. He'll have to stay in Goose Bay because we'll be full, but I'm sure Jack can ferry him out here for a tour of the property." She heard Jack's footsteps coming into the living room even as she spoke. They paused briefly outside the registration area when he heard his name mentioned, then continued on into the kitchen.

"It would be nice if he could stay there for a night or two."

"Tim, I'm not going to bump a paying guest out of their room so some rich corporate executive can decide whether or not he wants to buy out my half of the business. He doesn't have to stay here. Most people shopping for a house don't sleep overnight in it before they buy it."

"Senna, this guy's a big-time outdoorsman. He hunts and fishes all over the world and has all kinds of game trophies hung on his walls. He e-mailed me some pictures of his lodge in Alaska. It's a pretty fancy place. I don't know how fancy your Labrador lodge is and I told him that, but he seems to know quite a bit about it already. I guess he knows the banker who gave your grandfather the construction loan, which doesn't surprise me because Hammel seems to have connections all over. I'm only telling you this because I think if he likes the place he'll buy it on the spot and he'd get a better feel for it if he could stay there."

"If he feels he must stay overnight, the earliest vacancy we have is at the beginning of September, when fishing season ends," Senna said, wondering what a rich corporate executive hunted for in Alaska, and what he would hunt here, and how he could possibly know the banker who held the lien on the lodge. If Hammel knew that much, he probably knew how deep in the red they were.

"It probably snows there in September," Tim pointed out.

"Probably. It snows here in June." Senna heard Jack's

footsteps returning. "I'll talk to Jack," she said, anxious to complete the call.

"Will you call me as soon as you know?" Tim asked, and just then Jack bellowed loudly, right behind her, as though calling the cows in from pasture.

"Senna, sweetings, time for dinner!"

Senna jumped to her feet, cupping her hand over the phone's mouthpiece, and glared out over the registration desk. Jack, dressed in his finest blue jeans and flannel shirt, grinned back at her even as Tim's voice came over the line, astonished. "Who was that?"

"My business partner," Senna responded, choking back the sudden urge to laugh as Jack turned and sauntered back toward the kitchen.

"He doesn't sound like he's in his seventies, and why did he call you sweetings?"

"Oh, Jack calls all the girls that," Senna said. "He's quite a card. I'll call you as soon as I know anything, Tim. But I know he's not going to sell out to Hammel."

Minutes later she was shooing Jack out of the kitchen, where he was busy removing the lids from all the pots on the stove in order to peek inside. She gave Wavey last-minute instructions. "Remember to serve from the left and remove from the right. Replace any used silverware when you clear. Refill water glasses as needed, and offer to do the same with any wines the guests might be drinking with their dinner. This is a trial run, but pretend it's the real thing and try your best. Okay?"

Jack was already seated at the table but he jumped up when she entered and ceremoniously held her seat for her. "Thank you," she said, unfolding her napkin into her lap with formal aplomb. "Prepare to be wowed."

"Oh, believe me, I'm ready and waiting." He sat back down and hitched his chair closer to the table.

"Where's Charlie?"

"Hiding out at the cabin. He figures it's safer there."

Senna waited a few minutes, and when Wavey didn't appear she sighed. "I'm sorry, but I'm too tired to get back up," she explained before raising her voice and shouting, "Wavey, *now* would be a good time to start dinner service!"

Jack grinned, clearly enjoying the performance before it even began. Wavey made her tardy appearance holding two salads. She put Senna's down first, which was proper, and then Jack's, but she served them both from the right, which was wrong.

"Remember what I told you, Wavey," Senna coached. "Serve from the left, remove from right."

It was hard to know what the girl was thinking, or if she even thought about anything at all except her romantically tragic non-relationship with Jack. Wavey left the room and reappeared almost immediately carrying two soup bowls, putting one in front of Jack's salad and the other to Senna's left.

"Wavey, you don't bring the soup in until *after* the guests have finished their salads and you've cleared their salad plates. And don't forget that our water glasses need to be filled. That's the very first thing you should do, after which you might ask if we would enjoy a glass of wine with dinner."

Wavey's frown turned into a full-fledged pout. She placed her hands on her hips. "I don't think it's fair that you should be sitting there eating while I work," she said. "I've worked all day long."

"Wavey, this is a practice run so you'll know how to do everything properly when the guests arrive."

"I still don't think it's fair. I worked hard today and I'm just as tired as you are."

"All right, then." Senna stood with a surge of frustration. "You may leave. I'll do the rest of the serving."

Wavey hesitated. "Don't I get to eat?"

"No. At least, not with us, and not the good stuff. Go back to your cabin and get some rest. You obviously need it."

Wavey drifted from the dining room and Senna plopped back into her seat with a moan, dropping her head into her hands. "Honestly, Jack. I don't see how it's going to work."

Jack tasted the spinach and strawberry salad. "This is great," he enthused. "Pistachio nuts. Very exotic." He stood, went to the dry bar, and procured a bottle of merlot and two wineglasses. "Shall I pour for you, poor exhausted young miss?" Senna laughed as he poured two glasses of wine. He set her glass down and gave her shoulder a reassuring squeeze. "Be patient," he said. "Wavey'll probably do great around real guests."

"We can only hope," Senna said, feeling her heartbeat leap at his touch.

The soup was a Portuguese kale with spicy jalapeno chicken sausage. Jack finished his salad in six huge forkfuls and then inhaled his soup. "Killer," he pronounced. "Can I request seconds? We should serve this soup every night."

"Our guests would get sick of it and no you can't have seconds." Senna cleared the salad and soup dishes and brought out the entrées. "Which would you prefer, the chicken or the beef?"

"I'm a meat-and-potatoes man," he said. She set the beef in front of him and returned to her seat.

Jack wolfed down his steak and vegetables. His plate was as clean as if a dog had licked it. "Unbelievable," he said. "I didn't know food could taste that good. Say, wedding planner, wanna full-time job?"

"Got one, thanks."

"What's for dessert?"

"Sorry. No time to make dessert, and I didn't want to use up one of the frozen pound cakes. They're great in a pinch."

Jack sat back in his chair with a satisfied sigh. "Two truths. That was the best meal I've ever eaten, and you're the best dinner companion I've ever shared a meal with."

"It helps that you're starving and lonely," Senna said, but she glowed at his words. "I'm optimistic that Gordina will be able to manage the simple preparations. Both the chicken and beef were easy entrées to make."

"Thanks for trying to make me feel better," he grinned. "More wine?"

Senna shook her head. "I'm so tired I'd fall asleep." She stood to clear the plates. "Coffee?"

He shook his head. "Hot tub."

"I'll help Gordina with the dishes and be right out."

"Gordina can manage without you. Meet me in five minutes."

"Do you think it's safe to get in a hot tub after a big meal?"

"I think it's mandatory. Besides, that wasn't a big meal. It was a delicious meal, but those portions were scrawny."

"Those are standard portions," Senna pointed out. "You're just used to huge lumberjack meals."

"Damn straight. A man puts in a hard day's work, he needs a lot of food."

"True, but the guests aren't going to be working like slaves the way you do. Most people don't."

Jack stood. "Five minutes. And don't be late."

JACK MADE TRACKS TO THE guides' cabin, where he rummaged frantically through his duffel for a pair of swimming trunks. He knew he'd packed them in the hopes of just such a scenario as this, but it seemed to take him at least five minutes to find them. Charlie paid him no heed, lying on his bunk absorbed in one of the admiral's books. Jack could see from the pan on the stove that Charlie had opened a can of beans for supper. "You should've eaten with us up at the lodge," Jack said. "It was damn good."

He hurried back to the lodge, flannel shirt unbuttoned, jeans pulled over his swimming trunks, boots unlaced on bare feet. His heart was pounding. He had to find the champagne and have it ready before Senna arrived at the hot tub. Stupid! Should've done this before supper. There wouldn't be enough time to chill it properly. He burst into the kitchen, where Gordina was cleaning up. "Gordina, you brought some of the stuff up from the plane yesterday, didn't you?"

Gordina nodded, lips pursed as though clamping a cigarette.

"A pretty bag with handles, holding a bottle of champagne and some nice cheese. I need it. Where'd you stash it?"

Gordina's expression became guarded. "I don't remember a pretty bag with handles," she said.

"It was right beside the pilot's seat," Jack prompted.

"I didn't see it in the plane when I unpacked this morning. You and Wavey brought some things up, where did you put them? There was a green bottle inside the bag with a pink flower painted on it."

Gordina stared down at the pan she was scrubbing and made no response, but her entire body had gone rigid. Jack felt his own do the same. "Where's the champagne, Gordina?" he asked bluntly.

"We didn't know it was special," she mumbled, not looking up.

Jack thought that if there were a moment in his life when he was going to go ballistic, this was it. "Tell me you didn't drink my hundred-dollar bottle of champagne."

Gordina kept her eyes down and made no response.

"I don't believe this!" he roared. "You drank my hundred-dollar bottle of champagne?"

Gordina cringed away as he advanced. "We didn't know."

"Dammit all!" Jack whirled and kicked the door behind him, sending it crashing back on his hinges. "I don't freaking believe it. That's it. *That's it!* Pack your things, you and Wavey both. Get all your gear together, you're leaving first thing in the morning. You hear me? Where's Wavey?"

Without waiting for an answer Jack burst out of the back door and charged toward Wavey and Gordina's cabin. He entered without knocking, surprising Wavey, who was sitting on the edge of her bunk brushing her hair. She froze when he came into the cabin, but her initial smile of greeting faded instantly as Jack spied the green champagne bottle with the flower painted on it.

He snatched it off the little table and upended it. Not a drop remained.

"Get your things together. I'm flying you and Gordina to Goose Bay first thing tomorrow," he said, his voice remarkably calm after his initial outburst at Gordina. He turned and walked back up to the lodge, feeling weak and sick to his stomach. He climbed the porch steps one at a time with a weary, defeated tread, and came face to face with Senna. She was wrapped in a robe, bareheaded and barefoot, and looked like an angel descended from heaven in the midst of a holocaust.

"What's wrong?" she said. "What was all that shouting about?"

Jack held up the empty bottle. "Wavey and Gordina drank our bottle of champagne," he said. "They found it in the plane yesterday, while I was searching for you, and they drank it. Every last drop. Gone."

Senna reached for the bottle. "My goodness," she said softly. "You certainly picked out an expensive vintage."

"It was for a very special occasion, a once-in-a-life-time moment. And for what it's worth, I paid for it myself, I didn't charge it to your account." He slumped against a porch post and ran his fingers through his hair. "I fired both of them. I'll fly them out of here in the morning."

Senna's gaze was sympathetic. "Jack, I realize you're upset and I don't blame you, but you can't run this place all by yourself."

He rallied at her words, pulling himself back together and putting a little swagger back into the moment. What the hell. A faint heart, and all that. "You're absolutely right, but I got you, babe."

"For another day…"

"You could call your aunt, get an extension. Tell her you got lost in Labrador and can't seem to find your way back to Maine. Two more weeks, Senna. Just give this place two more weeks. I know we can get the lodge up and running, just the two of us, if we have to, and that will give me time to hire more help. Better help."

She hesitated and he braced himself for the head shake and the negative words. "All right," she said.

He stared in disbelief. "You mean you'll stay?"

"I can't say that I blame you for firing Gordina and Wavey, and I'm sure in two weeks time we'll be able to find help somewhere, even if it's just some high-school kids looking for an adventurous summer. I'll stay. I owe you that much, Jack. Of course I'll stay."

SENNA WAS FLOATING IN A euphoric daze. It was a delicious sensation to be immersed chin-deep in a tub of hot water, in the middle of a big wilderness, right next to a man who was like no other man she'd ever known. She was sitting so close to him, in fact, that she could reach out and touch the rounded muscle of his shoulder with her fingertips. His skin was smooth, his shoulder as hard as iron. She was amazed at her own temerity, but smiled at the look he gave her. For once he wasn't studying her as if she were a scientific specimen, and for once he was speechless.

"You know something, John William Hanson? I happen to think you're pretty damn wonderful," she said, dizzy from the wine, the heat of the water, and the cumulative exhaustion of the past two weeks. Everything conspired to make the words flow easily. "I think you're a wonderful man, and that's exactly why my grandfather made you his business partner, but I still don't understand why he left his half of the business to me."

Jack refilled her glass from the wine he'd fetched to replace the champagne and set the bottle back on the tub's edge. "Because he wanted you to have it."

It was nearly dark enough that she could almost see the stars, but she wasn't searching for them. She could only look at Jack. She wondered if this was what true love felt like, this strange, scary heart-sick longing, this lonely, empty pang deep down inside that only that one person could ever fill. Was she in love with John Hanson? She'd never felt this way about Tim.

"Tell me about Tim," Jack said suddenly, as if reading her thoughts.

Senna took another sip of wine and frowned. "He wondered why you called me sweetings."

"I call all my girls sweetings when I summons them to supper."

"Liar."

"He left a message for you at the lake house," Jack said.

"Why didn't you tell me?"

"It didn't seem all that important. He just wanted you to call him when you got a chance. He was worried about you."

Senna eased her sore muscles in the soothing water, leaned back and closed her eyes.

"Are you in love with him?"

Jack's abrupt question put a damper on Senna's floating euphoria. She opened her eyes, sat up straight, and drew a deep breath. "Tim's a very dear friend. He's only trying to help me settle my grandfather's estate."

"Who's this buyer he found?"

"You were eavesdropping on my phone conversation?"

"Damn straight."

"He's found a *potential* buyer," Senna said. "His name is Earl Hammel and he wants to stay here when he comes to look at the place, so I told Tim our first vacancy wasn't until the beginning of September. If he wants to come sooner, he'll have to stay in Goose Bay."

"And I'm supposed to ferry him back and forth on your behalf?" Jack prodded.

Senna felt a wild tumble of emotions assail her. "I can't see bumping a paying guest just because someone wants a tour of the property," she said.

"No, that would hurt occupancy, hurt the numbers, hurt the bottom line." His voice had become flinty and Senna wished she could steer the conversation away from selling the lodge.

"That's right, and I'm not anxious to do that. If he wants to come when we're fully booked, he'll just have to stay elsewhere. He can hire Thunder Air to fly him back and forth. I'm sorry I volunteered you. Tim says that Mr. Hammel wants to buy the lodge for his own personal use, and I made him aware that you don't want to sell your share of the business." There, that should calm him.

"And he still wants to come? Does he think he can talk me into selling my half? And by the way, if you don't mind my asking, what's the price you're asking for your grandfather's dream? Or were you planning to withhold that information from me, as well?"

She heard the caustic barb in his words and winced inwardly. "I haven't named a price. I wanted to talk to you first."

"That's mighty white of you, pard. When were you going to do that?"

Senna sat up so abruptly that water sloshed out of the hot tub and onto the deck. "Look, I'm sorry I didn't tell you about this right away. I know I should have, but I..." Suddenly she felt as if she'd hit a brick wall. She slumped back, overcome by a wave of dizziness so strong she was afraid she was about to pass out. Lights flashed and stars exploded. She felt Jack take the wineglass from her hand. "I started to tell you, but I just..." she began again, trying to gather the threads of what she wanted to say, but the words she wanted so desperately to speak aloud whirled silently inside her head, a mishmash of scrambled gibberish.

"It doesn't matter," she heard him say as he rose to his feet. "I was sure you'd fall in the love with the place and change your mind about selling, but I was wrong."

She wanted to tell him that he wasn't wrong, he was right, that she *had* fallen in love with the place but even more than that, she'd fallen in love with him. She wanted to tell him, but she could only lean helplessly against him as he lifted her out of the tub, wrapped her in the robe she'd worn over her bathing suit and carried her as if she weighed no more than a child. She curled her arms around his neck, rested her head against his chest and heaved a tormented sigh. She was very tired, no doubt moderately drunk, incredibly confused, and oh, so grateful that he was taking care of her.

Tomorrow. She would tell him how she felt about him first thing in the morning....

CHAPTER TWELVE

AT 6:00 A.M. SENNA WOKE with a start, unsure of where she was. For a moment she thought she was in Jack's cabin, lying in his bunk, but then she realized she was in her own room at the lodge, with Chilkat curled at the foot of her bed, and disappointment washed over her. She vowed that the next time she and Jack treated themselves to long soak in the hot tub, there would be no talk of work or of selling the lodge, and with any luck she wouldn't pass out from a potent combination of hot water, wine and exhaustion.

The next time?

Senna sat up, not surprised by the dull headache at her temples, but very surprised to see a mug of coffee on her bedside table, holding down a note in Jack's unruly scrawl. "Left for Goose Bay with G. and W. at five o'clock. Should be back by nine or ten. Enjoy a lazy morning all to yourself. Charlie's at the cabin if you need anything. Jack."

She threw back the coverlet and swung her legs over the edge of the bed. Lazy morning? Was he out of his mind? Now that there were only the three of them, there would be even less time to sleep. Three of them to open up a lodge at full capacity in just one more day. Twelve guests to cook for, clean up after, entertain and guide.

Impossible! Even more impossible was the idea of enjoying a lazy morning.

Her mind raced as she dressed. Without Wavey or Gordina, she would have to revise the menu plan. She'd set up the meals buffet style on the sideboard, and the guests could help themselves. Daily room service would be minimal and would include fresh towels and making up the bed. Forget turn-down service in the evening and chocolates on the pillows. She'd barely be able to keep up with the cooking and cleaning. Maybe she could teach Charlie to do the laundry? Senna stifled a laugh at the thought. If Charlie could just keep the woodbox filled and help Jack with the guiding, he'd be doing all right.

Chilkat raised his head, regarded her steadily for a moment, then yawned hugely and flopped back onto his side. "Yeah, me too," Senna agreed, "but unfortunately I'm not a dog. I just work like one." She was still sore, but the long soak in the hot tub had helped enormously. Oh, if only the night had ended differently. If only she'd said what she wanted to say to Jack instead of mumbling incoherently. If only she hadn't been so exhausted, hadn't drunk that third glass of wine.

If only…

She pulled on a pair of jeans, clean wool socks, a T-shirt for when the day warmed up and a thick fleece pullover to thwart the early-morning chill. She tasted the coffee from the mug Jack had set beside her bed. Still vaguely warm. Bless him. Bless his enduring strength, his sense of humor, and his patience with her.

In the kitchen she reheated the coffee and poured herself another cup, sitting down at the work station to make out the list of things to do. She still had to create and print up a mission statement to put into each guest room, a welcoming and informative one-page introduction to the lodge, including some rules regarding the fishing. Jack strongly believed that catch-and-release fishing was paramount, and the guests should be limited to one kill a week, a philosophy that Senna shared. The Wolf was an Atlantic salmon river, and the wild salmon fishery was in jeopardy. According to the lodge's rules, no salmon at all could be kept, only brook trout and pike.

Senna also wanted to give each of the guest rooms the name of a popular salmon fly to distinguish between them. She took a swallow of hot coffee and frowned. Forget all the frills for now. Rework the menu with a slant toward the sideboard buffet. Streamline the laundry. Get everything ready from the housekeeping perspective. Six guest rooms a day would take her about three hours to clean properly, prepping for and preparing three meals would take another five or six. The lodge itself, the grounds and gardens, doing the laundry, socializing with the guests…there would be little time for a luxury like sleep for the next two weeks, but in spite of the prospect of more grueling work, Senna was excited and glad she was staying.

Start-ups were hell, but they were the best kind of hell when the shake-down run went smoothly from the guest's perspective, even if the back of the house was involved in multiple crises. There was soul-deep satisfaction in pulling it all together and having the guest say, upon departure, "We had a wonderful time! Couldn't have been better. See you next year."

That's what she was hoping for.

Only time would tell what she and Jack would

achieve in the next two weeks. Meanwhile, she'd move out of the main lodge and into the cabin Gordina and Wavey had vacated, clean the room she'd been staying in, and put the finishing touches on all the guest rooms and public areas. Then she had to start prepping the food. Jack would be picking the first guests up tomorrow afternoon. She could do a lot of baking today. Sweets, mostly. Cookies and brownies. Get the sourdough starter working for the breads and pancakes. One of the guests was a diabetic with special dietary needs.

But the very first thing on the agenda was to call her aunt and tell her she wouldn't be back for another two weeks, something she wasn't looking forward to doing. The inn was in its busy season. Being short-staffed in the sales department would create a hardship for everyone else. But they'd get along. It was only for two more weeks. She took another sip of coffee and gazed down at the wild, lonely river tumbling over the rapids before dropping down into the pool in front of the lodge and felt a pang deep inside at the beauty of this place…and an even deeper pang at the thought of leaving it.

JACK WAS NOT HAVING a good morning. Gordina and Wavey definitely had something to do with it, making him feel like the lowest creature in the universe when he deposited them back in Goose Bay. "I'll drive you home in Goody's car," he said to Gordina.

"I'll walk. It ain't far and I don't want to put you out any. I suppose me and my poor sick sister will starve now, with you to thank," Gordina said, starting up the dock with her little suitcase in hand. She stopped for one last parting shot over her shoulder. "And all because we drank a bit of your bubbly, as if we didn't deserve it after all the work you made us do!"

"No, Gordina, that's not the entire reason, although you drank all of the bubbly, not just a bit of it, and it cost me dear. The real reason is because you stole that bottle of champagne and then you lied about it. I'm sorry it didn't work out, and I'm sorry if you and your sister starve, but what you did was wrong."

Gordina dropped her suitcase, pulled a pack of cigarettes out of her coat pocket, and lit up. Her eyes glittered through the blue smoke. "The hell with you, mister," she said, then picked up her suitcase and stalked off.

Wavey was weeping quietly and had been all morning. "I don't know what I'll do, with Goody gone and no job," she said, clinging to his arm as he walked her up the dock to the gravel path that led to Goody's house. "Me, all alone in that house."

"You'll figure something out," Jack said. "You can always go stay with Granville if you get too lonely. He's your grandfather. He'll take you in."

"What'll I tell Goody when she asks why I left the lodge?"

"Tell her the truth," Jack said, unlocking the door and handing Wavey the key, setting her suitcase just inside. He left immediately, ignoring Wavey's pleas for him to stay for a cup of tea, at least, and instead nabbing Goody's car for one last ride to the hospital to check on George Pilgrim.

George had been moved to a ward and was looking less than enchanted with hospital life. He was sitting up in bed and staring blankly at the television mounted high on the wall when Jack arrived. "Good to see you, bye," he said, his face brightening. "Have you ever seen the likes of what comes out of that box?" he said, indicating the television. "No wonder the world's gone crazy. If I watched for another day or two, I'd go crazy myself. Never seen such sorry, shameful trash."

"How the hell are you, George?" Jack said, dropping into a chair beside the bed and shaking George's hand. For the first time in his life, George was looking his age. "You ready to come out to the lodge with me?"

"They tell me I got to have some treatments," he said, "but I wonder if I shouldn't just go with you now, and to hell with modern medicine."

"I'll take you out of here if that's what you really want, George, but if you need more work, maybe you should stay."

"My daughter tells me the same thing, but she's not lying here in this bed, y'see, and you aren't either." George sighed in defeat. "I told you about the steel-workers' strike in Lab City, then?" Jack nodded. "Well, she's shaping up bad. They say it'll be a long one, and times'll be tough. Even the women are on the picket line now, supporting their men, but soon they'll have to support them in other ways. My daughter told me she'd come out there, to your lodge. She'd work hard, that one. She'd do anything. Her little ones are all growed but she still has bills to pay and a husband who's out of work, so that's something for you to think about, bye, if you'd still be needin' help. And I've a grandson who'd help with the guidin'. He's in Gander now but he c'n be here in two weeks after he gives his notice at the gas station. He's missin' the woods."

"Would you happen to have their phone numbers?" Jack said, seeing a bright light at the end of the tunnel.

Any relative of George Pilgrim would be worth their weight in gold. "I'll call them both right now. I just fired both my cook and my housekeeper. The cook couldn't boil water and the housekeeper couldn't do anything at all."

George laughed, then winced with the pain of it. "Eh, bye. I'll give you both numbers. My daughter probably has friends, too, looking for work, but if the strike ends tomorrow, I don't know where that'd leave you."

"No worse off than I am right now," Jack said, as George scrawled the numbers on a piece of scrap paper and handed it to him.

"I told her I'd be going out to the admiral's lodge myself, so she'd have her old daddy to goad. Give her a call. And don't forget about me."

Jack stood. "I won't, George. I'll be here an hour after you call for me, guaranteed. Here's the phone number to the lodge, in case you misplaced it. Keep it right by your phone."

Jack shook George's hand one last time and felt bad leaving him behind in the hospital, even if it was just for a few more days. He phoned George's daughter from the pay phone in the hospital's lobby and was relieved when she answered. Her name was Mary and she was glad to hear from him. George had told her all about the admiral's remote fishing lodge, and she was very interested in the job.

"I'll be wanting to meet you," she said. "I'm interested in the job. Me and a good friend, if you could use her help, too."

"When?" Jack said.

"Negotiations between the mining company and the

union have come to a halt," Mary said. "If you have work for us, we'll be needing it, and soon."

"Can you meet me at Tanya Lake at noon?"

"We'll be there with bells on," Mary promised.

Jack then called George's grandson, who assured him that he could be there in less than a week and that George had taught him a lot about guiding. He left the hospital feeling hopeful that George's daughter and grandson might bail him and Senna out of an almost impossible scenario. He climbed into the plane, and moments later had shaken free of the water and was heading for Labrador City, where members of the Steelworkers' Union were on strike and their wives were desperate for work.

NOON, AND JACK STILL hadn't returned. Senna took a break from cleaning and baking and walked down to the guides' cabin, Chilkat at her heels. Charlie was splitting wood and had made surprisingly good progress on the pile. He was happy to accept the sandwich she'd brought, and the cold lemonade. She gave the crackie a pat on the head and a piece of beef left over from supper the night before. "Charlie, did Jack tell you when he'd be back?"

"He left early," Charlie said around a mouthful of chicken sandwich, "but the note on the table said nine or ten o'clock, and to keep splitting wood until the job was done then wheel it up to the lodge and stack it on the porch."

Senna felt a coil of fear tighten in the pit of her stomach as she walked back to the lodge, determined not to let herself dwell on the worst-case scenario. No doubt there would be some reasonable explanation why Jack was late getting back, and it wouldn't have anything to do with that old plane crashing. She continued baking an assortment of sweets, enough to last out the week, and in between mixing and baking she worked on the in-room booklet and kept thinking about that old plane going down somewhere between the lodge and Goose Bay. She kept imagining that Jack was hurt and needed help. She had a very bad habit of always imagining the worst.

Twelve dozen cookies and three batches of brownies later, Senna shut down the big oven, moved out of the warm kitchen and into the registration area, and began inputting the lodge's mission statement into the computer. Her fingers flew over the keyboard and her eyes never left the computer screen, but she was seeing the twisted wreckage of a plane and remembering her father's funeral. At 5:00 p.m. she walked down to feed the sled dogs, and while she scooped out the food, Charlie watered. By the time she'd finished, Senna's anxiety level had reached an all-time high.

"Charlie, I'm a little worried that Jack's so late. He was due back seven hours ago. Does this happen often?"

Charlie shrugged. "Sometimes. Once, he was gone for two days. When he came back, the admiral hollered at him. Hanson told him he went to the big city to see the tall buildings and visit a friend."

"Terrific," Senna muttered. "Then I guess we'll just hope he shows up for opening day."

She returned to the lodge and was climbing the porch steps when she heard Jack's plane approaching. Her heart leapt and she raced down the ramp, feet hitting the dock at about the same time the plane touched down. Moments later the old aircraft taxied around the river bend into sight and pulled up beside the dock. The engine cut out, the prop feathered to a stop, and the plane's side door popped open. Jack jumped out onto the pontoon, looking as if it were just another sunny day. He flashed her a brief grin over his shoulder as he secured the plane to the dock.

"I come bearing tidings of great joy," he announced.

"We were getting a little worried about you," Senna said, struggling to keep her voice calm. After all, he didn't owe her an accounting of his day. "You said you'd be back by ten."

"Sorry I'm late, but I have good news. Great news."

In spite of her resolve to remain cool-headed, Senna felt perilously on the verge of tears. "You're seven hours overdue. I don't suppose you have any idea what it's like, waiting for someone who's flying around up in the air in an ancient plane. I was beginning to think something bad might have happened."

"Well, I did have to make an unexpected landing on the way back home and it took me a few hours to get the old girl up and running again, but Senna, listen to this. I went to see George Pilgrim in the hospital. His surgery went pretty good, I guess, but he needs some treatments and can't come out right away. It turns out he has a daughter in Lab City—" Jack stopped talking and his eyes narrowed. He reached out and grasped her shoulder. "Are you crying? What's the matter? What's wrong?"

"*What's wrong?*" Senna wiped her palms over her cheeks. "You're standing there talking to me as if nothing had happened, even though you just told me you had to crash-land that old derelict. You're such an idiot, John Hanson. Such a fool!"

Jack looked bewildered. "I'm sorry I'm a little late, but I'm not used to having anyone worry about me. I would've called but there wasn't a pay phone near the lake I landed in, and it wasn't a crash landing. As a matter of fact, it was a pretty damn good landing, for a beautifully built vintage aircraft whose engine unexpectedly quit." He stepped onto the pontoon, reached inside the plane and drew forth a box filled with plants. "I brought you some purple petunias," he said, holding them out as if they were a peace offering. "And some herb seedlings, for the kitchen garden."

Senna stared at the big box of plants and felt the hot prickle of tears again. She whirled and raced back up the ramp before she could make a fool of herself for the second time. She was churning with anger and frustration and relief. She knew Jack didn't understand why she was behaving this way and she also knew that no amount of explanation would enlighten him. She wasn't sure she *could* explain, because her reaction had taken her as much by surprise as it had him. She had to get a grip on her runaway emotions. Crying, for heaven's sakes! She never cried! And of course he wouldn't understand *why* she was crying because he didn't know how she felt about him.

She fled to the cook's cabin she'd moved into that morning and collapsed on the bunk, taking advantage of the privacy to vent all those hours of pent-up anxiety. Gradually she got herself under control and was blotting her tears and blowing her nose when a shadow darkened the doorway. She glanced up to see Jack standing there, one hand braced on the doorjamb, the thumb of the other hand hooked in the rear pocket of his jeans. He slouched that way for a few moments before stepping inside. "Look, Senna, I didn't mean to upset you," he began tentatively, as if he were afraid she would start crying again.

Senna rose to her feet, crossed to the wash basin, and splashed cool water on her hot face. She dried off with a towel, then turned to look at him. "I'm sorry I carried on that way. It won't happen again. At least not today," she added with a shaky laugh. "I don't know what came over me. I guess I'm just tired."

"I saw all the baking you did and sampled some of it, too. Maybe we should have a cup of hot tea and sample some more."

"Or maybe I should lock the sweets up to keep you and Charlie from devouring everything before the guests arrive," Senna said, leading the way back to the lodge where she put the teakettle on to heat and arranged a plate of cookies and brownies on the kitchen table. She sat down. "Go ahead and tell me the good news. I could use a little about now."

Jack picked up a cookie, leaned against the counter, and took up where he had left off. "George has a daughter in Lab City who's married to a guy who works in the iron-ore mine. The miners all belong to the Steelworkers' Union, and the union's on strike." He bit into the cookie with a smug look.

"So George's daughter's husband is no longer working."

"Correct. And George's daughter is looking for a job to help pay the bills. So I flew to Lab City to meet with them—"

"What?" Senna interrupted, the dreaded emotions surging back. "That's a long flight! You might have called the lodge and told me you were going, or are you

going to tell me that all the phone lines were down in Goose Bay?"

Jack turned off the burner under the boiling water and filled two mugs. He set the teakettle back on the stove and plopped a tea bag in each mug, placing one in front of Senna. He leaned against the counter again, picked up another cookie and continued as if she hadn't spoken. "Mary, George's daughter, met me at Tanya Lake with a friend of hers. We talked business. Those two gals know how to cook and clean, Senna. They both raised big families. They're hard workers, good people. I told them how much work there was, how hard it would be, and how long the days were, and it didn't phase either of them. I'm picking them up next Wednesday. They said they needed that much time to take care of loose ends. And we have another guide. George's grandson can start in less than a week. So there you have it. Three more full-time workers that'll do anything you tell them to do."

"Until the strike is over," Senna pointed out.

"The feeling is that this strike is going to last a long time and things are going to get pretty grim. Money's already tight."

"How much did you promise them?"

"They asked for nine dollars an hour, plus room and board."

"That's equitable. There'll be gratuities, too, on top of that." Senna dunked her tea bag up and down in the mug, watching him. "The next time you decide to change your flight plan, Hanson, please call me first? That's only fair, especially if I have to tell you when I'm going into the woods searching for wolves."

"Okay."

"What was wrong with the plane's engine?"

"Fuel filter was clogged."

"Does that happen often?"

"Nope. Never happened before. Believe me, that plane is properly maintained." Jack finished off the second cookie.

Senna hesitated. "Jack, I think we should contact Thunder Air Service and have them fly our clients in."

Jack's expression became carefully neutral. "There's nothing wrong with the Cessna."

"Nothing wrong? You just had to make an emergency landing. Maybe you're okay with that, but our clients might feel otherwise. Thunder Air uses brand-new Twin Otter float planes that can carry six passengers and all their gear, and their rates are competitive."

Jack said nothing for a few moments but she could tell from the set of his jaw that he was getting hot. "I take it you've already inquired."

Senna nodded, still dunking her tea bag and judging the negativity of his reaction. "Your plane can only carry four passengers. We have twelve people arriving tomorrow. Granted, they're not all coming at the same time, but you'd spend the entire day ferrying them to the lodge then turning around and going back for the next group. That's three heavily loaded trips in a very old aircraft."

"The Cessna can handle it, but go ahead and call the flying service, if that's what you want to do," he said, stalking out of the kitchen without touching his tea. His anger with her was so great that he didn't come up to the lodge to see if she'd cooked anything for supper, and long after sunset she could hear him down by the guides' cabin, splitting wood with a vengeance. Senna knew that she'd insulted his beautiful plane, but he had to face reality. They had a business to run, and there was no contingency in place for emergency landings in a plane old enough to be hanging from the ceiling of an air and space museum.

She phoned Thunder Air Service and made the arrangements for three trips the following day, the first arriving at 2:00 p.m. and the last guests just before supper. She gave them her credit card number to cover the charges and added that to her little notebook, wincing at the rapidly climbing total.

That detail taken care of, she kindled a fire in the woodstove that heated the hot tub and made sure that the stove was cranking before filling the firebox to the brim. Back in the kitchen she set up the sourdough starter and put it in a warm place to work overnight. She put the meat for the following day's dinner into a marinade and then tucked it back into the refrigerator. Then she worked in the garden, a small plot she'd turned over just outside the back door. She planted the herb seedlings Jack had bought and potted the petunias in the two rustic planters Charlie had hewn for her from two sections of spruce log. The planters flanked the base of the main porch steps, and even though the seedlings were small, they'd soon fill the space with a mass of bright color. She gave everything a good drink of water, then washed up in the kitchen and made a stack of sandwiches and a pitcher of iced tea and carried them, along with two beer mugs, down the path toward the sound of an angry man at work.

Jack had stripped down to his undershirt, and although the evening was chilly, he was sweating. He spotted her and split the piece he had just placed on the stump, then sank the ax into the stump and put his hands on his hips as she approached. He was studying her like a frowning scientist again, and she counterattacked with what she hoped was a calm and pleasant expression.

"I thought you might be hungry," she said, setting the plate on a wall bench outside the cabin door. "Has Charlie eaten?"

"Eaten and gone to bed, which is where you should be. Tomorrow's a big day."

"I know, but I thought a 10:00 p.m. snack might be good after all the work you've been doing. Sit with me. Please, Jack, don't be mad."

Jack picked his flannel shirt off a nearby tree branch and pulled it on, wiping his brow on the sleeve. "I'm not mad," he said. "I'm too damn tired to be mad." He sat down with a weary sigh and leaned against the cabin wall. "And you're right. Probably not many guests would appreciate the plane breaking down en route to the lodge…not that she ever would. That clogged fuel filter was just a freak thing." He took the cup of iced tea Senna handed him and drank it down without stopping. She refilled it and he emptied it again almost as quickly. His breathing slowed as he gradually relaxed. He drank the third mug more slowly, then picked up a sandwich, contemplating the river. "She's a good reliable plane."

"Maybe you could use her for ferrying clients to those nearby lakes you told me about, the ones loaded with ten-pound brook trout and giant landlocked salmon, but I really think we should let the commercial airlines fly the guests and their gear to and from the lodge. It's a liability thing, and I don't know what kind of insurance we carry on that plane."

"Never thought about that," he admitted. "She's insured, but not as a commercial carrier. That'd probably be pretty expensive."

"*Wicked* expensive."

He looked at her, then gazed back down at the river and uttered a short laugh. "You think about all the details, wedding planner. Every last undesirable one."

"That's my job. Now eat your sandwich, Hanson, because if you feel up to it, the hot tub should be just about ready."

He stopped just short of biting into the sandwich and looked at her again, meal forgotten. "Say again?"

"I just thought, after splitting all that wood, that you might enjoy one more soak before we open for the season. Unless, of course, you're too tired, in which case I completely understand. Last night I was too exhausted myself to really appreciate it."

Jack dropped the sandwich on the platter and lurched to his feet. "Good God, woman, no red-blooded man on this planet could ever be that tired. I'll be there just as soon as I get cleaned up and changed."

JACK WAS HUMMING UNDER HIS breath as he took his swim trunks down from the peg on the cabin rafter. He was singing arias as he ran to the river and plunged into the icy water to scrub the sweat of hard work and frustration off him. He was walking on air as he headed back to the guides' camp, picked out a clean flannel shirt and pair of jeans, towel-dried his hair, scraped off his five o'clock stubble, and brushed his teeth for good measure. "This is your lucky night, Hanson," he told the reflection in the little mirror above the sink. "Don't blow it."

Jack turned away from the mirror, his self-confidence flagging. He reminded himself that Senna's "very dear friend" had found a buyer for the lodge, the lodge that Senna's grandfather had dreamt into being and Senna had brought to life. Secretly Jack had hoped all along that she'd decide not to sell, that she'd decide that being partners with him was the best of all options, but she hadn't. She'd only agreed to stay for another two weeks. Still, that was two weeks more than he'd expected to get, and that gave him two more weeks to convince her that this was where she belonged. Senna would get the lodge through its maiden voyage. She'd make it happen, and she'd make it happen the right way, the way the admiral had envisioned. And who knows? Maybe in two more weeks she *would* fall in love with the place and change her mind about going back to Maine and that very dear friend of hers.

Holding that thought, Jack started up toward the lodge. He climbed the steps onto the porch and stopped abruptly, feeling his heart give a strong kick. Senna had placed votive candles in glass holders around the hot tub's deck, lighting the area in a soft, muted glow that captured the wraiths of steam rising into the cold night air. She was definitely planning a romantic interlude. He checked the hot tub's stove, added a few sticks of firewood, shucked out of his shirt, jeans and boots, and lowered himself into the tub. Perfect temperature. He sank down, trying to act nonchalant, as if this sort of seduction happened daily in his self-imposed monastic lifestyle, but by now the unsteady kick of his heartbeat had given way to the strong rhythmic pound of a war drum. He took several deep breaths and wondered what she'd say when she appeared.

Maybe she wouldn't say anything. Maybe she'd just

give him a sultry stare as she let the robe fall off her shoulders, only instead of the bathing suit she'd worn the night before, this time she'd be wearing nothing at all. She would stand there for a moment while he admired her sensual beauty, then she'd slip into the tub, slide up against him, sigh his name in his ear... He wondered what their first kiss would be like, and above all, how the night would end.

Tipping his head back, he imagined the possibilities. The sky was at its darkest, but its brightest as well, because the aurora borealis, rare in June, was dancing across it, igniting faint streamers of greens and reds and yellows that stretched across the broad-reaching twilight of the northern sky.

Howl, wolves, Jack silently willed the Naskaupi pack. *Howl for my beautiful woman, and this night will be perfect.*

He heard a soft footstep approaching from behind. Of course. She wouldn't be coming out of the lodge. She was staying in the cook's cabin now. Jack shifted his position in the hot tub to watch her. She wore a robe wrapped around her, the same as last night, and her hair was pinned loosely atop her head. She paused in the soft glow of the candles and smiled as she let the robe unfold from around her.

She was wearing the same bathing suit as the night before. It was a nice bathing suit. Pretty. And she looked gorgeous in it, but...

"What do you think about the candles?" she said. "I thought we could leave them around the tub and light them every night for the guests. They're pretty safe in the votive holders and they throw just the right amount of light."

She slipped into the hot tub while he was still struggling for some response, overcome with disappointment that the candles hadn't been a prelude to a romantic tryst and that when the robe fell around her ankles she hadn't been naked.

"I think the candles are a nice touch," he managed.

"I'm sorry if I insulted your plane."

"What plane?"

"I spent most of the day hating that old relic because I thought it had killed you, and hating myself for not having the courage to say the things to you that I wanted to say, so I'll say them to you now, before I lose my nerve." She drew a deep breath. "I want to thank you for befriending my grandfather, because if you hadn't, he never would have made you his business partner, and if he hadn't done that, I never would have met you. I wouldn't be here right now, staring up at a sky like I've never seen before in a land so wild a wolf walked up and looked me in the eye." She watched him as she spoke and in the flickering candlelight her eyes were dark and mysterious. "No matter what happens, I want you to know that I'll always remember this special time I spent here with you."

Jack felt a lurch of anxiety and sat up straighter. Good God, what kind of sentiment was that for her to be expressing? "That special time doesn't have to end," he said, trying to think of something profound to say, something that would make her realize that her time here could last forever, if she wanted it to.

Ah. There was the key. *If she wanted it to.* And up to this point, she definitely hadn't.

"All things come to an end, Jack," she said with a gesture of her hand through the steam rising from the tub.

"Tomorrow, this place will belong to the guests who arrive here, and we'll belong to them, too, for as long as they're here. That's why tonight's so special. This is the last night you and I will have this place all to ourselves."

Damn! It was as if she was ending everything before it even had a chance to begin. The desperation that swept through him was like nothing he'd ever felt before. Jack struggled for the right words, but he'd never been much good at expressing himself and tonight was no exception. It had always been easier to build walls than bare the soul. *If you stayed I could teach you to fly your half of the plane, and run a team of sled dogs. You could study the Naskaupi wolf pack, write a paper to educate the public, and help the wolves to survive in a world that doesn't begin to understand them. We could follow the George River caribou herd when it migrates through in winter, run the lodge together in summer. We could be happy here and have lots more nights like this all to ourselves.*

The silence that followed his unvoiced plea was long, and then Senna said, in a soft and wondering voice, "Listen. Do you hear that? Maybe it's my grandfather's black wolf. Maybe it's Raven."

Sure enough, in the distance, as deep and as haunting as the wilderness itself, came the long mournful howl of a lone wolf, and the sound embodied the very torment in Jack's soul.

CHAPTER THIRTEEN

THE ARCTIC TWILIGHT GAVE OVER to the pale-yellow gleam in the east that heralded the dawn, but not just any dawn. For the first time ever, the sun would rise on the Wolf River Lodge as an operating concern, and it would set on twelve guests settling in for a week of wilderness fishing. Senna knew she should be up and about, seeing to last-minute chores, putting the final polish on the lodge, but she lay still, unable or unwilling to move from the bed. Just a few minutes more…

She stretched in the dim quiet of the cook's cabin, shifting beneath the blankets and reflecting on the night before, and how quiet Jack had become after she'd declared her feelings for him…or tried to. She'd never been very good at that sort of thing. Still, even if she'd bungled it, she'd expected some sort of response, yet he'd said nothing after his first encouraging utterance about their time together not having to come to an end. After that, he'd clammed up. They'd shared the tub in silence while the northern lights ran wild against the sky, and then the admiral's wolf had howled. That moment had been so mystical. Hadn't he felt any of the magic? Wasn't he suffering from the same strange symptoms as she'd been having for the past week? Wasn't he the least little bit in love with her?

Apparently not, or else last night would have ended differently.

Footsteps approached on the cabin path and the door opened after a light tap as Senna sat up, sheet drawn to her chin. Chilkat raised his head from his paws as Jack appeared in the doorway, carrying a pot of coffee and one mug. He set the coffeepot on the table after filling the mug. "Thought you might need this to jump-start your day," he said, handing her the cup.

"Thanks. That soak in the hot tub last night relaxed me so much I'm afraid I overslept," Senna said. "But I enjoyed it. That was very special."

"Better enjoy another few minutes of peace and quiet," he advised over his shoulder as he headed out the door. "This is the last you'll get until Mary and her friend arrive."

Senna stared as the door closed behind him and his footsteps faded into silence. She uttered an incredulous laugh. For cripes sake, the man was clueless. Should she have tried to seduce him last night? Seduction was not something she was particularly experienced with. In fact, as far as men went, she was very much inexperienced. The first real relationship she'd ever had was with Tim, and he was the only man she'd ever slept with. No, she was definitely not up to speed as a seductress. Besides, she'd given Jack every opportunity to make the first move. Was she that undesirable? She brooded as she sipped the strong coffee and then, as the caffeine kicked in, she became swept up with the energy of the new day and the excitement of the date itself.

"To hell with men in general and Jack Hanson in particular," she said. "I have a lodge to open up."

She jumped out of bed, donned her swimsuit, and ran

barefoot down to the river. The water was ice-cold and her breath left her with a whoosh as she dove into the deep pool, no doubt startling a myriad of underwater creatures as she swam and splashed and kicked her way back to shore. She rushed back up the path to the cabin, dried off and dressed, vowing to take a hot shower before the first batch of guests arrived. She and Jack barely had time to acknowledge each other, which was fine with Senna. Breakfast was forgotten as they each attended to small last-minute chores. Charlie was moving wood up onto the porch, making much clatter and noise as he stacked it near the door.

By noon, they were sharing a rushed lunch of peanut butter sandwiches and tea with lots left to do. Senna took a quick shower then changed into decent twill slacks, a pale peach linen blouse, and a warm lime-colored cardigan. She pinned her hair in a French twist, pulled on soft comfortable shoes, and returned to the lodge. Jack was coming up the ramp, toolbox in hand. "The generator is now officially up and running for the summer." He paused beside her and gave her a brief glance. "You look real nice," he said.

Senna shook her head as he continued past. What a romantic. At 1:00 p.m. the satellite phone rang and Senna ran from the kitchen to answer it. It was Thunder Air Service, confirming pickup of six passengers, departing Goose Bay in thirty minutes. She felt a thrill of nervousness as she replaced the receiver. The phone rang again before she could leave the reception area. This time the caller was Tim.

"Senna?" he said. "I'm sorry to call you again, but I spoke with your mother and she told me you weren't coming home for another two weeks. I was wondering if you'd gotten an answer from your business partner about selling the lodge."

"Tim, Jack really doesn't want to sell his half of the business so I'm afraid that deal with Mr. Hammel is off."

"Not necessarily. I told Earl that your partner didn't want to sell, and he wants to talk with him about that very subject. The thing is, he's going to need a caretaker for the property and was actually amenable to the idea of Jack retaining half ownership, since Earl will only be using the property a few weeks out of the year. He even thought it would be a good idea to continue to operate it as a commercial lodge because it would be a great tax write-off for him, and Jack would have free rein to run the place as he sees fit. It seems to me that both he and Jack might benefit from this arrangement."

"Maybe," Senna said. "I'll run it by him, Tim, but today isn't a good time. It's opening day, and we have no help at all. We lost our two new hires, and twelve guests will be arriving in a matter of hours…"

"You mean it's just the two of you running the place?" Tim's voice was incredulous.

"Three, counting Charlie. At least until Wednesday, when we get two more replacements who'll need to be trained. I've agreed to stay on for another two weeks to get the lodge opened up, and we're right out straight."

"Is there anything I can do on this end to help?"

"No, but thanks for the thought. I have to go, it's time to get tea ready for our first guests. I'll talk to Jack about Earl Hammel's offer. I promise."

Senna hung up the phone and sat for a few moments, filled with confusion. She didn't want Earl Hammel to come to the lodge. She didn't want him to talk with Jack.

She needed to talk with Jack herself and tell him… Tell him what?

That she'd decided not to sell? *Had* she decided? Could she afford not to sell? How much more debt could she accrue before having to declare bankruptcy? And did the money problems really matter more than how she felt about Jack? Most important of all, how did Jack feel about *her?*

He chose that moment to duck his head into the registration area. "I was in the kitchen and couldn't help but overhear," he said.

"You mean you were eavesdropping again." Senna stood. "That was Tim, as you know. The prospective buyer, Earl Hammel, apparently doesn't mind the idea of having a business partner. He'd be happy buying out my half of the business as long as he could use the property when he wanted, and he liked the idea of operating it as a commercial lodge because it would give him a good tax write-off."

"Huh," Jack said, his expression stony. "And you told him you'd talk to me about it, so you're talking to me. But you're not telling me how you feel about selling to Earl Hammel. So tell me. How do *you* feel?"

Senna drew a deep breath and broached the dreaded money subject. "Earl Hammel is a very wealthy man. He could keep the lodge afloat until all the debts have been paid off and it starts to turn a profit. He'd make a better business partner than I would. My bank account is pretty near empty, my credit cards are maxed out and I don't even know how we're going to pay the hired help. I'm scared. That's what I'm telling you. That, and we have six guests about to arrive and I have to fix afternoon tea, so the rest of this conversation is going to have to wait."

Stomach churning, she slipped past him and returned to the kitchen. After a long pause she heard Jack's heels drumming his anger down the length of the porch in the direction of the guides' cabin. The last-minute chaos of the day soon swept her into a flurry of activity, and the sound of a twin-engine plane arriving caused her stomach to flip-flop. She placed the assortment of cookies on the sideboard and lit the Sterno under the tea urn to keep the tea nice and hot, gave one last critical look around the public spaces, then went down to meet the arrivals.

The plane was bigger than Jack's, and much newer. Senna greeted the guests as they disembarked and welcomed them to the lodge. Jack came down the ramp, shaking hands as everyone introduced themselves. The pilot wore a grim expression as he off-loaded the luggage. He took Jack aside and Senna overheard him saying, "Helluva tight takeoff run you got on this stretch of river. Not too bad for landing, and unloaded, we won't have a problem getting out, but I dunno about flying out of here with a full load."

To which Jack replied, "Well, if you can't do it, I will." Senna guessed that this was routine macho pilot talk, after which the Thunder Air pilot laughed, returned to his plane and took off with lots of room to spare.

Jack and Charlie were in charge of handling the luggage, and Senna had tagged each suitcase and duffel with the room number so they'd get placed in the proper rooms but Jack had already abandoned the plan in favor of assisting Mrs. Ida Snell, the diminutive wife of one of the fishermen. Mrs. Snell was a tiny woman in her late sixties or early seventies with vivid blue eyes, an infectious smile and beautiful snow-white hair pulled into a bun on the nape of her neck. She had a pair of binoculars around her neck and a husband who was as huge as she was tiny and apparently not up to the task of steadying her up the steep ramp.

"Now, Bert," she cautioned her husband as Jack took her arm. "This young man has graciously offered to help me to the lodge. I don't want you straining your heart. You know what the doctor said after your heart surgery. Light exercise."

Dear God, Senna thought. A big man in his seventies, borderline obese, with a heart condition that had required recent surgery. She stepped up beside Ida. "I'll help you up the ramp, Ida. Jack will make sure your husband doesn't overdo it."

Ida chatted as they climbed side by side, Senna's arm encircling Ida's waist to steady the elderly woman. "I brought my bird book and my binoculars. Bert tells me the insect life in Labrador is amazingly healthy, so there must be birds."

"Oh yes, many," Senna reassured her.

"Then this week will be a joy. How I love to bird watch!"

When Ida was safely ensconced in the living room and enjoying a cup of tea, Senna raced back down to the dock to lug a couple of bags up and deposit them in the guests' respective rooms. Jack, she noticed, was navigating Bert Snell up the ramp, pointing out landmarks and talking fishing, progressing at a sedate pace guaranteed not to stress his heart. Senna entered the living room out of breath but pleased to see that the five guests were talking amiably amongst themselves as they took

in the lodge. Some had already helped themselves to tea
and cookies. In no time she'd registered them and distributed the room keys. She showed them the hot tub out
on the deck and when Jack arrived with Bert Snell she
gave them some rudimentary information.

"This is a casual place, but when the dinner bell
rings, it's time to eat. Supper's served at 6:00 p.m. Hors
d'oeuvres will be set out at five in the living room, and
you're welcome to help yourself from the dry bar. Tea
and refreshments will be available from three to four
daily, also set out in the living room, lunch is promptly
at noon unless you're out fishing, in which case we'll
provide you with a box lunch, and breakfast is served
at seven. If you're an early riser, coffee and fresh pas-
tries will be on the sideboard by 5:00 a.m.

"The library in the living room is for your reading
pleasure, and we ask only that the books remain here at
the lodge, as they belonged to my grandfather. There's
a satellite phone available in the registration area if you
need to stay in touch with the outside world. Cell phones
don't work out here. As far as fishing goes, both Jack
and Charlie are first-class fishing guides and our boats
can accommodate four people. There are wading pools
just below the lodge, and above the lodge, at the foot of
the rapids, there's good deep holding water that you can
cast to from shore.

"As you no doubt know, the Wolf is a salmon river,
and this lodge is located approximately twenty miles
from the Sea of Labrador. The salmon spawning
grounds are another eighty miles upstream. We want to
remind you to practice catch-and-release fishing. The
Atlantic salmon are a magnificent but endangered spe-
cies, and we want both this lodge and the salmon to be

around for a long, long time. You'll also be catching brook trout and pike, and Jack can fly you into several nearby lakes if you want to hook into some trophy-sized brookies in the ten-pound range."

Senna gestured that she was through with her little introductory lecture and smiled. "Other than that, folks, the only rules are that you relax and enjoy yourselves. My name is Senna McCallum, and please don't hesitate to let me know if there's anything at all you need to make your stay more comfortable."

Most of the guests dispersed to settle into their rooms. Senna spoke to Bert as he started for the guest wing, clutching his room key. "I'll see that Ida gets another key to the room, Mr. Snell, as I'm sure you'll be out fishing every day."

Bert, who was still a bit out of breath from the climb, gave her a quiet smile as he mopped his forehead with a big handkerchief. "Oh, it's my wife who's here to fish," he said. "I'll be spending most of my time perusing your library and admiring your grandfather's books. That's quite a fine collection he has."

Minutes later she encountered Jack in the kitchen, pacing back and forth with an anxious expression. "What's wrong?" she said.

"Wrong? One of our very first guests has a heart condition and could barely make it up that ramp. He's here for a week of fishing and I'm not sure I can even get him in or out of a boat. And what if he has a heart attack?"

"He'll be fine," Senna said. "You'll be relieved to hear that it's his wife who's the outdoorsperson. Bert intends to spend his days relaxing on the porch with a good book. Better go get the rest of the luggage. The next batch of guests will be arriving shortly, and I have hors d'oeuvres and dinner to prepare."

The second planeload arrived by four-thirty, and at five all twelve guests were in the living room, enjoying drinks and Senna's modest assortment of hors d'oeuvres. Conversation was so lively the room reverberated like a crowded pub at happy hour, and they hardly took notice of Senna laying out the dinner buffet on the dining-room sideboard until the aromas of the food began peaking their interest. When she rang the dinner bell there was a veritable stampede. Senna had put four bottles of wine on the table, two red and two white, and a wineglass at each place setting. She'd never given service like this before, being used to the formal pass and serve of plated hors d'oeuvres, the taking of drink orders, the individual preparation of dinners, but so far the self-serve wilderness lodge routine seemed to be working quite well.

The guests settled in at the table, and she poured their first glass of wine. Their round-table conversations continued, featuring their non-stop fishing sagas and past adventures all around the world. The fire crackled in the fireplace, they ate, they drank, and they seemed quite happy to be there. Senna breathed a sigh of relief in the privacy of the kitchen, where Jack was repairing a broken tip top on one of the guest's fly rods in between bites of food.

He glanced up from heating a glue stick with a cigarette lighter. "The table looked great tonight, and I can personally vouch for the excellence of the food. Good job, pard."

"Where's Charlie?" she asked, firing up the dishwasher in preparation for its first real workout.

"Hiding out at the camp," Jack muttered, smearing the softened glue on the end of the rod, sliding the new tip top over and adjusting it precisely before the glue hardened. "I think the big crowd scared him off. I'll bring him down a plate of food and feed the dogs as well, just as soon as I've finished with this rod. I told the guests in advance they'd need at least 250 yards of backing on their reels, but from the conversations I've already had, I know a few of them didn't pay any attention. I'll need to make a quick trip to the lake house to get more backing, and also get the admiral's fly-tying desk. Should've thought to bring it before. We can put it in the corner of the living room for the guests to use. I'll bring his fly rods, too, as back-ups in case anything breaks." He glanced up questioningly. "If that's okay with you."

"Bring anything you think we'll need. I'm sure the admiral would approve. When will you leave?"

"After supper. I'll be back well before dark. Maybe then we can finish that conversation we started earlier today."

THE DISHES WERE DONE, the kitchen was clean, breakfast foods prepped and stored, coffee set up and ready to go, pastry dough refrigerated. Senna wiped down all the surfaces, wrung the dishcloth out in the sink, and draped it on a peg to dry. She eased a cramp in the small of her back and walked out onto the porch. Most of the guests were gathered in the living room near the big fireplace, some playing cribbage, others just relaxing with after-dinner drinks and talking softly amongst themselves.

Senna wandered down to the dock to sit in solitude

and listen to the river. Fish were rising in the pool just below the lodge, and she marveled that none of the guests had inquired about plying the waters.

Jack should be back very soon. She'd stay right here and help him lug her grandfather's fly-tying desk up the ramp. She lay back on weather-bleached boards still warm from the sun and let the sound of the water lull her.

Time lost all its civilized dimensions out here in the wild. The last colors of sunset faded gradually from the sky. True dusk, the blue twilight hour, had arrived, and still no Jack. Senna sat up, brushing her hair back from her face. Damn the man, was she fated to spend the rest of her life worrying about him? The thought gave her pause. The rest of her life worrying about Jack? What on earth was she thinking of? He was as much of a loner as the wolf that had howled its heart out to the northern lights last night. He was a bachelor through and through. No woman would ever tame the wild heart of that man. Certainly not in a few short weeks…

Senna gnawed on a fingernail and stared at the black ribbon of water that rushed past the dock. The idea of staying in Labrador had been on her mind pretty nearly constantly during the past two days. But how could she? Even if she did decide to keep her half of the business, she'd need to return to Maine and work pretty much nonstop to earn the money just to help keep the lodge afloat for the summer. The construction debts weren't all paid off yet, the monthly bank payment was hefty, the summer money hadn't started to trickle in, operating costs would be high, and her grandfather's life insurance policy and medical bills might be a long time getting paid by the insurance companies. She couldn't count on that to bail them out.

If she decided to remain partners with Jack, she'd have to leave. If she decided to sell to Earl Hammel she'd have to leave. Whatever she decided, she'd be heading back to Maine, and the thought scared her. She'd only been here two weeks, but already she couldn't imagine life without Jack. The fact that he didn't seem to feel the same way only added to her dilemma.

The roar of his plane thundered into hearing range and she pushed to her feet, craning her eyes in the deepening murk, but the plane touched down before she ever saw it and taxied around the river bend toward the dock. The side door opened and Jack jumped out. "I brought along a surprise for you," he said, bending to tie the plane off and then reached inside to help someone out. "Senna McCallum, meet Goody Stewart," Jack said as he handed a stalwart woman in her late sixties or early seventies safely onto the dock. Goody was squarely built with dark-gray hair pulled back in a tight bun and a hardworking, no-nonsense Scottish look about her. She was wearing dark slacks, black rubber boots, and, over her sweater, a red-and-black wool Filson jacket like the old-time woodsmen wore. She looked perfectly capable of handling just about anything.

Senna was so happy to see her that she nearly flung her arms around the older woman. "I'm so glad to meet you at last," she said, stepping forward to take the older woman's hand. "And I'm so glad you're here. I've heard so many wonderful things about you."

"And I you, m'dear," Goody replied warmly, her dark eyes sincere. "Your grandfather spoke very highly of you. He told me that one day you'd come here, and once you saw it you'd never leave."

Senna stared at the older woman. "He said that?"

"Aye, he did, and you're just as beautiful as he said you were."

"He said I was beautiful?"

"Smart and beautiful. Meant a great deal to him, that you had such a keen mind. Jack tells me you'd be needing some help around here, with the cooking and such. The admiral was counting on me, and though he's gone, God rest his dear soul, I feel as if I still belong here. And tha' knows, too, I miss my coopies."

"Please, come up to the kitchen and I'll fix you something to eat."

"I've eaten, m'dear, but I'd share a cuppa. It's been a long day. I brung something for ye, though," she said, turning back toward the plane. "It'd be in my satchel." Jack reached back into the passenger compartment and handed out a big, soft-sided embroidered bag with sturdy handles, setting it on the dock with a heavy thump. Goody opened it and drew forth a dark wooden box with brass hinges and a brass hasp. She handed it to Senna. "It's your grandfather's ashes," she explained. "I picked them up at the crematorium, like I promised him I would."

Senna took the box in her hands, shocked into speechlessness both by the unexpected weight of the box and what it contained.

"He wanted them scattered here, y'see," Goody said. "I promised I'd see to that, too, and so I brung him along with me. I hope you don't mind."

Senna shook her head, hoping she didn't appear too

rattled. "No, no, of course not. That was very thoughtful of you."

"Aye, well, I promised. I'll be goin' up to see my kitchen, then."

When Goody started resolutely up the ramp, moving spryly for a woman of her years, Senna stared back down at the box. "You might have warned me," she murmured beneath her breath.

"I told you I had a surprise."

"I thought you meant Goody Stewart."

"I did," Jack admitted. "I had no idea she was going to haul the admiral's ashes out of her satchel. Sorry about that." He gave her shoulder a squeeze. "You okay?"

Senna nodded. "Yes. I'm glad she brought him. I think he'd want to be here on opening day. But...where shall I put him?"

Jack took the box from her and set it back in the plane. "His ashes will be safe there until you decide where to scatter them. Besides, the admiral always loved flying in this plane."

"Shouldn't you and Goody be the ones who decide where to put his ashes?"

"We'll talk about those details later. Help me unload the desk."

"How did you manage to bring Goody with you?" Senna asked as the two of them eased the fly-tying desk out of the plane's passenger door.

"I got back to the lake house and listened to phone messages. The very first one was from Goody, saying she'd left her job in St. John's, was back in Goose Bay and ready to go to work at the lodge, so I loaded up the desk and the supplies and picked her up. Good timing, huh?"

"Pretty damn wonderful, as a matter of fact." Senna spoke with heartfelt enthusiasm.

Within minutes of Goody's arrival Senna understood Jack's undying pledge of love for the woman, and Charlie surprised everyone by showing up, sneaking in the kitchen door and flinging himself into the buxom woman's arms in an astonishing display of affection. "Ah, bye, I've missed ye, too, and that much!" Goody said, returning the boy's hug. She held Charlie at arm's length and scrutinized him with a beaming smile. "You've been toeing the line, then?" Charlie nodded. "Aye, that's good. Where's that wonderful small dog of yours? Ah, there she be, under the table waiting for scraps, just like always. She's been behavin', too, then?"

"Ula's a wonderful dog," Senna said as Charlie fidgeted, no doubt thinking about the missing coopies his crackie had eaten.

"Good, good. I've missed your storytelling, bye." Goody glanced at Senna. "It's me eyes, y'see. They've gone blotty and I can't read like I used to, but Charlie, here, he'd sit in the kitchen and read aloud from the admiral's books while I fixed supper. It was a wonderful thing, and I've missed it sore."

Senna poured mugs of tea for everyone and they gathered near the woodstove for warmth while Goody asked questions about the lodge, the meal preparations and the two women Jack would be bringing in to help her that week. "Jack tells me he'd never have managed the start-up without ye, and he's not one for admittin' he needs help," Goody said. "The admiral used to say that Jack was all wool and a yard wide without an inch of quit, which is why he liked having him for a partner." She took another sip of tea. "Jack tells me you'll be stayin' on for another two weeks, then?"

Senna caught Jack's brooding glance across the room and looked away, rising abruptly from her chair to tidy things that weren't messy. "I thought I might."

"It was awful good of you to come and help young Jack," Goody said. "As strong and capable as he is, every man needs a good woman to point him in the right direction. And now I'm going to have to excuse myself. I left St. John's only this morning and it's been that long and tiring of a day." She set aside her cup and pushed to her feet. "If you could show me where I'll be staying, I'd be that grateful."

"Charlie, take Goody's satchel and show her the cook's cabin," Jack said, and when the two of them had left the kitchen he picked up the mugs and carried them to the sink. "Imagine that. Three hired women. First a famine, then a feast," he said.

"We'll still need another guide, even after George Pilgrim's nephew arrives," Senna pointed out.

"George will fit that bill perfectly."

"He just had surgery and told you he needs treatments. Guiding can be pretty strenuous work, can't it?"

"Nah. Guiding's easy. Nothing to it. You don't know these native Labradorians, Senna. They're the toughest people on the planet, and if anything can cure George, it won't be any fancy treatments given in any fancy hospital. It'll be living out here in this wild place. I'll call him first thing in the morning." He shut the water off, wiped his hands on a dish towel, then turned and leaned against the counter, crossing his arms. "Now, about the rest of that conversation we started this afternoon…"

Senna sighed. "I didn't mean to whine about money matters. I'm just worried, that's all."

"Don't forget, at the end of the week we'll have a chunk of change coming in when these guests settle up. Things'll look different then. And the admiral's life insure payment is bound to help, when it arrives. I know how much money you've sunk into this place already and I know how it feels to watch your life savings vanish overnight, but it'll all be worth it, Senna. I swear to you. You'll get your money back and then some. And in the meantime you get to live in this beautiful peaceful place. That's worth a whole lot, isn't it?"

Before she could respond, Jack straightened and crossed to where she stood, closing his hands on her shoulders. "To hell with Earl Hammel and his need for big tax write-offs," he said, his gaze intense. "Keep your grandfather's dream. Don't sell your future down the river just because you're scared today. We can make this work. I know we can. Have a little faith in me."

"And just how *are* we going to pay the hired help in the meantime? With I.O.U.'s and faith?" Senna regretted the words the moment she spoke them, but it was too late to take them back. Jack's hands dropped from her shoulders and he abruptly took his leave.

Two HOURS LATER, she was lying in the top bunk of the cook's quarters rehashing her last conversation with Jack, during which he still expressed no personal interest in her other than as his business partner, and listening to Goody Stewart. She'd never in her life heard anything remotely like the snores that dear woman was producing. There was no way she was going to get a wink of sleep, and in a few more hours it would be daylight and time to get breakfast going. Each time she thought Goody was going to stop, the silence lasted only moments before the snoring began again, even worse than before. No doubt about it, her grandfather must have lost his hearing in his later years...or maybe that was the real reason why he hadn't married her. If she were going to be of any use at all in the morning, Senna needed to get some sleep.

Senna climbed out of the bunk, pulled on her clothes in the darkness and gathered up her blankets. Chilkat was waiting by the door when she opened it as if he knew her intent and shared her sentiments. Together, the two of them slunk out into the chill night air and made a beeline for the lodge, where they adjusted themselves on the big couch in front of the fire, sighed simultaneously with relief, and fell instantly to sleep.

To be awoken moments later by Jack touching her shoulder and saying quietly, "I've started the coffee and I took the pastry dough out of the refrigerator to rise. Is that okay?"

"No, no it's not okay, it's way too early, it's not morning yet. I only just started to sleep," Senna protested. But when she focused her eyes, lo and behold, she could see the gray light of morning and Jack standing beside the couch, looking concerned.

"Are you sick?" he said.

"Don't worry. I can still cook breakfast and clean rooms." Senna pushed herself up on one elbow and brushed her hair back from her forehead. "Goody's a dear woman but she snores."

Jack grinned. "When she stayed at the lake house, God love her, I slept on the floor out in the workshop. Grab a few more winks. I'll give you another wake-up call in half an hour, after I feed the dogs. Meanwhile, let the coffee perk and the dough rise."

After he'd gone she lay back on the couch for a few minutes more, wishing love wasn't quite so painful.

JACK'S FIRST MORNING of guiding went well. After breakfast he took out a party of two, with Charlie taking the second boatload of clients and the remaining fishermen donning their waders and plying their lines in the pools above and below the lodge. Charlie might have put the dyed-in-the-wool fly fishermen off with his undeniable youth, but none of them, with all their worldly experience in all the highest-class resorts in the world, could hold a candle to his uncanny knowledge of the river and the fish they sought to catch. Predictably, when the two boats converged at the dock for lunch, Charlie's clients were euphoric about their morning's experiences. Not to say that his own weren't, but to see the transformation of doubting Thomases to believers gave him a satisfying kick in the gut. "Good job, Charlie. I'm proud of you," he said to the boy as they trailed their clients up the ramp.

"They talk a lot," Charlie said, "but they can't fish too good."

Jack clasped the boy's shoulder. "That's why they have you along."

Senna and Goody had prepared a veritable feast which everyone set to with great enthusiasm. Charlie and Jack ate in the kitchen, where Jack could watch Senna as she worked, breathing the scent of her hair when she passed near him and wondering what she'd do if he suddenly jumped off his stool, took her in his arms and kissed her silly. Slap him, probably. Might be worth it, though. Might make her realize what she'd be missing if she left here. Might make her realize that money wasn't everything.

Though undoubtedly it helped. He had no idea how they were going to pay the hired help as well as the bank note and the vendors.

Senna came in from the dining room for the fourth time carrying an empty chafing dish. "Ida Snell is asking to see you," she said. "She spent the morning bird-watching but was wondering if she could join a fishing party this afternoon for an hour or two, since Bert will be napping."

"Sure. Not a problem. I'll get the boat ready. Oh, before I forget again, there were two messages on the lake house phone yesterday. One was from your dear friend, Tim. He wants you to call. The other was from Granville. He's found an important letter and he's keeping it for you in his office, and the papers you need to sign have come. Just in case I should happen to drown this afternoon, I wanted you to know."

"Thank you. I appreciate that."

"Glad to be of service," he said, walking out the door.

Twenty minutes later he was starting the small but reliable four-stroke Honda and pointing the skiff downriver, with Ida on board and nobody else, because as it turned out most of the others were napping, too, after Senna and Goody's huge lunch. Ida was wearing a nifty felt hat over her white head of hair and her ever-present binoculars were dangling around her neck. She was euphoric to have him all to herself. "I appreciate this, more than you'll ever know, young man. This is my dream of a lifetime, and you're making it come true. When my husband made the reservation, he told Admiral McCallum that he'd just had open heart surgery and we were both in our early seventies, and the admiral told him that all who wished to fish this special river were welcome to fish it, regardless of their gender, age, color or religious persuasions."

Jack let the boat drift downstream with the current. "The admiral died a short while ago."

"Yes, I was sorry to learn of that, but obviously his dream lives on in you and his granddaughter. This place of yours is a priceless treasure. Now let's find some Atlantic salmon to catch and set free. Let's shine a little light on this blue and green planet, so God can find it in the dark chaos of these troubled times."

In the next hour Jack listened as Ida told him about the job she'd held prior to her retirement. "It was awful timing, really," she said as he tied a black bear green butt to her line, having had no luck with the streamer. "I was two months short of retirement when it happened. I worked for a big life insurance company in New York City, and after September 11, I had to deal with a great many close relatives of the victims over the phone, trying to sort out the awful paperwork. They told me stories about their loved ones and some of them cried. Emotionally, that tipped me right over the edge.

"I went into a terrible depression and every night the nightmares would come back. Then one day my dear husband said to me, 'Ida, you've always wanted to go on a fishing trip in a really wild place, and I think I've found the perfect spot.' It's amazing how planning for this trip has changed my life. So here we are, Mr. Hanson, and I can't thank you enough for making my dream come true."

Ida had no luck with the second fly, either, but not

because she couldn't fly-cast. She was really quite skilled, but every time she saw a bird she would fumble for her binoculars and hand the fly rod to Jack. Clearly, she was torn between two loves. Then, as the little Honda powered them slowly around a curve in the river, she spied the mouth of a tributary on the far bank. "Let's try over there, Mr. Hanson," she said. "What's the name of that stream?"

"Black Duck Brook." Jack steered a new course to take her to the mouth of the brook, and she alternately fly-cast and bird-watched happily for another half hour before deciding that he should really go up the stream a little ways.

"I bet there's a big brook trout waiting up there with my name on it," she said.

"The water's deep right here, but she'll shallow up fairly quickly," Jack pointed out.

"Then we'll just turn around when it does. Thank you for this adventure, Mr. Hanson. I don't care if I catch a fish or not, being here is enough all by itself. Just wonderful."

Jack steered the nose of the skiff up Black Duck Brook. Thirty feet across at the mouth, the brook soon narrowed to half that width and the current had strengthened significantly. Ida threw her line out every once in a while but seemed content just to peer ahead and call out the details of the journey. "Oh, did you see that beautiful bird? A northern three-toed woodpecker!" she said. "I've never seen one before, but then again I've never been this far north." Then, a little farther along, she said, "Listen, I think I hear rapids!" and sure enough, another turn brought them face to face with an impressive fifteen-foot-high waterfall tumbling into a deep pool at its base. Ida pointed with her fly rod. "Right at the base of those falls is where my big brookie awaits. I can feel it in my old bones."

Jack motored as close as he dared to the base of the falls and Ida cast out her fly. The cast was a pretty one, and by God, she hooked a fish right off, and not just an ordinary fish. By the flex of her fly rod, Ida had caught a monster of a brook trout. "I think it's a big one, Mr. Hanson! I can hardly hold the tip of the rod up!" The fish leapt out of the water, thrashing madly, and Jack backed the boat as it made a run toward them.

"Better take in some line," he advised.

Ida's reel hummed as she cranked as fast as she could.

"Keep the tip of your rod up."

She jerked it higher with great effort.

"The fish is making a run. Give it some line…."

She gave it some line, her expression fierce with concentration beneath the brim of her felt hat.

"Watch it, he's coming at you, take in any slack now and keep the tip up…. By damn, Mrs. Snell, I do believe you've hooked yourself a trophy fish."

She looked back at him, eyes sparkling with excitement. "My very first arctic fish, at that," she said. When the time came to net the trout, Ida admired it briefly then gave him a pleading look. "Please release it quickly, Mr. Hanson. Such a beautiful wild thing belongs in this beautiful wild place. I hope I haven't hurt it."

"You tired it out a little, that's all, Mrs. Snell."

"Then we're even. I'm played out, too. How much do you think it weighs?"

"A brookie that long and that fat would go about ten

pounds. That really is a trophy fish. I don't know if I've ever seen finer."

Jack carefully handled the trout in the water beside the skiff as he slipped the hook from its jaw. He held it cradled in his palms just beneath the surface of the water for a few moments until it regained its vitality and with one swift surge disappeared in the cold dark water. He glanced up and was deeply moved to see Ida's cheeks wet with tears. She gave him a trembling smile as the sunshine splintered through the black spruce and spangled her face. "This has been such a wonderful day, Mr. Hanson. I can't thank you enough."

Had Jack been paying closer attention he would have noticed that the aluminum boat had drifted out of the calm eddy and into the swift current, but the vision of Ida Snell's emotional reaction to catching the trout, and then begging him to let it go unharmed, riveted him. Most clients would have killed a fish that size and had it mounted to hang on their den wall back home. Ida's compassionate generosity was a rare thing. She was a beautiful woman, and he knew that Senna would be as beautiful as Ida when she reached her older years, still full of zest and a love of life, still seeking and appreciating the healing power of the wild places. He felt a painful thump in his chest when he realized that he wanted very much to be there as Senna matured and grew old, and knew he wouldn't be.

Almost at the same moment he felt another painful thump that knocked him against the gunnel as the boat ran up hard against a large boulder and spun sideways as the current swept them downstream.

CHAPTER FOURTEEN

JACK INSTANTLY GUNNED the throttle to straighten the boat out and steered into calmer water. "Are you all right?" he said to Ida, who had dropped her fly rod to grip both sides of the boat when they hit the rock.

"I'm fine, Mr. Hanson," she said. "Are we sinking? My feet are getting wet."

"We seem to have sprung a little leak. I'll get you ashore and then bail her out."

He made for the nearest landing spot and Ida was able to scramble ashore before the water had risen to ankle depth in the bottom of the boat. By the time Jack had secured the Lund and joined Ida on the bank, the water level had risen to mid-shin. The impact of the hull against the boulder had cracked a bottom seam, and that crack, from what Jack could see, was a good twelve inches long. He stood on the bank beside Ida and stared down into the boat.

"Well," Ida said matter-of-factly. "I hope you brought some duct tape along."

"Never travel without the stuff," Jack said with a laugh. "I'll make a fire and put the billy can on. You can have a cup of tea while I fix the boat."

Ida sighed. "Tea sounds wonderful. What an adventure this is turning out to be! Do you think the boat will get us back to the lodge or will we have to walk? I love to walk, you know. Doesn't bother me a bit, though it'll take us a good deal longer. I can't wait to tell Bert about that beautiful brook trout and the three-toed woodpecker."

"Not to worry, Mrs. Snell. This boat'll get us home in jig time. I still have a few tricks up my sleeve." After he'd kindled a little fire, made Mrs. Snell comfortable under some mosquito netting and put the billy can on, Jack withdrew the tarp he packed to use as a lean-to on foul days and a spool of parachute cord. The tarp measured fifteen by twenty feet and was barely large enough to do the job.

"Okay, Ida, here's what I'm going to do," he narrated, unfolding the tarp in the water at the stern of the boat. "I'm going to work this tarp under the boat and draw it up around both sides, stem and stern, and lash it through the grommets to secure it."

"Wrap the boat up like a present, sort of," Ida observed from her seat near the fire.

"That should seal off the leak by creating a temporary outer hull. How's our tea coming?"

"Just fine. It'll be ready when you are, young man."

Jack waded into the icy water and began the painstaking process of trying to slide the tarp under the grounded boat. The boat was resting on a sandy strand, which helped enormously. The last thing he wanted to do was rip a hole in the tarp. He did the side farthest away from the bank first, lashing the tarp and fastening the lengths of cord to the thwarts, then working first at the bow, then at the stern, rocking the boat as little as possible as he gradually slid the bulk of the tarp beneath the hull, using the slack at the bow and stern to lever the remainder of the tarp into place. He had to lift the flooded stern with all his strength to shift it enough to get the tarp all the way under the boat, and then do the same in the bow. By the time he pulled the tarp up the near side of the boat and lashed it taut with the lengths of parachute cord, he was wet to the waist and shaking with cold and fatigue.

Jack climbed back into the boat and began to bail, slinging the water as fast as he could over the gunnels. After five minutes of steady bailing, he felt the boat lift off the stream bottom. In another five minutes the water was only ankle deep. "That's got her, I think," Jack said as he bailed down to the hull. "I'm ready for that cup of tea now, Mrs. Snell, and then we'll head for the lodge."

Ida poured him a cup from the billy can and he warmed himself by the fire while he drank the strong, dark, rejuvenating tea. "Well, young man," she said. "I must say, I envy your lifestyle. You and your lovely wife certainly work hard, but it's a good kind of work, far away from the madding crowds."

Jack felt a jolt to the soles of his feet. *Wife.* He'd sworn never to walk that path again, but when Ida referred to Senna as his wife it had sounded…good.

"Senna's not my wife, Mrs. Snell. She's my business partner."

Ida gave him a look he couldn't quite fathom across the smoke of the little fire. "Well, you couldn't have picked a better one. She's a dear, and she knows more about birds than I do. More about plants, as well, and I always thought of myself as quite an expert on both."

"She's a wildlife biologist."

Ida nodded. "That doesn't surprise me a bit. She certainly loves it here, and you're lucky to have her."

"I couldn't agree with you more," Jack said. "I only wish she felt the same."

"Oh?" Ida's eyebrows raised. "What do you mean?"

"She came to Labrador to settle her grandfather's estate and is only staying a few weeks. She plans to sell her half of the business in the fall, and nothing I've said has changed her mind. Believe me, I've tried."

Ida studied him over the rim of her cup. "Maybe you shouldn't try so hard," she said. "Sometimes letting go of someone you love is the only way to keep them."

Love? Ida's words startled Jack yet again. He stared into the embers of the fire and rubbed his jaw.

Was he in love with Senna McCallum?

SENNA WAS DETERMINED not to worry just because Jack was a little late getting back with Ida. No doubt if they went very far downriver, the trip back up against the swift current would take quite a bit longer. But by suppertime, when they hadn't arrived, she sent Charlie out in the second boat. The guests were on dessert when she heard both boats motoring toward the dock. She felt a strong rush of relief as she cleared the table, served dessert wine to those who wanted it, refilled coffee cups, shared in the easy banter, smiling, always smiling, until one of the guests, watching out the window as the boats approached, said, "What the hell? That's gotta be one of the strangest sights I've ever seen."

Everyone, Bert included, got up and tramped out onto the porch, where they stood for a moment speculating amongst themselves before descending the ramp to find out what had happened. By the time Senna reached the dock, Ida had been assisted out of the boat by a multitude of helping hands and everyone was examining the Lund with its makeshift outer hull. Senna could only imagine the story behind that.

"You're a little late for supper, Ida," Bert said, concerned. "Are you all right?"

"Oh, I'm fine. Our boat sprung a little leak, but we had a fine time, didn't we, Mr. Hanson?"

"The best of times," Jack nodded.

"Mr. Hanson let me use his secret dry fly," Ida said. "Bert, you should have seen the size of the brook trout I caught! It was twenty inches long and Mr. Hanson said it would probably weigh close to ten pounds! It was simply beautiful, and the spots on its side were so vivid and bright."

"Why didn't you keep it?" someone asked.

"Keep it? Why on earth? It belongs in the water. That's where I caught it and that's where I left it. I'll keep the memory of catching it, and maybe someone else will have that same thrill some day."

"What was the fly you used, Jack?" one of the guests asked.

"Top secret. If I told you that, I'd have to kill you," Jack replied.

"You must be hungry, Ida," Senna said. "Let's go up to the lodge."

While Jack helped Bert Snell up the ramp as before, one slow and easy step at a time, Senna settled Ida in the living room for a before-dinner drink and to tell her story in front of the fire. Then she sat at the dining-room table for over an hour and a half reveling in the magic of her day, describing to Bert the birds she'd seen in great detail, and Senna was left wondering why Jack had abruptly disappeared after delivering Bert to the living room.

At 9:00 p.m. Goody shooed her out of the kitchen with a firm, "Better go on down and check on the byes," and Senna, who had finally figured out that byes meant boys, was able to carry a plate of food down to the cabin. Charlie was sitting outside on the wall bench, the natural light still bright enough to be able to read by. "Hanson's asleep," he said as she approached. "I fed the dogs for him."

"Thank you, Charlie. That was good of you." Senna entered the cabin and set the plate onto the table. Jack was sprawled face down on his bunk like a dead man, but at least he'd changed out of his wet jeans before hitting the mattress. "Jack?" He mumbled something unintelligible but didn't move. She shook his shoulder. *"Jack!"*

His eyes opened. He blinked, then rolled slowly onto his back with a low groan. "Do you know how much a sixteen-foot aluminum boat weighs when it's full of water? Just shoot me," he said. "Put me out of my misery."

"My goodness, Jack. Wasn't it just yesterday you told me that guiding wasn't a hard job? Sit up. I brought you something to eat. Charlie!" she shot over her shoulder. Charlie appeared in the doorway. "Is there any whiskey in this cabin?"

Charlie pointed to the open shelf behind the stove where all the dry goods were kept, then went back outside. Senna retrieved the bottle, poured a slug into a coffee cup and pressed the cup into Jack's hand. He sat slumped over the edge of the bunk, shoulders rounded and head ducked. "I screwed up. I wasn't paying attention and we ran onto a rock."

"Drink the whiskey," Senna said.

"I screwed up," he repeated.

"Nobody's perfect," Senna said. "Besides, you gave Ida the adventure of a lifetime."

"She's a sweetheart of a woman and I could have killed her. She might have drowned and if she had, her husband would have died, too, because they're so in love I doubt one could live without the other."

"Oh, Jack." He looked so forlorn that as Senna took the cup from him she had to resist the urge to kiss him. "She didn't drown, she had a wonderful time and she told me she can't wait to go fishing with you again."

He moaned. "You should see the size of the crack in the bottom of the Lund. I'll have to fix it before tomorrow morning. We don't have a spare boat and everyone'll want to fish the dawn hatch. I have to fix the damn thing tonight."

"First you have to eat." She set the cup of whiskey on the table beside his plate of food. "Come on. Set to it before it gets cold."

LATER, LYING ON HER BUNK and listening to Goody's thunderous snores, Senna wondered how Jack planned to mend the boat's hull. If he couldn't, that would leave them with another problem; all those clients to take fishing and only one boat. At 1:00 a.m. she left the cook's cabin and headed for the lodge's couch, but turned when she heard a thump down on the dock. A glowing lantern revealed Jack working on the boat. He'd hauled it out of the water and was squatting on his heels and doing something to the hull.

She altered course and walked down the ramp. He glanced up at her approach. "Almost done," he said.

"How did you fix it?"

"I was going to rivet the seam back together but I taped it instead with aluminum aircraft tape. Should be good as new until I hit another rock. What the hell are you doing up at this hour?"

"Heading for the couch again."

Jack rose to his feet, wiping his hands on a rag. "No doubt your job in Maine will seem like an endless vacation after the past few weeks. Not only are you working sixteen hours a day, but you can't even get a good night's sleep." He sounded discouraged, which surprised Senna.

"I'll survive. It's only for a little while longer."

He stared at her. In the lamplight his eyes were dark hollows in his face. "Ida and Bert Snell have been married for fifty-two years."

"I know. She told me."

"And they're still as much in love as they were in high school."

Senna smiled. "True love really does exist."

"If she'd fallen out of the boat…"

"Jack, she didn't. You've had a rough day. Things'll look better in the morning."

"Hell, woman, it *is* morning. In a few hours we'll be doing it all over again, and what for? If this Earl Hammel wants to buy you out, maybe you should let him. Be a whole lot easier for you, and it'll bail you out of your financial woes. But if you decide to sell, just make good and goddamn sure he pays you what it's worth." He threw the rag onto the dock and walked up the ramp, leaving her to ponder the darkness of his mood.

FOUR HOURS LATER Senna and Goody were in the kitchen preparing breakfast. Senna was mixing up a

batch of blueberry muffins when Jack trailed in, looking in a marginally better mood than he'd been in the
night before.

"What day is this?" he asked around a yawn.

"Monday." Senna handed him a big mug of strong
coffee.

"Monday. Good. I'll call George, see if he feels up
to guiding. He oughta be fully recovered by now. He's
had two whole days of rest."

"Do you mean George Pilgrim, then?" Goody asked,
tying on her apron. "I went to school with George. Quite
a hell raiser, he was. I was sweet on him, but so were
all the girls, he was that handsome. He went off to the
war and when he came back he married Petra Gillard
and took to rangering." Goody reached for a big mixing bowl, plunked it down on the counter, and began
cracking eggs into it. "He'd be a good guide." She nodded. "Nobody knows the land any better than George."

Jack carried his coffee out onto the porch and when
Senna had slid the muffin tin into the oven she poured
herself a cup of coffee and joined him. "Stolen moments of peace," she said, sitting on the bench beside
him. "Sometimes they're the sweetest."

"I'm sorry I was so short with you last night," he said,
staring at the river.

"That's all right. You were tired."

"I was wrong," he said bluntly. "I've been wrong all
along. I've been trying to make you see that this is
where you should be. I've been force-feeding you on my
own dreams and on the dreams of your grandfather, but
you have your own life to live. I was wrong to try and
make you stay."

Senna was taken aback by the grim delivery of this

statement. She sat for a moment in silence, trying to fathom his sudden change of heart. "Are you saying you *want* me to sell my half of the business to Earl Hammel?"

He turned his head to look at her. "I want you to do what *you* want to do, whatever that may be."

Senna drew a breath. It was time to tell him just how she felt about him, no matter how vulnerable that made her. "Jack, I…"

"Good morning, you two early birds!" a bright voice said. Ida Snell appeared in the kitchen doorway cradling a cup of coffee and came out onto the porch to join them. "I was hoping I'd find you here, Mr. Hanson. Do you think we might go fishing again this afternoon? I could bring my camera along, and take a picture of my next trophy trout."

AFTER THE FIRST ROUND of clients went off in the boats, the others donned waders and worked the pools above and below the lodge. Bert and Ida sat side by side on the porch enjoying the early sunlight while Senna began cleaning the rooms. By the time she finished that chore and was halfway through the laundry it was time to help Goody with lunch. They were setting the platters onto the sideboard when she heard both boats approaching the dock and then another sound that drowned out all others; that of a twin-engine plane. Strange, they weren't expecting visitors, though Jack had called the hospital earlier and found out George Pilgrim was being released the following morning. Jack had promised to pick him up, but perhaps George had jumped the gun and signed himself out of the hospital a little sooner.

The plane made three slow flyovers of the lodge before landing on the river and taxiing to the dock. Senna stood at the top of the ramp, shielding her eyes against the sun and watching while the pilot of the plane jumped out and secured it. Two men disembarked. Two bags were deposited on the dock. Senna felt a sharp stab of foreboding, especially as the shorter of the two men turned and looked up toward where she stood. She drew a sharp breath and her heart skipped a beat.

Tim. And other man could only be Earl Hammel. Jack was tying his boat up to the other end of the dock and helping his clients out. He would know without even being told who those two men were and what was happening. He would think she'd called Tim and told him to bring Earl Hammel to the lodge because she'd decided to sell. She could almost see the rigid set of Jack's shoulders from here. Tim had spotted her and was raising his hand in a wave, but Senna was so shocked she couldn't respond. There was no place for them to stay. Tim knew they had no room, yet the pilot was depositing two more bags, accepting what Senna assumed was a tip from the taller man, then climbing back into the plane and starting the engines up.

Tim waved to her again. "Senna!" she heard him call.

Her legs felt rubbery as she walked down the ramp. Tim was smiling as he moved toward her and met her halfway, his broad, friendly face earnest.

"I'm sorry," he said. "I know this is a surprise, but Earl was going to come with or without me. I thought it would be better if I could at least introduce you."

"But Tim, I told you several times that we have no room here. He can't stay. And…and the thing is, he shouldn't have come. He's wasting his time. I've decided that I don't want to sell my half of the business, either."

Tim glanced over his shoulder to where the tall, distinguished-looking man watched the fishermen disembark from the boats. He looked back at her with a shrug. "Well, he's here. At least listen to what he says. He's prepared to offer a lot of money, Senna. Just give him a tour of the property and let him make his pitch. Then if you still don't want to sell, don't sell. It's your decision and you have nothing to lose making an informed decision."

Earl Hammel was younger than Senna had imagined, in his early fifties, with the bronzed complexion and athletic physique of one who spent much time out of doors, except for the diamond the size of a grape flashing in his ring. He shook her hand as Tim introduced them. "I'll tell you straight off that I like the place already, from what I saw from the air," he said. "And Jack here tells me the Atlantic salmon fishing on this river is outstanding."

"Then you've already met my business partner, Jack Hanson. You'll have lunch with us, of course," Senna said. She knew she was supposed to smile, always smile, but she'd never felt less like smiling as she studiously avoided Jack's gaze and led Tim and Earl up the ramp to where guests were already converging in the dining room and exchanging fishing stories. This was hardly the time to be discussing business, and she was grateful that Tim and Earl Hammel joined the other guests at the table and allowed her to help Goody with the midday meal. She was taking a pan of fresh biscuits from the oven when Jack walked past the kitchen window, heading toward the guides' camp. She yearned after him, filled with a peculiar sickness that made her tremble all over.

"Here, now, lass, you'll burn yourself, standing there with that hot pan," Goody warned, and Senna set the pan on the counter.

"I'll be right back," she promised, dashing out the door and racing down the porch steps. "Jack!" she called out. "Jack, wait, we need to talk!"

He paused in mid stride and waited for her to approach. "You don't need to say anything," he said. "Just do what you have to do."

"I didn't know they were coming. I'm sorry," Senna said, her heart aching at the stoniness of his expression.

Jack shrugged. "It would have happened, sooner or later. Today, tomorrow, what difference does it make? This place is special and there are people out there who would snap it up in an instant. There's just one thing I'd ask. Let the summer run itself out. Don't close on the property until we've finished up the season. Don't disappoint Ida Snell. She was counting on going fishing with me this afternoon."

"Jack, wait!" Senna said as he turned and continued on. She rushed after him, reaching for his arm, and was startled by the vehemence of his response. He spun around and raised both hands in a warning gesture.

"Don't," he said. "I can't do this. I told you before, you have to decide what you want. I can't make you buy into this dream. I was wrong to think I could. I was wrong to try."

"No, no, you weren't. I didn't want Hammel to come here. I don't want to sell to him!"

He stared. "You don't?"

"No, but he's here so I'm going to listen to what he has to say, and then I'm going to tell him how I feel."

"If you really meant that about keeping your half of the business, Senna, you'd tell him before lunch," Jack said, turning on heel once again. This time he didn't stop when Senna called his name. She knew he wouldn't. She also knew he was right. She should march over to the lodge and call Thunder Air to come pick Tim and Hammel up. But why did Jack tell Hammel that the Wolf was a first-class salmon river? Why? Why would he want Hammel to like the place?

Feet dragging and heart on the ground, she returned to the lodge to help Goody with the rest of the meal. She felt numb as she moved between the kitchen and the dining room. Smiling, always smiling, pleasant to the guests in spite of her inner agony. Did Jack want to get rid of her? Was he hoping that she'd sell to Hammel?

Senna arranged fruit on one platter, cookies and other assorted sweets on another, and was heading for the dining room when Jack crossed by the kitchen window again, on his way back down to the boats. He had a duffel bag slung over his shoulder, and she stood at the window long enough to watch him toss it inside his plane. The sick feeling in the pit of her stomach intensified.

She carried the desserts into the dining room and set them on the sideboard, but when she returned to the kitchen she couldn't see Jack on the dock, nor did she see him after lunch, except to catch a glimpse as he and Charlie loaded the next group of clients and their gear into the boats. Ida had opted out of the afternoon fishing to play cribbage with Bert. Goody had retired to the cook's cabin for her restorative afternoon nap and Tim dogged Senna's footsteps as she cleaned up the kitchen and prepped for afternoon tea.

"I'm really sorry about showing up this way," he said again. "I didn't realize how much work this was for you. I just want you to know that we brought a tent. We don't expect to sleep at the lodge."

"That's wise of you, since there are no rooms," Senna said. Her patience with Tim was running thin.

"Earl would really like to go out on the river after the tour of the lodge. He'd like to experience the fishing first-hand before he makes any solid decisions."

"Right now we're short on guides, Tim. There isn't anyone who can take him. And what decisions? I'm not selling."

"Talk to him first, Senna," Tim pleaded. "He's waiting in the living room. Just talk. That's all. Earl's really a nice guy. I realize you've been through a lot in the past few weeks. You've been run ragged, that's plain to see. Take ten minutes to sit down and listen to him."

"I have to get things ready for tea," Senna said.

"Ten minutes," Tim said. "Then, if you don't like what you hear, we'll leave in the morning. Senna, I only want what's best for you. For what it's worth, I'm only trying to help you settle your grandfather's estate in the fastest and most profitable way."

"I know that, but…"

"Ten minutes," Tim repeated, and after a long pause, Senna gave a reluctant nod.

THE AFTERNOON SEEMED ENDLESS to Jack, plying the boat through the lower rapids and into good, deep holding water, advising the clients on which flies to use, pointing out the most promising pools, holding conversations about Atlantic salmon, arctic char, grilse, pike, and brook trout, trying to be engaging when all he could think about were Tim and Hammel showing up at the lodge unannounced, flying in as if they already owned the place and making themselves to home. And Senna, pretending she knew nothing about it. Did everything they'd shared together in the past two weeks mean nothing to her at all?

No way in hell was he hanging around to watch her entertain them. He'd fly to the lake house, spend the night there, and pick up George first thing in the morning. While his thoughts churned, one of his clients hooked into a twenty-pound Atlantic salmon and played it to the net, holding it up briefly for a picture before releasing it back into the clear, swift water. Fly rods whipped back and forth with great enthusiasm after this. The hours dragged on. Tim and Senna were back at the lodge together. Talking. Or maybe not talking. Maybe they were making up for a two-week dry spell.

Queasy thought.

The sun lowered ever so slowly. Happy hour finally beckoned, and he motored his clients back upriver to the lodge, helped them onto the dock, and was dismayed to see Tim and Earl coming down the ramp as the guests ascended. Earl Hammel didn't beat around the bush.

"I've had the tour of the lodge and I'd really like to try the river before sundown," he said. "I'll pay you three hundred bucks, American, for two hours of your time."

"Does that cover both of you?"

Tim shook his head. "I don't fish."

Great. Tim would stay behind with Senna. The bastard knew how to sink the knife deep and twist it. Jack wanted to refuse but he knew he couldn't. Earl Hammel wanted to buy the lodge, and if he'd been given a tour and was standing here asking to go out on the river, apparently Senna, in spite of her statement to the contrary, must have decided to sell. "All right," Jack said, more curtly than he intended. "We'll go out right after supper."

After they left to join the other guests for drinks in the living room, Jack neatened the boat, readied the gear, filled the gas tank. He puttered around on the dock feeling about as low as he ever had, then wandered back to the guides' cabin to feed the dogs. Charlie had beaten him back with his own boatload of clients and was reading on his bunk. When Jack entered the cabin he glanced over. "Five big salmon, two huge pike," he said around an exaggerated yawn.

Jack scowled. "You win only because I was distracted. I don't suppose you fed the dogs."

"Not yet. I was about to."

"Yeah, right." Jack fed and watered the dogs, cleaned the dog yard, returned to the cabin and poured himself a hefty shot of whiskey. He drank it sitting on the wall bench outside the cabin, staring bleakly down at the river. Senna would be in the kitchen with Goody, getting supper ready to go, and no doubt Tim was hanging with her. Jack wasn't sure if it was the whiskey that burned in his stomach or his own bitter jealousy. He didn't go up to the lodge for a plate of food, but shared a can of beans with Charlie, then pushed away from the table and pulled on his hat. "I'm taking a client out for a couple of hours, then I'm heading for the lake house. I'll spend the night there and bring George Pilgrim back in the morning. Can you feed the dogs?"

"Sure," Charlie said, not glancing up from his book.

"I mean, really feed them?"

"I'll feed them and water them," he promised.

Earl Hammel was waiting on the dock, fly rod in hand. Not just any fly rod, but a custom made Thomas and Thomas. Everything Hammel wore or carried was of the finest quality. He didn't talk much as Jack turned the skiff upriver, opening the throttle and picking his way through the rapids, into a broad, calm stretch, then around several bends to a place where ledges hemmed both sides and the current was swift.

"Try under that shallow rock overhang there," Jack said, throttling back just enough to keep the boat moving slowly forward until he could set anchor.

"That doesn't look like a very promising spot to me," Hammel commented, but he stripped off some line and made a cast. Ten minutes later, after a long and tiring fight, he landed and released a twenty-eight-pound Atlantic salmon. Jack continued up the river to a deep holding pool at the foot of another set of rapids, where Hammel hooked into five different big fish in an hour of casting. He was a cool customer, but in the end he couldn't contain his enthusiasm when he heard the distant howl of a wolf echoing across the black spruce forest.

"By God, this beats Alaska," he expounded, exhilarated. "Wilder country, better fishing and that lodge is a much finer piece of work than I expected. Look, I know you and the lady are business partners, but man to man, I want to make a deal with you. As I understand it, she wants to sell and you don't, so here's the deal. I was going to try to convince you to sell out as well, but I could use a caretaker to watch over the property when

I'm not here, that would be a salaried position , of course, and when I am here, I could use a good guide, too, especially when I bring friends and corporate clients. You can run the place any way you want as long as the lodge is at my disposal when I want it to be. I told the lady I'd give her one million dollars, American, for her share of the business, and that includes the lake house, the plane, everything. What do you say?"

"The lady's name is Senna McCallum, and what did *she* say?"

"She was helping Tim set up the tents. She said she'd think about it. What about you?"

"I'll go along with whatever Senna decides to do, but if she decides to sell, you'll have to buy me out, too, and my price'll be a whole lot higher."

It was nearly dark by the time they returned to the lodge. Hammel shook his hand, thanked him, and tried to press three crisp one-hundred-dollar bills into his hand but Jack firmly refused. Afterward he wasn't sure why he had. He definitely could use the money, but he didn't want to take anything from Hammel. Not one damn thing. He secured the boat and was doing a preflight on the plane when he remembered he'd left the lake house keys up in the lodge, hanging on one of the key hooks just inside the kitchen door. Dammitall. He'd wanted to sneak away without having to make any explanations, but it was not to be.

He climbed the ramp and the steps that ran up the back porch near the kitchen door, hoping Senna wouldn't be there. But when he opened the door, not only was Senna there, but so were Earl Hammel and Tim Cromwell, and Jack guessed from Senna's expression that Hammel might have just upped his offer to buy out her half. Maybe he'd just offered her one and a half million. Her stunned look gave way to a guarded expression as Jack entered the room.

"Sorry to interrupt. I forgot my keys," he said.

"Ah, there you are," Hammel said with a satisfied nod. "Good. I was hoping you'd stop in. Perhaps you'd like to join us in this discussion."

"No, actually, I wouldn't," Jack said, reaching for the keys and turning immediately to go.

"Wait!" Senna said. "You can't just walk out now. This decision has as much to do with you as it does with me." He met her intense gaze only briefly before turning away again. Even at the end of a long and arduous day, she was as beautiful and full of promise as the dawn. The very thought of a dawn without her in it hurt like hell but there was nothing he could do about that except bow out of the picture as quickly as he could and keep what dignity remained. "I'd like to hear what you have to say about Mr. Hammel's offer, Jack," she said quietly. "I'd like to hear it directly from you."

Jack glanced at her, the pain intensifying. "It's your decision, Senna. I already told you that. I'm spending the night at the lake house. I'll pick George Pilgrim up first thing and be back in time to take clients out." Before she could respond he was out the door, escaping into the gathering darkness, cursing himself for his weakness and cursing all women for making men weak. He heard the kitchen door open behind him before he'd taken four steps.

"Jack?" Senna's voice, her footsteps quickening on the porch, followed after him. "Damn you, Jack, wait up!"

He descended the ramp in record time, feet hitting

the dock hard even as he heard Tim calling out Senna's name from the porch. He jumped onto the pontoon, wrenched open the plane's door, and hoisted himself inside, but before he could slam and latch the door Senna pried it back open. "What the hell do you think you're doing?" he said, refusing to let her in. "You have an important business deal to discuss and important company to entertain."

"You can't just fly off like this," she shot back. "Doesn't what we've shared here for the past few weeks mean anything to you at all? Please, please, I'm begging you, Jack, let me in. We need to talk."

CHAPTER FIFTEEN

THE FLIGHT TO THE LAKE HOUSE seemed endless, and Senna spent that long hour in silent turmoil trying to compose her thoughts, trying to structure exactly what she was going to say and how she was going to say it, but the moment the pontoons grazed the surface of the lake a sense of panic began to overwhelm her. Jack taxied to the dock, secured the plane, helped her down, all without speaking a word. He started for the lake house while she stumbled along behind him in the gloaming. He unlocked the door and held it open for her. She stepped past him, reaching automatically for the light switch but he caught her hand in his to prevent her from illuminating the moment. They stood in the dim silence, listening to each other's ragged breathing and gripping each other's hands tightly. Senna realized that she was trembling all over.

"I didn't think you'd accept Hammel's offer of partnership," she said, her voice choking up around the last word.

"I didn't," Jack said. "I didn't think you'd sell your half to him."

"I told him I wouldn't, but then he told me that you told him…"

"I told Hammel it was up to you," Jack interrupted,

his voice hard. "Whatever you wanted to do. A million dollars is a lot of money."

"He upped the offer to a million five, and he said you were all for it." She drew another painful breath. "What do *you* want, Jack?" Dangerous question. She felt dizzy and breathless as she agonized over what his answer might be. "What did you really tell Hammel?"

"I told him that if you sold your half of the business to him, he's going to have to buy me out, too. That's what I told him."

"You did?" Hope surged in her heart.

"I did."

"You'd leave this place if I sold out?"

"I would."

"Hammel hunts wolves in Alaska from airplanes," Senna burst out.

"I believe it."

"He thinks his money will buy him anything he wants."

"That's because it probably does."

"Well, it isn't going to buy our lodge. We'll tell him no."

His grip on her hand tightened even more. "Are you sure that's what you want? It might be a while before another buyer comes along. And what about Tim?"

"What about him?"

"You're involved with him, aren't you?"

"No. I mean, I was at one time, but not anymore. Tim's a dear friend, he always will be, but I don't love him and I realize now that I never did." Senna felt the masculine strength of the hand that held hers, a hand that had worked unimaginably hard to make her grandfather's lodge a reality, a hand far more calloused and blistered than her own. She could barely speak past the fierce surge of emotion that overwhelmed her. "The only man I've ever been in love with is you. I don't want to sell the lodge to Hammel or to anyone else. I want to stay here with you. I want to follow the wolves and the caribou with you. I want to learn to fly your plane and run a team of dogs." She swallowed past the tight burn in her throat and drew a quivering breath. "I love you, John Hanson, and if you don't feel the same way about me then I guess it's my turn to suffer, but I can't help how I feel."

There. She'd said it. She listened to the sound of his harsh breathing and waited for his response, her whole body tense with dread and vibrating with hope.

"God almighty, woman," he said. "Why didn't you tell me this sooner?"

"I thought you knew. I thought you felt the same way. At least I hoped you did. But you never said anything about how you felt, and then when you started talking about being wrong to try and make me stay, I..." He swore beneath his breath and his head lowered as he kissed her very gently, with reverent ardor, effectively ending the conversation. He swept her up in his arms, kicked the door shut behind him, and carried her up the stairs, his kisses intensifying as he ascended. At the top of the stairs he lowered her to her feet and pulled her up against his lean, hard body while she struggled dizzily to catch her breath.

"My room or yours?" he asked, a superfluous question since they never made it to either, and Senna reflected afterward that it was a good thing there was a thick wool rug on the landing. In the early morning hours Jack carried her to his bed and she awoke with her head pillowed on his chest, listening to the strong rhythmic beat of his heart and feeling the steady rise and fall of his breathing. She nestled closer when she heard the loons out on the lake, calling back and forth in a lonesome, tragic way.

"You're wrong, you know," she murmured to them. "Life isn't always sad and lonely. It can be wild and crazy and wonderful, too."

And at that very moment, as if on cue, one of the loons gave a wild and crazy laugh.

"I think they've struck a pretty good balance," Jack said.

The rumble of his deep voice surprised her. He slept more lightly than she. As his arms encircled her in a warm, protective embrace Senna smiled with sublime happiness. "I think we have, too," she said, and kissed him as the loons called the morning in and the Labrador wilderness awakened to the new day.

Later, after sharing a very early pot of coffee out on the porch, Jack helped Senna divide the admiral's ashes, so that some could be distributed at the lake house that morning, and the rest later at the lodge, the two places he loved the most. It was an emotional experience, and Senna was glad that Jack was a part of it.

IN GOOSE BAY, JACK DROPPED Senna off at Granville's office while he went to the hospital to fetch George Pilgrim. Granville met her at the door, letter in hand. "Good morning, m'dear, I'm glad you called, and I don't mind a bit opening the office early. Come in and I'll fix us a some tea." He handed her the sealed envelope and motioned her inside, where he set about heating the pot of water on a hot plate and readying the mugs. "I'm sorry about the letter, took me forever to find it because it wasn't here in the office, y'see. Your grandfather gave it to me at the pub where we shared our last drink together, and I put it in the pocket of my overcoat because it was a nasty, rainy day. I wore that coat again just three days ago, and found the letter right where I put it. Quite a relief, too. I was beginning to think it was gone for good. Another thing, the life insurance company sent along this mail. I hope it's the payment on your grandfather's policy. How are things out at the lodge?"

Senna tucked the letter inside her purse to read in private, then opened the documents from the insurance company. She breathed a sigh of relief at the sight of the check. The money was more than enough to cover all the outstanding bills and pay the employees for the summer. She signed all the appropriate papers while she filled Granville in on all that had happened in the past few weeks. Listening to herself speak she was filled with a sense of wonder at how life could lead a person down such strange and unexpected paths. That her grandfather's death could, just by coincidence, unite her with the man she would spend the rest of her life with was a humbling thought. She relayed none of her innermost feelings to Granville, but shook his hand with genuine fondness when she took her leave.

"You'll be going back to Maine soon, I expect," he said as he walked her to the door.

"Only temporarily, until I can pack my things and move back here. I'm staying, Mr. Granville. I've decided to remain business partners with Jack. We're going to run the lodge together."

He seemed quite surprised by this, and pleased. "I'd

like to see that lodge someday. The admiral talked about it so much. Maybe when the busy season's over, I could get a few days away…."

"We'd love to have you come."

Jack was waiting in Goody's car and another man sat in the back seat, an older man who looked as fit as Goody, if a bit more worn by the ravages of his recent surgery. "George Pilgrim, Senna McCallum," Jack said.

She reached over the seat to shake his hand. "I'm so glad you'll be staying with us, George."

"I won't be much help to you, y'see, not at first. But when I gets me strength back, I'll be taking the byes fishin', and showin' 'em what Labrador has to offer." He spoke the words with a gruff and almost desperate affirmation of his own worth, in spite of everything that had transpired to trip him up in his twilight years.

"Don't worry about the fishing just yet, just concentrate on getting well," Senna said.

"Oh, it won't take me long to come to the front. All the medicine I needs is out there," George said, indicating the wild spaces beyond the tight clutch of civilization. "Jack tells me that Goody Stewart is at the lodge, too. That's good to hear. She's a grand gal, that Goody. We raised some hell together back in the old schoolhouse days. It'll be fine to see her again after all these years."

Back at the plane they loaded some last-minute groceries and supplies into the back and made sure George had everything he needed. George was settled in the passenger compartment and Senna was about to climb aboard when Jack's hand on her arm stilled her. She turned toward him, eyebrows raised.

"Something to think about," he began, looking suddenly serious.

"Don't worry." She gave him a reassuring smile. "I'll take care of everything when we get back. I'll tell Hammel we've decided not to sell, but that he's welcome to come back any time and enjoy the world-class fishery at the Wolf River Lodge."

Jack took her shoulders firmly in his hands and his keen gaze held her captive. "That's my brave and courageous woman, but that's not exactly what I was talking about," he said.

"Oh?" Senna looked up at him, puzzled. "Just what *are* you talking about?"

"I'm talking about us. You and me. I'm talking about the future. Twenty, thirty, forty years from now. I'm talking about the possibility of the first wedding held at the lodge being ours. Yours and mine."

Senna's heart thumped hard once and then skipped two full beats as she grappled with this unexpected statement. "I think that sounds like a finc idea," she said. "When?"

"The lodge is dead empty the second week in September. Betcha we could fill it with wedding guests."

"I bet we could, too," Senna said as his arms closed around her.

"Is that a yes, wedding planner?"

"That's a definite yes, but only if you promise never to call me that again."

"It's a deal, but only if you promise to be the one who plans our wedding."

Senna wondered, as he bent his head to kiss her, how she could have ever doubted Jack's feelings for her and what George Pilgrim must think about all these last-minute goings-on.

But when they finally climbed into the plane, he was beaming.

SENNA REACHED FOR HER grandfather's letter as soon as they were airborne, having waited for this private hour of flight time to come to grips with all that it might portend. She broke the seal on the official envelope and drew forth the single sheet of paper, glad to see that the letter was written in the admiral's own hand but dismayed that the message was so short. She'd been hoping for a long explanatory treatise, and had received but three brief sentences. Foolish of her, to think the admiral might loosen up just because he was dying. His handwriting was tight, formal and regimented, and she felt a painful pang as she began to read, noting the date and realizing that he'd written it just two days before he died.

Dear Senna,
If you are reading this letter, then you've seen the lodge and lake house and met your business partner, John Hanson. He's hard-working and trustworthy. I hope you like him, I hope you like Labrador, and I also hope you'll forgive this surly old man for meddling in his granddaughter's affairs.
Best of luck,
Stuart Anderson McCallum

Senna folded the letter and replaced it in the envelope. She sat back in her seat and gazed out at the wild expanse unrolling beneath the plane's wings, dazed both by the letter's succinct brevity and the dawning realization that her grandfather had planned this whole business partnership just to get her together with John Hanson after he died. Her surly old grandfather had been playing matchmaker!

She shook her head, torn between laughing and crying. She looked across at Jack, studying the handsome profile of her future husband and life mate as he piloted the old plane back toward the Wolf River Lodge. "I love the man you chose to be my business partner, I like Labrador more by the moment, and I forgive you for meddling in my life. I do, I do and I do," she said softly beneath the roar of the plane's engine, knowing in her heart that her grandfather heard…and approved.

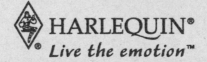

If you enjoyed what you just read,
then we've got an offer you can't resist!

Take 2 bestselling love stories FREE!

Plus get a FREE surprise gift!

Clip this page and mail it to Harlequin Reader Service®

IN U.S.A.
3010 Walden Ave.
P.O. Box 1867
Buffalo, N.Y. 14240-1867

IN CANADA
P.O. Box 609
Fort Erie, Ontario
L2A 5X3

YES! Please send me 2 free Harlequin Superromance® novels and my free surprise gift. After receiving them, if I don't wish to receive anymore, I can return the shipping statement marked cancel. If I don't cancel, I will receive 6 brand-new novels every month, before they're available in stores. In the U.S.A., bill me at the bargain price of $4.69 plus 25¢ shipping and handling per book and applicable sales tax, if any*. In Canada, bill me at the bargain price of $5.24 plus 25¢ shipping and handling per book and applicable taxes**. That's the complete price, and a savings of at least 10% off the cover prices—what a great deal! I understand that accepting the 2 free books and gift places me under no obligation ever to buy any books. I can always return a shipment and cancel at any time. Even if I never buy another book from Harlequin, the 2 free books and gift are mine to keep forever.

135 HDN DZ7W
336 HDN DZ7X

Name	(PLEASE PRINT)
Address	Apt.#
City	State/Prov.	Zip/Postal Code

Not valid to current Harlequin Superromance® subscribers.

Want to try two free books from another series?
Call 1-800-873-8635 or visit www.morefreebooks.com.

* Terms and prices subject to change without notice. Sales tax applicable in N.Y.
** Canadian residents will be charged applicable provincial taxes and GST.
  All orders subject to approval. Offer limited to one per household.
  ® are registered trademarks owned and used by the trademark owner and or its licensee.

SUP04R   ©2004 Harlequin Enterprises Limited

Artist-in-Residence Fellowship— Call for applications

She always dreamed of studying art in Paris, but as a wife and mother she has had other things to do. Finally, Anna is taking a chance on her own.

What Happens in Paris

(STAYS IN PARIS?)

Nancy Robards Thompson

HARLEQUIN *Super Romance*

HOME TO LOVELESS COUNTY
Because Texas is where the heart is.

MORE TO TEXAS
THAN COWBOYS

by Roz Denny Fox

Greer Bell is returning to Texas for the first time since
she left as a pregnant teenager. She and her daughter
are determined to make a success of their new dude
ranch—and the last thing Greer needs is romance,
even with the handsome Reverend Noah Kelley.

On sale January 2006

Also look for the final book in this miniseries
The Prodigal Texan (#1326) by Lynnette Kent
in February 2006.

Available wherever Harlequin books are sold.

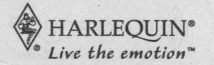

HARLEQUIN®
Live the emotion™

HARLEQUIN *Super Romance*

COLD CASES: L.A.
Giving up is not an option.

AND JUSTICE FOR ALL
by Linda Style

With three unsolved murders and only one suspect,
Detective Jordan St. James demands justice. He's
convinced the suspect, a notorious mob boss, also
killed his mother. What St. James doesn't know is
that he's putting his source, Laura Gianni—and
her daughter—in terrible danger.

On sale January 2006

Available wherever Harlequin books are sold.

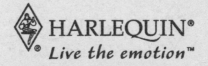

HARLEQUIN®
Live the emotion™

www.eHarlequin.com

HSR